The screen went hostile and nearly took Cardenas with it.

Wind erupted into the offices, blasting his thin hair across his head. On screen the visual had gone berserk, bereft of logic and organization. A dull roaring pounded in his ears.

Something was coming out of the wall.

A full-sense hallo, a monstrous alien shape, thick white slime, an oozing mass of biocircuitry-generated false collagen, bristling with raw neural connectors that reached for him.

As it drew near, it became mostly mouth, a dark, bottomless psychic pit that extended back into the wall, lined with teeth that were twitching, mindless biogrowths.

Cardenas stumbled backward. The expanding mouth was ready to swallow him, the steady roar from its nonexistent throat like the approach of a train inside a tunnel.

Hit the release. The voice that screamed at him was a tiny, fading squeak. His own. He extended a shaky hand . . .

★   ★   ★

BOOKS BY ALAN DEAN FOSTER

The I Inside
Krull
The Man Who Used the Universe
Pale Rider
Shadowkeep
Starman
Cyber Way
Glory Lane
The Damned Trilogy
Flinx of the Commonwealth
Codgerspace
Midworld

THE SPELLSINGER SERIES:
Spellsinger*
The Hour of the Gate*
The Day of the Dissonance*
The Moment of the Magician*
The Paths of the Perambulator*
The Time of the Transference*
Son of Spellsinger*
Chorus Skating*

*Published by
WARNER BOOKS

ALAN DEAN FOSTER

MONTEZUMA STRIP

ASPECT

WARNER BOOKS

A Time Warner Company

WARNER BOOKS EDITION

Cover design by Don Puckey
Cover illustration by Colorspace

Warner Books, Inc.
1271 Avenue of the Americas
New York, NY 10020

W A Time Warner Company

Printed in the United States of America

First Printing: August, 1995

10 9 8 7 6 5 4 3 2 1

For Sebastian Horsley,
Who, much as he decries the travel time required
to get to the end of the Journey,
Seems to be enjoying the trip nonetheless.

Contents

Introduction

Alan Dean Foster

SEX and Money.

I happen to think they're the two prime motivating forces of human existence. Always have been, are now, always will be. Somewhat but not entirely interchangeable in that you can use the former to acquire the latter, but it's much easier to use the latter to obtain the former. Give someone enough money and the sex will follow. The reverse isn't always true.

There are a lot of magazines out there. Quite a few deal with sex, and not only the overtly pornographic, or the covertly pornographic (like *Playboy* and *Penthouse*). Picked up a copy of *Cosmopolitan* lately? How about *Reader's Digest*? Yep, **the** *Reader's Digest*. I've noted with academic interest that each month's cover of America's favorite magazine (excepting perhaps *TV Guide*, which is equally obsessed) now contains at least one article about matters sexual.

And now that I've managed to get you to read this far, I can tell you that the tales in this tome don't arise from an interest in sex. Though they did originate because I subscribe to a certain magazine.

It's called *The Economist*.

British-based, I happen to think it's the best news magazine in the world. At least, it's the best I've come across. Appears weekly and contains more sheer information in each issue than any two issues of *Time* and *Newsweek* put together. Funnier writing, too. There are times when I'm convinced that Basil Fawlty's elder brother has an advisory position on the editorial board.

Not that every article in the magazine is about money. It's just that, as in the real world, money inspires, relates to, or impinges on every subject the magazine tackles. If it's soccer, we're sure to hear about the World Cup champion Brazilian team trying to smuggle a few million in American purchases past sharp-eyed hometown Customs officials. If the subject is art, it's the financial ill health of major orchestras, or festivals, or operas, you're likely to read about. If technology, it's how new developments might inspire new businesses. These in addition to articles on banking, international financial dealings, and so forth.

Which brings me to The Border.

I use the caps because if you live in my quarter of the United States, there's only one border, and that's the one we share with Hispanic America. Not just Mexico, though sheer physical proximity gifts (or curses) our Mexicano neighbors with the majority of the press. I refer to all the people who live south of the line, from Tijuana to Tierra del Fuego.

Some of them would like to work here. Not necessarily live, as the headlines would have you believe, but just work. Make a living. Support the family. A few make it. Most do not. But thanks to developments in international economics, they now have a real choice between staying home and immigrating illegally.

It's called the *maquiladora*.

Over the past twenty years, hundreds of industrial facilities have been constructed on the Mexican side of The Border. These plants assemble components fashioned elsewhere into finished products for export not only to the U.S. but to Europe and even Asia. Hundreds of *Norteamericano* companies large and small have found that you don't need to have your product assembled in Taiwan, or Indonesia, or Malaysia, or even China. Not when there's a vast pool of willing labor, cheap and skilled or unskilled, just down the road.

The result is that tens of thousands of poor Hispanic Americans have crowded into border towns and provinces, seeking a steady wage and a better life in the communities that are growing up around these plants. Growing, hell; they're exploding, erupting, bursting at the seams. But much more is happening because of them than mere economic integration.

A whole new culture is coalescing along The Border, one comprised equally of *Norte* and Hispanic American influences. Especially since the passage of NAFTA (North American Free Trade Agreement), trade between the U.S. and Mexico has increased at an even faster pace than it had been previously. The consequences are dramatic, and not all of them are blatant.

In Arizona and southern California in particular, thousands of retirees and folks on fixed income travel across the border for medical services; everything from pills to dental work. They're passed by hordes of increasingly well-off southerners who prefer to shop the clean, better-stocked malls of San Diego and Tucson than those of Tijuana. In Texas it's long been nigh impossible to tell where the city of El Paso ends and Ciudad Juarez begins. Literally cross a street and you're in another country. But not another culture. You can buy excellent Mexican food in El Paso, and get your McDonald's fix in Juarez.

People who live along the border are generally conversant in English, Spanish, and Spanglish. The latter deals with economics especially well. Why? Because trade and money are the first things people learn to talk about. Sometimes the money is legal, sometimes not, but it's all business.

I've tried to imagine what this region, stretching from the Pacific to the Gulf of Mexico, might be like in a hundred years, more or less. New York and Los Angeles and Mexico City and Tokyo and Singapore and more, all linked and stretched out from sea to sea, with individual towns and cities forming blobs and bulges along the wandering line like pearls on a string. Some glistening, some dirty, all fascinating, as marketplaces invariably are.

Science-fiction writers don't claim to predict the future. For one thing, we're not especially good at it. But we're sure no worse than anyone else. One thing I *can* predict about new developments, whether they involve science, or sport, or religion, or art, or education, or anything else. Sex, too.

In the future as in the present, if someone can make money off it, someone will.

So why don't more science-fiction writers employ economics as the basis for their stories? More do than most people believe. It's just that the tenets are usually invisible behind the gloss of the tenants. Philosophy trails protagonists. Death rays grab the reader's attention fast, especially if they're wielded by someone svelte, young, and preferably inadequately clad.

While reading such stories it sometimes occurs to me to wonder who designed, manufactured, and sold the death ray. Who's paying the shootist. What do those skimpy clothes cost. All of this is integral to the schematic of any future. It's just that such details are wont to find themselves abandoned by the wayside as the plot screams forward.

There are exceptions where the prime motivating force of money, cash, moolah, and credit are given their due. William Gibson, the astute reader will quickly point out. Kudos to Bill for paying (no pun intended) attention to what really pushes people forward through a frantic future (and plot). But who remembers the work of Mack Reynolds? Fewer than have kept company with Poul Anderson's Nicholas van Rijn, I expect.

Everyone's a van Rijn to a great or lesser extent. Why should folks in the foreseeable future be any different? Morals intervene, and other desires, but who wouldn't sacrifice for a chance to be Scrooge McDuck? Not many science-fiction stories explain how much simpler it would be to buy out one's enemy, or give them jobs, than to blow them away. War boosts short-term dividends, but in the long run it's bad for business. Interstellar war would be worse.

That's why there was no Third World War, in case you didn't know.

The Border's a busy place now. It's going to get busier in the immediate future. A *lot* busier. Strange things will happen there, and most of them, I expect, will orbit around money.

I've tried to give the matter some thought.

Sanctuary

"*H*EY, Cardenas, don't you retire today, man?"

"Chief's got it in for you sure today."

"Naw, he's gonna fire Cardenas and promote the dog!"

He smiled as he walked past their desks, the laughter lapping against him in friendly, cool waves before falling away behind him. Occasionally he replied, brief verbal jousts with those he knew well that left no one injured. He always gave as good as he got. When you were the oldest sergeant on the force, not to mention the smallest, you had to expect a certain amount of ribbing.

"Don't sweat it, Charliebo," he told his companion. "Good boy."

At the mention of his name the German shepherd's ears cocked forward and he looked up curiously. Same old Charliebo. The laughter didn't bother him. Nothing bothered him. That's how he'd been trained and the years hadn't changed him.

We're both getting old, Cardenas thought. Jokes now, but in another year or two they'll make me hang it up no matter what. Then we double the time in front of the video, *hoh*. Just you and me and the ol' TV, dog. Maybe that's not such a bad idea. We could both use some rest. Though he had a hunch the chief hadn't called him in to talk about rest.

A visitor might've found the big dog's presence in the ready room unusual, but not the Nogales cops. The dog had been Sergeant Cardenas's shadow for twelve years. For the first six he'd also been his eyes. Eyes that had been taken from him by a frightened nineteen-year-old ninloco Cardenas had surprised in the process of rotoing an autofill outside a Tucson hydro station. Pocket change. Pill credit.

Cardenas and his partner had slipped up on the kid without expecting anything more lethal than some angry words. The ninloco had grabbed his pants and extracted an Ithaca spitter. The high-pocket twenty-gauge shattered Cardenas's partner and made jelly of the sergeant's face. Backup told him that the ninloco had gone down giggling when they'd finally expiated him. His blood analysis showed .12 spacebase and an endorphin-based expander. He was so high he should've flown away. Now he was a memory.

The surgeons plastered Cardenas's face back together. The drooping mustache regrew in sections. When he was recovered enough to comprehend what had happened to him they gave him Charliebo, a one-year-old intense-trained shepherd, the best guide dog the school had. For six years Charliebo had been Cardenas's eyes.

Then the biosurges figured out a way to transplant optic nerves as well as just the eyeballs and they'd coaxed him back into the hospital. When he was discharged four months later he was seeing through the bright perfect blue eyes of a dead teenager named Anise Dorleac whose boyfriend had turned him and her both to ground chuck while drag racing a Lotusette at a hundred ninety on Interstate Forty up near Flag. Not much salvageable out of either of them except her eyes. They'd given them to Cardenas.

After that Charliebo didn't have to be his eyes anymore. Six years, though, an animal becomes something more than

a pet and less than a person. Despite the entreaties of the
guide dog school Cardenas wouldn't give him up. Couldn't.
He'd never married, no kids, and Charliebo was all the family
he'd ever had. You didn't give up family.

The police association stood by him. The school directors
grumbled but didn't press the matter. Besides, it was pretty
funny, wasn't it? What could be more outré than a short,
aging, blue-eyed Tex-Mex cop who worked his terminal with
a dog guarding his wastepaper basket? So they left him alone.
More important, they left him Charliebo.

He didn't pause outside the one-way plastic door. Pangborn
had told him to come right in. He thumbed a contact switch
and stepped through as the plastic slid aside.

The chief didn't even glance at Charliebo. The shepherd was
an appendage of the sergeant, a canine extrusion of Cardenas's
personality. Cardenas wouldn't have looked right without the
dog to balance him. Without having to be told, the shepherd
lay down silently at the foot of Cardenas's chair, resting his
angular gray head on his forepaws.

"*Como se* happening, Nick?"

The chief smiled thinly. "*De nada*, Angel. You?"

"Same old this and that. I think we wormed a line on the
chopshop down in Nayarit."

"Forget it. I'm taking you off that."

Cardenas's hand fell to stroke Charliebo's neck. The dog
didn't move but his eyes closed in pleasure. "I got eighteen
months before mandatory retirement. You pasturing me
early?"

"Not a chance." Pangborn understood. The chief had five
years left before they'd kick him out. "Got some funny stuff
going on over in Agua Pri. Lieutenant there, Danny Mendez,
is an old friend of mine. They're oiled and it's getting uncomfortable. Some real specific gravity on their backs. So he
called for help. I told him I'd loan over the best Intuit in the
Southwest. We both know who that is."

Cardenas turned and made an exaggerated search of the
duty room outside. Pangborn smiled.

"Why not send one of the young hotshots? Why me?"

"Because you're still the best, you old fart. You know why."

Sure, he knew why. Because he'd gone six years without eyes and in that time he'd developed the use of his other senses to the opto. Involuntary training but unsurpassingly effective. Then they'd given him back his sight. Of course he was the best. But he still liked to hear it. At his age compliments of any kind were few and far between, scattered widely among the ocean of jokes.

Under his caressing fingers Charliebo stretched delightedly. "So what's skewed in Agua Pri?"

"Two Designers. Wallace Crescent and a Vladimir Noschek. First one they called Wondrous Wallace. I dunno what they called the other guy, except irreplaceable. Crescent was the number one mainline man for GenDyne. Noschek worked for Parabas S.A."

"Also mainline design?" Pangborn nodded. "*Que* about them?"

"Crescent two weeks ago. Noschek right afterward. Each of them wiped clean as a kid's Etch-A-Sketch. Hollow, vacuumed right back through childhood. Both of them lying on an office couch, relaxed, Crescent with a drink half finished, Noschek noshing on a bowl of pistachios. Like they'd been working easy, normal, then suddenly they ain't at home anymore. That was weird enough."

"Something was weirder?"

Pangborn looked uneasy. That was unusual. It took a lot of specific gravity to upset the chief. He'd been a sparkler buster down Guyamas way. Everybody knew about the Tampolobampo massacre. Late night and the runners had buffooned into an ambush laid by local spitters trying to pull a ripoff. By the time the cops arrived from halfway across Sonora and Sinaloa the beach was covered with guts the waves washed in and out like spawning grunion. Through it all Pangborn hadn't blinked, not even when older cops were heaving their insides all over the Golfo California. He'd just gone along the waterline kicking pieces of bodies aside looking for evidence to implicate the few survivors. It was an old story that never got old. Decaders liked to lay it on rookies to see how green they'd get.

But there was no record of Pangborn looking uneasy.

"Nobody can figure out how they died, Angel. Parabas flew their own specialists up from Sao Paulo. Elpaso Juarez coroner's office still won't acknowledge the certification because they can't list COD. Both bodies were clean as the inside of both brains. No juice, no soft intrusions, no toxins, nothing. Bare as Old Mother Hubbard's cupboard. Inviolate, the reports said. Hell, how do you kill somebody without intruding? Even ultrasound leaves a signature. But according to Mendez there wasn't a damn thing wrong with either man except nobody was home."

"Motives?"

Pangborn grunted. "Tired of small talk? Working already?"

"Aren't I?"

The chief scrolled crunch on his desk screen, muting the audio. "Money, schematics, razzmatazz, who knows? Parabas and GenDyne Internal Security immediately went over homes, friends, and work stations with good suction. Nothing missing, everything in place. Both men were straight right up and down the lifeline. No alley-oops. GenDyne's frizzing the whole Southwest Enforcement Region. They want to know how as much as why. They also want to know if anybody's going to be next. Bad for morale, bad for business." He scratched at his prosthetic left ear. The real one had been chewed off by a ninloco ten years ago and the replacement never seemed to quite fit.

Cardenas was quiet for a long moment. "What do you think?"

Pangborn shrugged. "Somebody vacuums two mainline Designers after penetrating state-of-the-art corporate security but doesn't steal anything insofar as anybody can tell. Both work files were checked. Both are regularly monitored and everything was solid. So nobody did it to steal crunch. Just a whim, but I think maybe it was somehow personal. Not corporate at all. You can't tell that to GenDyne or Parabas. They don't like to hear that kind of stuff."

"You'd expect them to go paranoid. Any connections between the two men?"

"Not that Mendez and his people have been able to find. Didn't eat at the same restaurants, moved in different circles entirely. Crescent was married, one wife, family. Noschek was younger, a loner. Separate orbits, separate obits. Me, I think maybe they were flooded with a new kind of juice. Maybe involuntarily."

"No evidence for that, and it still doesn't give us a motive." Pangborn stared at him. "Find one."

Cardenas was at home in the Strip, a solid string of high-tech that ran all the way from LaLa to East Elpaso Juarez. It followed the old and frayed USA-Mehico border with less regard for actual national boundaries than the Rio Grande. Every multinational that wanted a piece of the Namerica market had plants there and most had several. In between were kilometers of upstarts, some true independents, others entrepreneurs spun off by the electronic gargantuas. Down amid the frenzy of innovation, where bright new developments could be outdated before they could be brought to market, fortunes were risked and lost. If you were a machinist, a mask sculptor, a programmer, you could make six figures a year. If you were a peon from Zacatecas or Tamulipas, a dirt farmer made extinct by new tech, or a refugee from the infinite slums of Mexico City, you could always find work on the assembly lines. Someday if you worked hard and didn't lose your eyesight to overstrain they might give you a white lab coat and hat and promote you to a clean room. Kids, women, anybody who could control their fingers and their eyes, could make hard currency in the Montezuma Strip, where First World technology locked hands with Third World cheap labor.

Spinoffs from the Strip extended north to Phoenix, south to Guyamas. Money brought in subcultures, undercultures, anticultures. Some of the sociologists who delved into the underpinnings of the Strip didn't come out. The engineers and technocrats forced to live in proximity to their labor and produce lived in fortified suburbs and traveled to work in armored transports. Cops in transit didn't rate private vehicles.

Cardenas squeezed into a crowded induction shuttle bound for Agua Prieta. The plastic car stank of sweat, disinfectant, Tex-Mex fast food. Other passengers grudgingly made way for Charliebo but not for his owner. The dog wouldn't take up a seat.

Cardenas found one anyway, settled in for the hour-long rock-and-ride. Advertising bubbled from the overhead speakers, behind spider steel grates. A ninloco tried to usurp Cardenas's seat. He wore his hair long and slick. The Aztec snake tattooed on his right cheek twitched its coils when he grinned. Cardenas saw him coming but didn't meet his eyes, hoping he'd just bounce on past. The other commuters gave the crazyboy plenty of room. He came straight up to Cardenas.

"No spitting, Tio. Just evaporate, *bien*?"

Cardenas glanced up at him. "Waft, child."

The ninloco's gaze narrowed. When Cardenas tensed, Charliebo came up off the floor and growled. He was an old dog and he had big teeth. The ninloco backed a step and reached toward a pocket.

"Leave it, leave you." Cardenas shook his head warningly, holding up his right arm so the sleeve slid back. The ninloco's eyes flicked over the bright blue bracelet with its gleaming LEDs.

"Federale. Hey, I didn't know, *compadre*. I'll jojobar."

"You do that." Cardenas lowered his hand. The crazyboy vanished back into the crowd. Charliebo grunted and settled down on his haunches.

Surprised at the tightness in his gut, Cardenas leaned back against the curved plastic and went through a series of relaxation breathing exercises. This ninloco wasn't the one who'd flayed him years ago. He was a newer, younger clone, no better and no worse. A member of one of the hundreds of gangs that broke apart and coalesced as they drifted through the length of the Strip like sargassum weed in the mid-Atlantic. The ninlocos hated citizens, but they despised each other.

Across the aisle two teenage girls, one anglo, the other spanglo, continued to stare at him. Only they weren't seeing him, he knew, but rather the vits playing across the interior lenses of the oversized glasses they wore. The arms of each set of lenses curved down behind their ears to drive the music home by direct transduction, straight to the inner ear. Cardenas didn't mind the music, but the vibrations were something else.

By the time the induction car pulled into Agua Pri station he'd completely forgotten the confrontation with the ninloco.

The flashman at GenDyne would've taken him through the whole damn plant if Cardenas hadn't finally insisted on being shown Crescent's office. It wasn't his escort's fault. A flashman just naturally tried to promote and show off his company at every opportunity. Wasn't that what sales-pr was all about? Even the police departments engaged flashmen. If you didn't have a professional to intercede for you with the media, they'd eat you alive.

That didn't mean you had to like them, and most people didn't. Cardenas thought they were one with the lizards that still scuttled across the rocks north and south of the Strip.

The GenDyne think tank was built like a fortress. In point of fact it was a fortress, the architecture inspired by Assyrian fortifications unearthed in Mesopotamia. Only instead of stone it rose from the desert whose sand it crowded onto on foundations of reinforced concrete. Its walls were bronze glass set in casements of white high-construct plastic. It was built on the southern edge of this part of the Strip, so the south-facing alcoves and offices all had views of once-hostile terrain. Expensive real estate. This was a place for a multinational's pets, its most privileged people. Designers and engineers, who conjured money out of nothing.

Crescent had been important enough to rate a top-floor work station, right up there with the modem mongers who swapped info and crunch with the home office in LaLa.

Through the window that dominated one wall could be seen the smog-shrouded heights of the Sierra de la Madera. Like a python dressed for Christmas the arc of the Strip curved around toward Laguna de Guzman and the new arcomplex of Ciudad Pershing-Villa.

The office itself had been furnished professionally. Thick, comforting chairs, a cabinet containing ice maker and drink dispenser, indirect lighting, everything designed to produce a work environment conducive to the sort of brainstorms that added fractions to a multinat's listing on the International Exchange. An expensive colorcrawl by an artist Cardenas didn't recognize lit the wall behind the couch, two square meters of half-sentient neon gone berserk. The pale orange and brown earthtone carpet underfoot was thicker than the upholstery on his furniture back in Nogales. It smelled of new mown hay and damp sandstone, having been sense recharged not more than a week ago. To cover the smell of death? But Crescent's passing had been neat. As the flashman spieled on, Cardenas studied the couch where the body had been found, calm and unstressed.

The desk was a sweep of replicant mesquite, complete to the detailed grain. The east wall was, of course, all screen. It was just a flat beige surface now, powered down.

"It's been scanned, scraped, and probed, but nothing except the, uh, body's been moved." The flashman finally saw him staring at the couch. The death frame. He wore a metallic green suit with short sleeves. The set of red lenses swathed his eyes. The other two primaries were pushed back atop his head, bracketed by the high blond crewcut. A hearsee stuck out of his right ear like a burrowing beetle. His green shoes were soled in teflink and he slid noiselessly across the carpet without slipping. Lizard, Cardenas thought.

Ignoring the mute workscreen, he strolled behind the desk. A couple of holos drifted a centimeter above the replicant wood, off to the left. He'd only been able to see them from the back. They were set to rotate every half hour. They showed a pretty young woman, two kids. The boy and girl were also pretty. Everyone smiled warmly. Crescent was in one of the holos. Images of a happy, content family on its way up. Soaring, if Crescent was half as brilliant as GenDyne's files had led Cardenas to believe.

In his mind's eye he conjured up the coroner's vit of the victim, the Designer sitting placidly on the couch, his body undamaged, heart pumping steadily. The eyes staring but not seeing because everything behind them that had been Wallace Crescent had been removed. This space for rent.

Who would do that to a man who according to every record had no enemies, had never bothered a soul, wanted nothing but to succeed at his job and take care of his handsome family? Cardenas felt sick. Nearby Charliebo whined, gazing up at his two-legged friend out of brown, limpid eyes.

The flashman's lenses dropped. "Something new? I know they used to train them to sniff juice, but that was a long time ago."

"Just a friend." Cardenas spoke absently, still inspecting the couch. "That's where they found him."

The flashman flipped up his reds. His eyes were pale, weak. Spent too much time relying on the lenses, Cardenas thought. No wonder he needed triples.

"Right there, on the middle cushion. Could've been sleeping except that his eyes were wide open."

Cardenas nodded and walked over to run his fingers across the upholstery. No blood, no signs of any kind. So sayeth the Official Inquiry. If it had been otherwise they wouldn't have called for help. He straightened and strolled back to sit behind the desk. Hydraulics cushioned his weight, all but silent. Crescent's body was being kept alive in a Douglas hospital. The family insisted on it, hoping against hope he'd return someday from wherever he'd gone to. They hadn't listened to the police. Crescent hadn't *gone*. He'd been moved out forcibly. There was nothing to come back. But the family wouldn't listen. Gradually the police stopped bothering them.

What had happened to this stable, incisive, innovative mind?

He let his fingers slide along the top of the desk until he found what he was searching for. A center drawer snapped open. He ignored the printouts, storage cubes, miscellania, and picked up the vorec. Small, the very latest model, a Gevic Puretone-20. It was slim and smooth, the size of a small hot dog, no bun. Twiddling it between thumb and fingers he slowly turned in the chair until he was facing the workscreen wall. He flicked a tiny button set in the polished metal surface. The east wall lit with a soft light. A barely perceptible hum filled the office.

The flashman took a nervous step toward the desk. "You can't do that."

Cardenas spared him a sideways glance. "I have to. I have to know what he was working on when he was vacuumed."

"I'll need to get you clearance. You can't open the box without clearance."

Cardenas grinned at him. "Want to bet?"

"Wait." The flashman was backing toward the door. "Please, just wait a moment." He hurried out.

The sergeant hesitated, continued to play with the vorec mike. Charliebo stared eagerly at the wall. He knew what was coming. This was something Cardenas did frequently. So far as he knew the dog enjoyed it as much as he did. It didn't matter whether he was rummaging through a personal box or a much larger one holding company records, it was always interesting to examine the contents. The mike in his hand was cool to the touch, uncontaminated.

The flashman came back with someone in tow. She didn't look pleased.

"Company policy. We need someone equally capable of interpreting data present when you go in." *So we're sure you don't pocket anything on the side*, was the unspoken corollary. "Senior Designer Hypatia Spango, this is Sergeant Angel Cardenas. He's over from Nogales to work on . . ."

"I know what he's here to work on. Why else would anyone be in Wally's office?" She stared evenly at him.

Straight on, Cardenas noted. No flinching, no deference,

certainly no worry. She was at least fifteen years younger than he. Handsome, not pretty. Black hair permed in tight ringlets that fell to her shoulders. Black eyes, too, but oddly pale skin. Body voluptuous beneath the white corporate jumpsuit. Mature. He wondered how much of her was held up by polymers and how much by herself. She was taller than he but it would've been unusual if she wasn't. Everybody was taller than he was. She wore a reducer cap over her right eye. When she saw him looking at it she removed it and dropped it into a pocket. Three chevrons on each sleeve of the jumpsuit. The woman carried some weight and not just in her pants.

Well, they wouldn't set a post-grad scanner to keep watch on him.

Reluctantly she advanced until she was standing on the other side of the desk. Then she noticed the gray-black lump near his feet. "Nice dog."

"That's Charliebo. He's nicer than most people."

"Look, I didn't want to do this but they insisted Optop. I don't want to like you either, but you've got a dog, so I guess I'm stuck there, too." She extended a hand across the desktop. Her grip was firm and full, not the half-dance tentativeness favored by most women. Her nails were cut short and clean, no polish, none of the rainbow insets currently in fashion. Soft but efficient. Working hands.

"You from around here?" He meant the Strip.

She shook her head tersely. The ringlets jangled silently. If they'd been made of metal there would have been music. "Iowa. Des Moines. It's a long story."

"Aren't they all, *verdad*?" He sat up straight and looked past her. "You can go now."

The flashman licked his lips as he fiddled with his lenses. They dehumanized him, if it was possible to dehumanize a flashman further. "I should stay."

Spango turned. "Waft."

He did.

She sat down without being asked, pulling one of the chairs up to the other side of the desk.

"How long you been with GenDyne?" he asked her.

"Is this being recorded?"

He tapped his breast pocket. *"Everything's* being recorded."

She sighed. "All my life. Univ in Des Moines, then three years graduate work. Vegas School of Design. Then GenDyne. Five promotions and two husbands along the way. Kept the promotions, lost the husbands." A shrug. "That's life. All of mine, anyway."

"And how long's that?"

A slightly wicked smile. "I'm not sure that information's pertinent to your investigation here, Federale."

It was his turn to grin. "Alright. Pax. How long did you know Crescent?"

"Ten years. All of it off and on. You know Designers. We spend most of our time inside the Box. Wally was friendly enough, knew everybody and they knew him. Except I don't guess anybody really *knew* him. His wife, Karen, a real quiet sweet gal. They made all the company picnics, reward trips, all the expected functions they were both there. Wally played high goal on the division socball team."

"Ever notice anything that would make you think he was an abuser?"

She shook her head. "As far as I knew he was clean as the box room. Of course, you never know what anybody does in private."

"No, you don't. How good was he?"

"As a Designer? The best. Wally knew how to use imagination *and* logic. He had a flair most of us don't, no matter how long we work at it. Talent, you know? I don't know what else to call it. He knew the inside of the box the way most of us know our own bodies.

"GenDyne knew it, too. The rest of us had to beg for a raise or an extra day off. All Crescent had to do was sneeze and he'd have the whole marketing department cleaning his shoes with their tongues. Are you familiar with the GS Capacitate?" Cardenas nodded. "That was Crescent's baby. Sensitized microbio circuit. Plug one into your screen, feed it, and it automatically replicates existing storage until you turn off the power. Gallium arsenide proteins are a lot cheaper in bulk than predesigned slabs. Revolutionized peripheral information storage."

Cardenas was impressed. "Crescent came up with that?" She nodded. "So obviously money wasn't a problem for him."

Spango leaned back in her chair. For a big woman she had small feet, he mused. "He wasn't independently wealthy but he made more than you or I'll ever see."

"Maybe he was onto something new. Something potentially as big as the GS."

"If so he was keeping it to himself. We couldn't find anything revolutionary in his section of the box. Of course, Crescent was a genius. The rest of us are just plodders. It could still be in there, tucked away where nobody but Wally himself could find it."

"Isn't that kind of unusual?"

"I see what you're thinking. Not only isn't it unusual, it's standard policy. The company understands and accepts it. I do it myself. Hey, if you don't protect your ideas from your good *compadre* next door, next thing you know he's accessed your storage and is presenting your hard-won innovation to the Board. How do you prove you thought of it first? It's tough to ident an idea."

"So there's serious competition even within a division. You sure he wasn't planning to sell to somebody else?"

"Outside GenDyne? How the hell would I know that? How would anybody? Is that what you think?"

"Right now I'm thinking of everything. You say he had plenty of money. But he wasn't independent. Maybe some other outfit was willing to set him up for life. Maybe he wanted something GenDyne couldn't or wouldn't get for him. Something nobody else knew about. Let's say that was the case only at the last moment he backed out. Got nervous, changed his mind, I don't know. The people he was dealing

with got angry. They argued, they sent someone in after him,
they vacuumed him to get what they wanted. No such thing
as selective vacuuming, of course. Not yet. Not that the type
another corporation would send to do something like that
would care. Why leave a witnessing consciousness around to
make noise afterward?"

"You make a good case but I think it's all idletime. You
didn't know Wally Crescent. Subside dealings weren't his
style."

"People are full of surprises." He twirled the vorec. "Time
to start digging."

She turned to face the wallscreen. "GenDyne Security's
already combed his storage. Nothing but what you'd expect.
You won't find anything, either."

"Maybe not, but I've got to start someplace. You want to
give me the access or you want to make me work?"

Those deep black eyes studied him. "Maybe I'll get you
to work some other time. You've already got the access."

He smiled. "What makes you think that?"

"Security wouldn't have asked you to look around without
giving it to you. Without access there wouldn't be anything
for you to look at. And if I knew it, then I'd be a suspect,
wouldn't I?"

"You're a suspect already. Everyone in this building's a
suspect."

She sniffed. "Can I stay and watch?"

He shrugged. "This kind of examination can get pretty
dull. Looking for useful concepts to swipe?"

"If there was anything readily extractable in there worth
stealing, Security's done it already."

He nodded and turned to face the blank wall, raising the
voice recognition mike to his lips. "Coordinate Hapsburg
Hollenzolleren Mermaid."

The wall seemed to disappear. He was looking across the
carpet down an infinite rectangular tunnel. Within the tunnel
tiny flecks of light and color swarmed like protozoa in pond
water. As he stared, the flecks began to coalesce to form a

simple holographic square, neatly lettered on all six sides. A musical female voice, the synthesized duplicate of a reconstructed nineteenth-century singer known as the Swedish Nightingale, spoke from concealed speakers.

"Welcome to the GenDyne box, Mermaid storage and files. You are not Wallace Crescent."

"Federales Security Special Forces Bomo Bomo Six." Cardenas withdrew a plastic card from a shirt pocket and slipped it into a receptacle in the side of the desk.

"Welcome, Sergeant Cardenas. Security clearance processed. Mermaid awaits."

Cardenas frowned. "That was too easy."

"Not if Crescent had nothing to hide. I told you company Security's already run this. Mermaid let them go anywhere they wanted to. If Wally'd been hiding something, they would've found a block."

"Maybe not, if this guy was as clever as you say. What better way to hide something than to let everybody look around for it?"

"You mean like hide it in plain sight? You can't do that in a box. If Crescent had tucked something into a seam, Security would've smelled it out even if they couldn't crack it. Besides, Crescent didn't design for Security. He was strictly heavy-duty industrial."

"How do you know what Crescent was and wasn't into?"

She had no reply for that.

He started in. He was methodical, efficient, experienced, able to skip whole blocks of information without so much as a surface scan. He pumped the vorec up to three times normal speed. It impressed Spango, though that wasn't his intention. That was just the way he worked. Within GenDyne itself nobody except the vorec Designers worked even double speed.

Sometimes he switched to printout when he wanted to be sure of something, reading the words as they formed in the void created by the screen, but most of the time he stuck with the faster vorec. Much of the time he kept his eyes closed as the Mermaid storage spoke to him. He did it because it helped his concentration. He was used to analyzing without being able to see. What he couldn't detect with his eyes shut was Hypatia watching him.

Not so very long ago people had wasted time tapping out their commands on keyboards. Nobody used keyboards anymore except hobbyists. With the perfection of voice recognition circuitry you just talked to your box and it replied in a voice of your choice. A whole industry had been created just to supply custom voices. Your box could reply in the measured tones of Winston Churchill, or Sheila Armstrong, or even Adolph Hitler. Or your dead father. Or your favorite seamyvit star.

He probed and dug and inquired without wondering who might be listening in. He took it for granted this room was smothered. GenDyne Security would've seen to that.

Mermaid was stuffed with notions, ideas incomplete, concepts partly rounded, files that dead-ended, rotating neural highways and biochem cylinders. Most of it was far above a cop's venue, but so far he hadn't encountered anything he couldn't recognize as incomplete. Even so he found himself glad they'd pushed Hypatia on him. If anything slipped past his notice she'd pin it for him. He didn't have to ask. Having been allowed inside another Designer's private sanctum, she was studying eagerly. But so far she gave no indication they'd stumbled into anything unusual or out of the ordinary.

Nothing worth vacuuming a man for.

"Hey?"

"Hmmm?"

"C'mon, Cardenas. Give it a rest. You're starting to put down roots."

He blinked. He hadn't been asleep, not really. Just dozing, his mind lazy and open to the steady flow of verbosity from the wall. He sat up and saw Charliebo resting his head in her lap. A glance the other way showed it was dark outside. He checked his bracelet. Tiny lights flashed accusingly at him. It was after nine. He'd been sponging for eight straight hours.

"I'm not tired."

"The hell you're not."

Slowly he eased out of the chair. His muscles protested. His bladder was tight as a slipknot.

"Where's the . . .?"

"Down the hall." She stood, grinning at him. "Come on, I'll show you."

"Show me what?"

"Just the door, man. Just the door."

She took him to a French restaurant. Cardenas had never been to a French restaurant in his life. Spanglish was near enough to French to enable him to read half the menu and Hypatia translated the other half. Ten minutes later he gazed helplessly across the table.

"Isn't there *anything* in this place that doesn't have some kind of sauce on it?"

"I'll take care of it." She ordered for both of them. The place was fancy enough to afford live waiters. Cardenas waited until the man left.

"What am I getting?"

"Poulet. Pollo. Plain. Don't worry, I wouldn't poison you with Bernaise or worse."

He pushed the menu aside. "The only thing I'm worried about is the bill."

"Don't. This was my invite so I'm paying." He went through the motions of protesting. "Look, my salary's five times yours. Don't go ancien-macho on me."

"Not a chance. Why the largess?"

"Suspicious little northie, aren't you?"

"Consider my profession."

"I'm doing it because you didn't ask me. Because even though you didn't want me around back in Crescent's office you still talked to me. Civil. Because you didn't make a pass at me. Because I like your dog. Enough reasons?"

"I'm too old to make passes at girls."

"That may be, but then I'm no girl. I haven't been a girl for a long time. Also, you spoke to my face instead of my chest."

"I wanted answers from you."

She giggled. It was an extraordinary and utterly unexpected sound, fluting up from the depths of that mature shape, as though for a few seconds it was suddenly home to a wandering seventeen-year-old.

"That's not what most men want."

Not knowing what to say next, he found himself looking toward the entrance. The curving plastic tunnel led up and out to the street above. They were down in fancy undersand, where corporate execs came to do business, where the flashmen sat selling and stealing, and sylphs sold themselves to worms from Asia and Europa. Occasionally the patrons ate.

"Worried about your dog?"

He looked back to her. "I could have brought him in with us. Claimed impaired vision. That's what Charliebo's trained for. Sometimes I do it."

"Unnecessary. He's fine in the checkroom. I told the girl there to filch him some kitchen scraps. She said she'd be glad to. Charliebo's a lover. He'll probably enjoy this dinner more than you will."

His eyebrows rose. "I didn't hear you say anything about scraps. Thanks."

Her eyes dropped. Beneath her forearms the thermosensitive Lexan tabletop changed color as the plastic responded to the subtle shifts in her body temperature.

"I like Charliebo. I've always preferred animals to people. Maybe because I haven't had much luck in my relationships with people." She looked back up at him. "Aren't you going to ask me about my wonderful marriages?"

"Hadn't planned on it."

"For a man you're pretty understanding. Maybe I should've kept away from the pretty boys. The first one was a Designer. Good, though not as good as me, not anywhere near Crescent's class. But he was slick. Did furniture. Did me, too. Designed me right out of his life. The second one lasted four years. I guess I went to the other extreme. Max had a body like a truck and a brain to match. After a while that got old. It was my turn to move on." She palmed a handful of shrimp crackers from a bowl. "That was ten years ago."

"Maybe you should have stuck with it awhile longer."

"You're one to talk." She looked around wildly. "God, I wish I had a cigarette."

"I saw a den up the block as we were coming down here." He did not offer the expected criticism.

"Can't anyway. Company doctors tell me I've got 'thin lungs', whatever the hell those are."

"Sorry. You get anything from what we saw and heard today?"

She shook her head sadly. "Typical cop. Can't you leave your business outside for a while?"

"I've done pretty good so far."

"I didn't sponge a thing. Nothing in Mermaid lively enough to prick a neuron. Oh, lots of fascinating design work, enough to awe just about anybody except Wally himself, but nothing worth killing for."

He found himself nodding agreement. "That's what I thought. I spent most of my time looking for what wasn't there. Blocks, wells, verbal codes, Janus gates. Didn't find any, though."

"I warned you. How can you sponge a code? Don't they sound the same as everything else?"

"To most people."

"What do you mean, 'to most people'?"

He met her eyes once more. "Hypatia, why do you think they put me on this case? Why do you think Agua Prieta had to bring somebody all the way over from Nogales?"

"Because you're good?"

"I'm more than that. Hypatia, I'm an Intuit."

"Oh. Well."

Her expression stayed carefully neutral. She didn't look at him like he was some kind of freak. Which of course he wasn't. He was just infinitely more sensitive to sounds and verbal programming than practically everyone else. But the sensationalist media delighted in putting their spotlights on anything that hinted of the abnormal. Intuits were a favorite subject.

Cardenas could hear things in speech nobody except another Intuit would notice. Previously that was something useful only to actors, lawyers, and judges. With the advent o⁻ ˙erbal programming it was recognized as more than a ˙ alent. It became a science.

In the late twentieth-century primitive machines had been devised that were crude mimics of natural Intuits. When the majority of information programming and storage switched from physical to verbal input, the special abilities of those people identified as Intuits were suddenly much in demand. Because people could hide information with delicate phraseology and enunciation. They could also steal. The impetus came from the Japanese who after decades of trying to solve the difficulty of how to program in characters leapfrogged the entire problem by helping to develop verbal programming.

Not all Intuits went into police work. Cardenas knew of one who did nothing but interview for major corporations, checking on potential employees. As living lie detectors their findings were not admissible in court, but that didn't prevent others from making use of their abilities.

Six years of blindness had only sharpened Cardenas's talent.

He'd attended a few Intuit conferences, where the talk was all about new vorec circuits and semantics. Little was said. Little had to be, since there were no misunderstandings between speakers. Among the attendees had been other cops, translators for multinats and governments, and entertainers. He remembered with special pleasure his conversation with the famous Eskimo Billy Oomigmak, a lieutenant with the Northwest Territories Federales. An Inuit Intuit would be an obvious candidate for celebrity status and Billy Oo had taken full advantage of it. Cardenas had no desire to trade places with him.

"Can you read my thoughts?"

"No, no. That's a common misconception. All I can do is

sense the real meaning of a statement, detect if what's being said is what's being meant. If somebody utilizes phraseology to conceal something either in person or through an artvoc, I can often spot it. That's why there are so many Intuit judges. Why do you think . . .?"

He stopped. She had a hand over her mouth, stifling a laugh. Obviously she knew Intuits weren't mind readers. She'd been teasing him. He pouted without realizing how silly it made him look.

"Why'd you take me out, anyway? Charliebo aside."

Her hand dropped. She wasn't smiling now, he saw. "Because it's been a long time since I was out with a real grown-up, Angel. I like children, but not as dates."

He eyed her sharply. "Is that what this is? A date?"

"Fooled you, didn't I? All this time you thought it was a continuation of business. Tell me: how'd they let somebody as small as you on the force?"

He almost snapped at her, until he realized she was still teasing him. Well, he could tease, too. But all he could think of to say was, "Because there's nobody better at breaking into a box."

"Is that so? You haven't proven that to my satisfaction. Listening and probing at triple verbal's impressive, but you still didn't find anything."

"We don't know yet that there's anything to find."

"If there isn't?"

He shrugged. "I go back to Nogales where I can't hear GenDyne scream."

"Dinner," she said as their main course arrived. Cardenas's chicken was simply and elegantly presented. He hadn't realized how hungry he was. Eight hours of sponging had left him drained. He hardly heard her as he reached for his silverware.

"Maybe later we'll see how efficient a prober you really are."

He intuited that easy, but didn't let on that he had. Steam hissed from the chicken as he sliced into it.

* * *

Each day he went into the GenDyne box and each evening he left the corporate offices feeling more baffled and disturbed than when he'd gone in. Not that Mermaid wasn't full of accessible, fascinating information: it was. It was just that none of it was of the slightest use.

Hypatia was of inestimable help, explaining where he didn't understand, patiently elaborating on concepts he thought he understood but actually did not. GenDyne assigned her to him for the duration of his investigation. It pleased him. He thought it might have pleased her. After a week even she couldn't keep his spirits up. He could be patient, he was methodical, but he was used to progressing, even at a creep. They weren't learning anything. It was worse than going nowhere; he felt like they were going backward. Nor could he escape the feeling that somebody somewhere was laughing at him. He didn't like it. Cardenas had a wry, subtle sense of humor, but not where his work was concerned.

Anything that smelled of potential he recorded for playback later at half speed, then quarter speed. His senses were taut as the high string on a viola. He listened for the slightest off pronunciation, the one quirky vowel that might suggest an amorphous anomaly in the data. He found nothing. Mermaid was clean, neat, tidy, and innocuous as baby powder.

On the eighth day he gave up. The solution to Crescent's murder wasn't going to be found in his files.

It was time to look for parallels. He'd spent too much time at GenDyne, but he was used to finding hints, clues, leads wherever he searched and this utter failure rankled. Perhaps the Parabas box would be more revealing. It was time to access Noschek's work.

Half on a whim he requested Hypatia's assistance. It was a measure of the importance GenDyne attached to his work that they agreed immediately. As for Spango, she was delighted, though she concealed her pleasure from the dour company official who pulled her off her current project to give her the news. It was like a paid vacation from designing.

When the people at Parabas were told, they went spatial. They'd sooner shut down than let a GenDyne Designer into their box. Important people in LaLa talked reassuringly to their counterparts in Sao Paulo. It was agreed that finding out what had happened to the two Designers was paramount. There were certain safeguards that could be instituted to ensure that Parabas's visitor saw only the contents of Noschek's files. Parabas consented. Agua Pri was overruled. Hypatia would be allowed in. But nobody smiled when Cardenas and his GenDyne "spy" were admitted to the dead Designer's office.

It was larger than Crescent's, and emptier. No charming domestic scenes floating above this desk. No expensive colorcrawl on the walls. Noschek had been a bachelor. Barely out of Design School, top of his class, brilliant in ways his employers hadn't figured out how to exploit before his death, he'd been the object of serious executive headhunting by at least two European and one Russian multinat in the three years he'd been at Parabas.

Hypatia'd read his history, too. As she looked around the spartan office her voice was muted. "Nobody becomes a Senior Designer before thirty. Let alone at twenty-five."

Cardenas called up the pictures they'd been shown of the vacuumed Designer. Noschek was tall and slim, still looked like a teenager, a beautiful Slav with delicate features and the soulful dark eyes of some Kafkaesque antihero. Something in all the holos struck Cardenas the instant he saw them but he couldn't stick a label on it.

The Parabas box was approximately the same size as Gen-Dyne's. Noschek's key was Delphi Alexander Philip. The voice of the wallscreen was deep and resonant, instantly responsive to his sponging, as he scanned the meteoric career of the young Designer. Parabas's Security team had been at work 'round the clock. Some of the information would reveal itself only when Hypatia was out of the room. The South Americans might be cooperative but they weren't stupid.

Each time Hypatia left she took Charliebo with her for company. She liked playing with the dog and the hair she scratched out of him gave Parabas's cleanteam fits. Each day brought them closer together. Her and Charliebo, that is. Cardenas still wasn't sure about her and himself.

It didn't matter whether she was present or not. Three days of hard sponging saw him no nearer any answers than when he'd stepped off the induction shuttle from Nogales.

On the fourth day the screen went hostile and nearly took him with it.

He was sponging off a hard-to-penetrate corner of Philip, down in the lower right corner of the box. Hypatia had gone outside with Charliebo. Biocircuits spawned the same steady, sonorous flow of information he'd been listening to for hours, revealing themselves via concomitant word streams and images on the wallscreen. If he'd been watching intently he might have had time to see a flicker before it declared itself, but as usual he was most attuned to aural playout. Maybe that saved him. He never knew.

Wind erupted into the office, blasting his thinning hair back across his head. On the screen the visual had gone berserk, running at ten speed through emptiness, reason gone, bereft of logic and organization. A dull roaring pounded in his ears. Dimly he thought he could hear Charliebo frantically howling outside the door. There was a hammering, though whether outside the screen-secured door or inside his brain he couldn't tell. He pressed his palms over his ears, letting the vorec spill to the floor.

Something was coming out of the wall.

A full-sense holo, a monstrous alien shape thick with slime and smelling of ancient foulness, an oozing shifting mass of raw biocircuitry-generated false collagen that pulsed slowly and massively, booming with each heave. Reflective pustles lining its epidermis bristled with raw neural connectors that reached for him. The hammering on the door was relentless now and he thought he could hear people shouting. They'd have to be shouting very loudly indeed to make their presence known through the sound-dampened barrier.

He tried to block out sight and sound of the ballooning

apparition. The door was security sealed to prevent unauthorized access. Where was the override? It was manual, he remembered. He fought the sensorial assault, tears streaming from his eyes, as he struggled to locate the switch.

Bits and pieces of the false collagen were sloughing away from the nightmare's flanks as it drifted toward him. The amount of crunch required to construct a projection of such complexity and reality had to be astronomical, Cardenas knew. He wondered how much of Parabas's considerable power had suddenly gone dead as it was funneled into this single gate.

As it drew near it became mostly mouth, a dark, bottomless psychic pit that extended back into the wall, lined with teeth that were twitching, mindless biogrowths.

He stumbled backward, keeping the desk between the projection and himself.

Near the center of the desk a line of contact strips were glowing brightly as a child's toy. The expanding mouth was ready to swallow him, the steady roar from its nonexistent throat like the approach of a train inside a tunnel.

Hit the release. The voice that screamed at him was a tiny, fading squeak. His own. *The yellow strip.* He extended a shaky hand. He thought he touched the right strip. Or maybe he fell on it.

When he regained consciousness he was lying on the floor staring at the ceiling of Vladimir Noschek's office. Someone said two words he would never forget.

"He's alive."

Then hands, lifting him. The view changing as he was raised. He broke free, staggering away from his saviors, and they waited silently while he heaved into a wastepail. When someone pressed a mild sting against his right arm he looked around sharply.

There must have been something in his expression that made the man retreat. His response, however, was reassuring. "No combinants. Just a pickmeup. To kill the nausea and the dizziness."

He managed to nod. The Brazilian turned to whisper to his companion. Like images drawn on transparent gels Cardenas saw collagen teeth bursting before his retinas as the afterimage of the monster continued to fade from his memory.

"You scared the shit out of us." Hypatia was watching him carefully. She looked worried.

Something heavy and warm pressed against his legs. He glanced down, automatically stroked Charliebo's spine. The shepherd whined and tried to press closer.

"What happened?" one of the medicos asked as he closed his service case.

Somehow Cardenas managed to keep down the anger that was building inside him. "It was a psychomorph. Full visual, audio, collagenic presence. The works. Sensorium max. *Why the hell didn't somebody tell me this was a tactile screen*?"

"Tac. . .?" Both medicos turned dumbfounded stares on the east wall. It was Hypatia who finally spoke.

"Can't be, Angel. Designers aren't given access to tactile. Nobody is. Uses too much crunch. Besides, that's strictly military stuff. Even somebody as valued as Noschek wouldn't be allowed near it."

The chief medico looked back at him. "No tactiles in Parabas S.A. I'd know, my staff would know. You sure it was a psychomorph?" Cardenas just stared at him until the man nodded. "Okay, so it was a psychomorph. I don't know how, but I'm not in a position to argue with you. I wasn't here."

"That's right, *compadre*," Cardenas told him softly. "You weren't here."

"You gonna be alright?" The same stare. The medico shrugged, spoke to his assistant. "So okay. So we'll sort it out later. Come on." They left, though not without a last disbelieving glance in the direction of the now silent wallscreen.

As soon as the door shut behind them and sealed, Hypatia turned on him. "What's going on here? That couldn't have been a psychomorph that hit on you. There isn't enough crunch in the whole Parabas box to structure one!"

"That's exactly what I've been thinking," he told her quietly. "But it was a psychomorph. The most detailed one I've ever seen. I do not want to see it again. It was a trap, a guard, something to wipe out the nosy. It almost wiped me."

She was watching him closely. "If it was as bad as you claim, how come you're standing there talking to me instead of lying on the floor babbling like a spastic infant?"

"I—felt it coming. Intuition. Just in time to start closing down my perception. I can do that, some. When you're blind for six years you get practice in all sorts of arcane exercises. I sidestepped it right before it could get a psychic fix on me and managed to cue the door. It must have cycled when you all came in. They can't fix on more than one person at a time. Takes too much crunch."

"I thought that kind of advanced tech was beyond you."

He met her gaze. "Did I ever say that?"

"No. No, you didn't. I just assumed, you being a duty cop and all—people do a lot of assuming about you, don't they?"

He nodded tersely. "It helps. People like to think of cops as dumber than they are. Some of us are. Some of us aren't. I don't discourage it."

"How old are you, anyway?"

"Fifty-three in two months."

"Shit. I thought you were my age. I'm forty-one."

"Part of it is being small. You always look younger."

"What kind of a cop are you, anyway, Cardenas?"

He was searching beneath the desk, straightened when he found the vorec mike. "A good one."

You just didn't brew a full-scale sensorium max hostile psychomorph out of a standard industrial box, no matter how big the company. Hypatia knew that. Not unless Parabas was into illegal military design and under questioning the company reps did all but cut their wrists to prove their innocence. Cardenas believed them. They had more to lose by lying than by telling the truth.

He was beginning to think brilliant was too feeble a word to use to describe the talents of the late Vladimir Noschek.

But Noschek had made a mistake. By slipping something as powerful as the psychomorph into Philip storage he'd as much as confessed to having something to hide, something to protect. Ordinarily that wouldn't have mattered because the sponger discovering it would have been turned to neural jelly. Only Cardenas's training and experience had saved him. With Hypatia at his side he continued to probe.

They solved the secret of the commercial wallscreen quickly enough. It was numb as a sheet of plywood—until you went someplace you weren't wanted. Then you tripped the alert and the screen went tactile. It was one hell of a modification, worth plenty. Cardenas could have cared less. He wasn't interested in how it was done as much as he was *why*. The camouflage was perfect.

A tactile screen could spit back at you. One that looked normal and then became tactile was unheard of. The Parabas executives went silly when the medicos made their report. They wanted to take the screen apart immediately, resorting to furious threats when Cardenas refused. Gradually they gave up and left him alone again. They'd get their hands on Noschek's last innovation soon enough.

If it *was* Vladimir Noschek's last innovation, Cardenas thought.

There was also the possibility that the dual tactical-numb screen wasn't the work of Noschek at all, that it had been set up by whoever had vacuumed him. The psychomorph could have been inserted specifically to deal with trackers like Angel Cardenas. Or it could be a false lead spectacular enough to divert any probers from the real answers.

Answers hell. He wasn't sure he knew the right questions yet.

They'd find them.

First he needed to know how a max psychomorph had been inserted into a conventional industrial box. Hypatia confirmed his suspicions about the requisite parameters.

"If you saw what you say you saw, then Noschek or whoever built the insert needed a lot more crunch than Parabas employs here in Agua Pri."

"How do you know how much crunch Parabas has here?"

"It gets around. No reason to keep it a deep dark secret."

"Assuming for the sake of discussion that it's Noschek's toy we're dealing with, could he have drawn on crunch from the home office?"

"Possible, but considering the distance it would've been mighty risky. Would make more sense to borrow locally."

"How much would he have had to steal?"

"Based on what you describe I'd say he would've needed access to at least one Cray-IBM."

"GenDyne?"

She laughed. "That's more crunch than our whole installation would use in a year. No way. Though I'd love to have the chance to play with one."

"So who on the Strip uses a Cribm?"

"Beats hell out of me, Angel. You're the cop. You find out."

He did. Fast, using Parabas's circuits to access the major utility files for the whole Southwest Region in Elpaso Juarez. His opto police security clearance let him cut through normal layers of bureaucratic infrastructure like a scalpel through collagen.

"Sony-Digital," he finally told her as the records flashed on screen. The wall's audio checked his pronunciation. "Telefunken. Fordmatsu. That's everybody."

She stared at the holoed info. "What now?"

"We find out who's been losing crunch—if we can."

They could. Word of what had happened at GenDyne and Parabas had made the corporate rounds. As soon as Cardenas identified himself and the case he was working on they had plenty of cooperation.

It was Fordmatsu. Their own Security was unaware of the theft, much less its extent, so cleverly had it been carried out. Cardenas sourced it, though. He didn't bother to inform them.

He was no accountant and he didn't want anybody sponging around until he'd finished what he'd come to Agua Pri for. Though no expert, he knew enough to admire the skill that had been at work in Fordmatsu's box. Everything had been done during off hours and painstakingly compensated for throughout the crunchlines. Neat.

"How much?" Hypatia asked him.

"Can't tell for sure. Hard to total, the way it's tucked in here and there. Weeks worth. Maybe months."

She stared at him. "A Cribm can crunch trillions of bytes a second. I can't think of a problem it couldn't solve inside an hour. There isn't anything that needs days of that kind of crunch, let alone months."

"Somebody needed it." He rose from behind the desk. "Come on."

"Where are we going?"

"Back to GenDyne. There are some sequences I ran here I want to rerun on Crescent's wall."

"What about the psychomorph?"

He put an arm around her shoulders. She didn't shrug it off. "I'm going to endrun that sucker so slick it won't have time to squeal."

It was all there in Crescent's Mermaid. If he hadn't tripped the psychomorph in Noschek's storage, they never would have found it. He leaned back in the dead man's chair and rubbed his eyes.

"Fordmatsu is out millions and they don't even know it. Somebody was running one gigabox of a sequence."

"Noschek?"

"Not just Noschek. Maybe he designed the sponge schematic, but they were both into it."

"Damn," she muttered. "What for?"

"Aye, there's the rub. That we don't know yet."

"But it doesn't make any sense. Why would a GenDyne Designer co-opt with somebody out of Parabas? You think maybe they were going to fracture and set up their own firm?"

"I don't think so. If that was their intent they could have

done it by entrepreneuring. Easier and cheaper." He leaned back in the chair and ran a hand down Charliebo's neck. "Besides, it doesn't fit their profiles. Crescent was pure company man, GenDyne do or die. Noschek was too unstable to survive outside the corporate womb."

"Then why?"

"I thought they might've been doing some work for somebody else but there's no indication of that anywhere. They did a hell of a job of hiding what they were up to, but no way could they hide all that crunch. You know what I think?" He gave Charliebo a pat and swiveled around to face her. "I think there's a box in here that doesn't belong to GenDyne."

"And Noschek?"

"Maybe there's one in Parabas, too. Or maybe the same box floating between both locations. With that much crunch you could do just about anything. *Quien sabe* what they were into?"

"So you're thinking maybe whoever they were working for vacuumed them for the crunch?"

"Not the crunch, no. Whatever our boys were using it for. Haven't got a clue to that yet." He found himself rubbing his eyes again.

She rose and walked over to stand behind his chair. Her hands dug into his shoulders, kneading, releasing the accumulated tension. "Let's get out of here for a while. You're spending too much time sponging. You try doing that and playing the analytical cop simultaneously, you're going to turn your brain to mush."

He hardly heard her. "I've got to figure the why before we can figure the how."

"Later. No more figuring for today." She leaned forward. He was enveloped by the folds of her jumpsuit and the heavy, warm curves it enclosed. "Even a sponge needs to rest."

It came to him when he wasn't thinking about it, which is often the path taken by revelation. He was lying prone on the oversized hybred, feeling the preprogrammed wave motion stroking his back like extruded lanolin. Hypatia lay nearby, her body pale arcs and valleys like sand dunes lit by moonlight. The ceaseless murmur of the Strip seeped through the down-polarized windows, a susurration speaking of people and electronics, industry and brief flaring sparks of pleasure.

He ran a hand along her side, starting at her shoulder and accelerating down her ribs, slowing as it ascended the curve of her hip. Her skin was cool, unwrinkled. Her mind wasn't the only thing that had been well taken care of. She rolled over to face him. Next to the bed Charliebo stirred in his sleep, chasing ghost rabbits that stayed always just ahead of his teeth.

"What is it?" She blinked sleepily at him, then made a face. "God, don't you *ever* sleep? I thought I wore you out enough for that, anyways."

He smiled absently. "You did. I just woke up. Funny. You spend all your waking hours working a problem and all you get for your efforts is garbage. Then when you're not concentrating on it—there it is. Set out like cake at a wedding. I just sorted it out."

She sat up on the hybred. Not all the lingering motion was in the mattress. He luxuriated in the sight of her.

"Sorted what out?"

"What Crescent and Noschek were doing together. It wasn't in the boxes and it wasn't in their files. No wonder corporate Security couldn't find anything. They never would have. The answer wasn't in their work. It was in them. In their voices, their attitudes, what they had in common and what they didn't. In what they didn't commit to storage. They shared their work but they kept themselves to themselves."

"A cop shouldn't be full of riddles."

"Have you got a terminal here?"

"Does a cow have udders?" She slid off the bed, jounced across the room, and touched a switch. A portion of wall slid upward to reveal a small screen while the vorec popped out of a slot nearby, an obedient metal eel. He walked over and plucked it from its holder, studied the screen. They were both naked, both comfortable with it and each other.

"Pretty fancy setup for a household."

"Think. I have to work at home sometimes. I need more than a toy." She leaned against him.

"Look, let me concentrate for a minute, will you?"

She straightened. He saw her teeth flash in the dim light. "Okay. But only for a minute."

He activated the screen, filled the vorec mike with a steady stream of instructions. It was slower than the Designer units he'd sponged at Parabas and GenDyne but far faster than any normal home unit. Soon he was running the files he needed from both companies. Then he surprised Hypatia by accessing Nogales. The problem he set up was for the Sociopsycultural Department at the U of A. It didn't take the University Box long to render its determination.

"There it is."

She stared at the screen, then back at him. "There *what* is?"

"Answers, maybe." He slipped the vorec back into its slot. The screen went dark. "Let's ambulate."

"What, now?" She ran fingers through her unkempt hair. "Don't you ever give a lady a chance to catch up?"

"You can catch up next week, next month." He'd found his pants and was stepping into them. "I think I know what happened. Most of it, anyway. The data make sense. It's what our two boys did that doesn't make sense, but I think they went and did it anyway."

She thumbed a closet open and began rummaging through her clothes. "You mean you know who vacuumed them?"

He fastened the velcrite of his waistband. The blue federales bracelet bounced on his wrist. "Nobody vacuumed them. They vacuumed themselves."

She paused with the velcrite catch of her bra. "Another riddle? I'm getting tired of your riddles, Angel."

"No riddle. They vacuumed themselves. Simultaneously,

via program. I think it was a double suicide. And by the way,
I'm no Angel. It's 'Ahn-hell,' for crissakes."

"That's Tex-Mex. I only speak anglo."

"Screw you."

She struck a pose. "I thought you were in a hurry to leave?"

Security let them back into GenDyne but they weren't
happy about it. There was something wrong about cops going
to work at three A.M. The guard in the hall took his time. His
helmet flared as the scanner roved over both nocturnal visitors.
Just doing his job. Eventually he signed them through.

They went straight to Crescent's office. It was the same as
they'd left it, nothing moved, unexpectedly sterile-looking
under the concealed incandescents. Cardenas found his gaze
returning unwillingly to the bright family portraits that hovered above the desk.

He flicked the vorec and brought the wallscreen online.
He warmed up with some simple mnemonics before getting
serious with the tactical verbals he'd decided to use. Hypatia
caught her breath as the wall flared, but no psychomorph
coalesced to threaten them. Cardenas was being careful, addi-
tionally so with Hypatia in the room. Charliebo cocked his
head sideways as he stared at the screen.

Five minutes later Cardenas had the answer to the first of
his questions.

"It's tactile. Same kind of concealed setup Noschek had
in his place."

"Jesus! You could warn a body."

"There's no danger. I'm not sponging deep yet. All surface.
There are ways. I was pretty sure I wasn't going to trigger
anything."

"Thanks," she said dryly.

He drove in, the words flowing in a steady stream into the
vorec as he keyed different levels within the main GenDyne
box. This time he went in fast and easy. He went wherever
he wanted to without any problem—and that was the problem.

After what seemed like fifteen minutes he paused to check his bracelet. Two hours gone. Soon it would be light outside.

Hypatia had settled herself on the edge of the desk. She was watching him intently. "Anything?"

"Not what I came for. Plenty Parabas would pay to get their hands on. I'm sure the reverse would be true if I was sponging their box like this." He shook his head as he regarded the screen. "There's got to be another box in there, somewhere. Or a section that's reading out dead."

"Impossible. You need full cryo to keep the box wet and accessible. You can't just set something like that up in the middle of an outfit like GenDyne without tripping half a dozen alarms."

"Alarms are usually set to warn of withdrawal, not entry."

"Any kind of solid insertion like that would have people asking questions."

"You can avoid questions if you can avoid notice. These guys were wizards at avoiding notice."

She crossed her arms. "I still say it's impossible."

He turned back to the wall. "We'll see."

He found it only because he had some idea what he was looking for. No one else would have glanced at it. There was no separate box. Hypatia was right about that. Instead it was buried deep within the basic GenDyne box itself, disguised as a dormant file for a biolight conveyor. When he sponged it Hypatia caught her breath.

"My God. A subox tunnel."

"I've heard about them," Cardenas murmured tightly, "but I've never actually seen one before."

"That's as close to being invisible as you can get and still be inside a box." She was standing close to the wall now, examining the holo intensely. "Whoever engineered this was half Designer and half magician."

Cardenas found himself nodding. "That's our boys." He studied the slowly rotating cylindrical schematic. "The key question is, where does it go?" He was set to start in when

Hypatia stopped him, walking over to put a hand on his arm and block his view of the screen.

"Maybe we better get some help. This is way over my head."

"And therefore mine, too?" He smiled. "You don't have to know how to build a plane to know how to fly one. I can handle it."

"More psychomorphs? And who knows what else."

"I'm ready for it this time. Hypatia, I can intuit *fast*. Anything starts coming out of that tube I'll just dry out."

"Man, I hope you know what you're doing." She stepped aside. Together they stared as he spoke into the vorec and started down the tunnel.

They encountered no traps, no guards. Smart. Oh, so smart, he thought to himself. Make it look like an ordinary part of the box. Make it look like it belongs. Normalcy was the best disguise.

They wouldn't put him off the track with that. Because even though he didn't understand the how yet, he knew the why.

Hypatia asked him about it again. "I still don't get this double suicide business."

"It's what they were." He spoke between commands to the vorec, waiting while the wall complied with each sequence of instructions. He was tense but in control. It was one lonnnng tube.

"Noschek particularly. He was the key. You see, part of the tragedy was that they could never meet in person. Security would have found out right away and that would have finished both of them. It meant they could only communicate through the joint Fordmatsu link they established. Like in the old times when people sent information by personal messenger. It was too complex, too involved, too *intense* for it to just be business. There had to be more to it than that. And then when I couldn't find any business at all, that clinched it."

"Clinched what?"

"The fact that they had to be lovers. Via the Fordmatsu link. Crescent and Noschek were homosexual, Hypatia."

She went dead quiet for several minutes before replying. "Oh, come on, Angel! Crescent had a family. Two kids."

"He was latent. Probably all his life. That's why I had to run double profiles together with what I suspected through the Sociopsycultural box up at U of A. It confirmed. I'm sure if we had time to go over their lives in more detail we'd find plenty of other clues.

"You told me Crescent was a trueglue GenDyne man. I'm sure he was. GenDyne's about as liberal as its multinat counterparts. Which is to say, not at all. Two Fundamentalists on its Board. Crescent knew if he strayed once it would put endo to his career. So he stayed in the closet. Covered himself thoroughly for the sake of his future. I've no doubt he loved his wife. Meanwhile everything proceeded the way he'd probably dreamed it might. Gradually his tendencies faded as he buried himself in his family and work.

"Then Noschek came along, possibly through a casual social hookup. A brilliant, wild young talent. Pretty to boot. And they got to know each other. Most relationships develop. This one exploded."

"So they 'related' through box links?"

He nodded. "Try to imagine what they must have gone through. It's all there in their voices, in the stuff I was able to sponge from the months before they vacuumed. They knew they couldn't meet. Crescent knew it would ruin him. I don't know if that bothered Noschek—he didn't seem to give a damn for social conventions. But he cared about Crescent. So they built this Fordmatsu link out of stolen crunch."

"They wouldn't need all that crunch just to maintain a private communication."

"Exactly. So they started discussing their problem, fooling around with all that excess crunch they had access to. Meanwhile their relationship just kept getting tighter and tighter at the same time as they were becoming increasingly frustrated with their situation.

"Eventually they found something. Noschek was the innovator, Crescent the experienced constructor. They discovered a way to be together. Always."

"Through mutual suicide?" She shook her head. "That doesn't bring people together. It doesn't profile, either. Noschek sure, but Crescent was too stable to go for that."

"How stable do you think he would have been if his wife had ever found out? Or his kids? The only way to spare them the disgrace was to make it look like a murder. That way our boys would be able to slip away untarnished and untroubled."

"So they figured out a way to vacuum themselves? Papier-mâché wings and brass harps and the whole metaphysical ensemble?"

"No. They're vacuumed, alright, but they're not gone. They're together, like they wanted to be. Together in a sense no one else can understand. I wonder if they fully understood it themselves. But they were willing to take the risk."

"That doesn't make any sense."

He took a deep breath. "Consider all the crunch they'd been siphoning from Fordmatsu. Then consider Noschek's hobbies. One of them is real interesting. You ever hear of MR?"

"Like in 'mister'?"

"No. Like in morphological resonance."

She made another face. "Gimme a break, Angel. I'm just a lousy Designer. What the hell is morphological resonance?"

"The concept's been around for decades. Not many people take it seriously. The scientific establishment has too much invested in existing theories. That doesn't put off those folks who are more interested in the truth than intellectual comfort. People like Noschek. When I found out he was into it I did some reading.

"A long time ago somebody ran a bunch of rats through a series of mazes in Scotland. The same mazes, over and over, for much longer than anyone would think necessary to prove a point. Each time the rats ran a maze they managed it a little faster."

"That's a revelation?"

"Consider this, then." He leaned forward. "Some folks in Australia decided to run the same maze. Identical as to size, distance, configuration, reward at the end, everything. The first time they tried it the rats ran the distance just a hair faster than the first time their Scottish cousins ran it. Then they repeated the experiment in India. Same thing. The Indian rats got off to a quicker start than did the Australians. What do you get from that?"

She looked bemused. "That Indian rats are smarter than Scottish or Australian rats?"

He shook his head impatiently. "It wasn't just done with rats and mazes. Other similar experiments were run, with identical results. For the scientific establishment that hasn't been conclusive enough. But it hasn't stopped theorists from making proposals."

"It never does."

"It was suggested that each time an intelligent creature repeats something exactly as previously done, it sets up a resonance. Not in the air. In—spacetime, the ether, I don't know. But it's there, and the more it's repeated the stronger and more permanent the resonance becomes, until it spreads far enough to affect the identical pattern no matter where it's repeated. That's where the rats come in. The theory holds that the rats in Australia were picking up on the resonance set up by the maze runners in Scotland. Then again in India. Which is why they ran the maze slightly faster at the start and progressively thereafter for the duration of the experiment. The resonance gave them a head start.

"MR's been used to explain a lot of things since it was first formulated, up to and including mankind's exponential progress in science and technology. According to the theory we're working on one hell of an expanding resonance. Each

time we come up with something new it's because we're
building on thought patterns or experimental methodology
that's been repeated in the past."

"What's all this got to do with our departed Designers?"

"You told me what a supercooled Cribm can do. Trillions of
crunch a second. Unthinkable quantity in an hour. Incalculable
content in a day. Cribms are used to crunch whole bushels of
problems. Suppose you set it to process just one problem,
instead of hundreds. Set it to run the sequence over and over,
trillions upon trillions of times. Think of the resonance you
could set up. Enough to last a long time without fading. Maybe
even enough to become permanent." He nodded toward the
flickering, flaring wallscreen.

"You could set it up in there."

She followed his gaze, found herself whispering. "Crescent
and Noschek?"

"Safe, together. As a dual resonance. Patterns of memory,
electrical impulses: what we call memory. Reduced to streams
of electrons and run over and over until brought separately
into being as a floating resonance inside a box. Not in formal
storage, exactly. Different. Independent of the box systems
and yet localized by them. So they'd hang together even
better. They reduced themselves to a program the Cribm could
process and set it to repeating the designated patterns, using
all that stolen crunch. They're in there, Hypatia. In a box built
for two."

"That's crazy." Her mouth was suddenly dry. For the first
time she felt uncomfortable in the cool office. The door, the
unbreakable window, were keeping them in instead of others
out. "You can't box a person."

"Resonance, Hypatia. Not a program as we conceive of
one. Repetition creates the pattern, brings it into existence.
You vacuum yourself into the Cribm and it repeats you back
into existence. As to whether that includes anything we'd
recognize as consciousness I don't know."

"If it's a pattern the Cribm can repeat, maybe it could be—
accessed?"

His expression was somber. "I don't know. I don't know how they're in there, if they're just frozen or if they have some flexibility. If they're anything more than just a twitch in spacetime, Hypatia, they've found immortality. Even if the power to the box fails the resonance should remain. It may be restricted in range but it's independent of outside energy. The resonance maintains itself. Don't get me started on thermodynamics. The whole thing's cockeyed. But it's not new. People have been discussing it for decades."

"Easier when they're talking about rats," she murmured. "You say they're restricted by the confines of the box. Can they move around inside it?"

"You've got the questions, I haven't got the answers. We're dealing with something halfway between physics and metaphysics. I don't know if I should consult a cyberneticist or a medium." He indicated the tunnel on the screen. "Maybe when we get to the end of that we'll find something besides a dead end."

She joined him in monitoring their progress. The tunnel seemed endless. By now it should have pushed beyond the confines of the GenDyne box, yet it showed no signs of weakening.

"They took a terrible chance. They worked awfully hard to hide themselves."

Cardenas stroked Charliebo. "Maybe all to no end. The theories I've enumerated might be just that. It's more than likely they're as dead as their physicalities."

"Yeah. But if there's anything to it—if there's anything *in there*—they might not like being disturbed. Remember the psychomorph."

"I'm pretty sure I can handle the screen if it goes tactile again, now that I've got an idea what to expect. I can always cut the power."

"Can you? You said this resonance, if it exists, would remain whether the power was on or not."

"Their resonance, yes, but cutting the power would deprive them of access to the system—assuming they're able to interface with it at all. They could have inserted traps like the psychomorph before they vacuumed themselves."

"And you think you can access this resonance?"

"If it exists, and only if it's somehow interfaced with the GenDyne box."

Three hours later the rising sun found them no nearer the end of the tunnel than when they'd begun. Thirty years earlier Cardenas could have hung on throughout the day. Not anymore. There were times when mandatory retirement no longer seemed a destination to be avoided. This was one of them.

He let Hypatia drive him back to her place and put him to bed. He fell asleep fast but he didn't sleep well.

A psychomorph was chasing him; a gruesome, gory nightmare dredged up from the depths of someone else's disturbed subconscious. Frantically he tried to find the kill strip to shut down the power, but someone had removed them all from the control panel in front of him. And there were screens all around him now, and on the ceiling, and beneath his feet, each one belching forth a new and more horrible monstrosity. He curled into a fetal ball, whimpering as they touched him with their filthy tendrils, hunting for his psychic core so they could enter and drive him insane. One used a keyword to open the top of his skull like a can opener.

He sat up in bed, sweating. Beneath his buttocks the sheet was soaked. A glance at the holo numerals that clung like red spiders to the wall behind the bed showed 0934. But it was still dark outside. Then he noticed the tiny P.M. to the right of the last numeral. He'd slept the whole day. His mouth confirmed it, his tongue conveying the taste of old leather.

"Hypatia?" Naked, he slid slowly off the hybred and stumbled toward the bathroom, running both hands through his hair. Water on his face helped. More down his throat helped to jump-start the rest of his body. He used one of her lilac towels to dry himself, turned back to the bedroom.

"Hypatia? Charliebo?"

She wasn't in the kitchen, nor the greeting room. Neither was the shepherd. Both gone out. Maybe she'd taken him for a walk. Charliebo was well trained, but his insides were no different from any other dog's. He'd go with her. Dog and Designer had grown close to each other this past week.

He knew she was worried about him. While he would have preferred to have spared her the concern, he was pleased. Been a long time since anyone besides Charliebo had really cared about Angel Cardenas, and Hypatia had better legs than the shepherd. Sure he was stressing himself, but he could take it. All part of the job. Experience compensated for the lack of youthful resilience. He could handle any traps Crescent and Noschek had left behind, even if she didn't think he could.

He stopped in the middle of the room. Concerned about him, yeah. About his ability to deal with another psychomorph or worse. Under those circumstances what would a caring, compassionate woman do? What could she do, to spare him another dangerous, possibly lethal confrontation? Couldn't an experienced, younger Designer follow the path he'd already found and thus keep him from possible danger?

Shit.

He was wide awake now; alert, attuned, and worried. He didn't remember getting dressed, didn't recall the short elevator ride to the subterranean garage. Sure enough, her little three-wheeler was gone. She wasn't out for an evening stroll with Charliebo, then. His lungs heaved as he raced for the nearest induction station. It would be faster than trying to call for police backup.

Besides, he might be getting himself all upset over nothing. If he was wrong, he'd end up looking the prize fool. If he was right, well, Hypatia was highly competent. But he'd much rather play the fool.

The only thing that saved him was his three decades on the force. Thirty years experience means you don't go barging into a room. Thirty years handling ninlocos and juice dealers and assorted flakes and whackos says you go in quietly. Go in fast and loud and you might upset somebody, and they might react before you had time to size things up.

Thirty years says Hypatia would have secursealed the door to the office. When he discovered it wasn't, he opened it as slowly as possible.

The lights were on low. The wallscreen was alive with flaring symbols and muted verbal responses. In the center was the tunnel, twisting and glowing like an electrified python. He picked out the desk, the muted holo portraits of Wallace Crescent's abandoned, innocent family.

Hypatia was on the floor. There was enough light to illuminate the figure bent over her. Enough light to show the still, motionless lump of Charliebo lying not far away.

Quiet as he'd been, the figure still sensed his presence. It turned to face him. The blend suit melted into the background but he recognized the triple lenses that formed a multicolored swath across the face instantly. All three primaries were down and functioning now.

Cardenas saw that Hypatia's jumpsuit was unzipped all the way to her thighs. A handful of secrylic had been slapped across her mouth, muffling her as it hardened. More of the so-called police putty bound her ankles and wrists. She tried to roll toward him but found it hard to move because the figure had one knee resting on her hip.

His gaze flicked to Charliebo. The shepherd's chest was still, the eyes vacant. Cardenas's vision blurred slightly and his teeth moved against each other.

"Don't," said the flashman. He didn't sound uncertain tonight. He glanced down at Hypatia, then smiled up at the federale. "Worried about baby? No need to. Maybe. Come in, close the door behind you. If I'd sealed it you would've gone for help. This way I only have to deal with you, right?" He leaned slightly to his left as if to see behind Cardenas.

"Right." Cardenas kept his hands in view, his movements slow and unambiguous. Hypatia stared at him imploringly. He saw that she'd been crying. Easy, he told himself. Keep it easy.

But it wasn't easy, it wasn't easy at all.

"You so much as twitch the wrong way, Federale, and

she'll be sorry." The flashman was grinning at something only he found amusing. "You should've stayed in bed, man."

No hurry. No emergency. Not yet. He moved off to his right. "Why'd you have to kill my dog?"

He didn't get the response he expected. The flashman let out a short, sharp laugh. "Hey, that's funny! You don't know why it's funny, do you? I'll tell you later, after I'm through here. Or maybe I'll let her tell you." He glanced quickly at the screen, not giving Cardenas any time. "Got to be an end to this damn tunnel soon."

"All I have to do," Cardenas said softly, "is shout, and Security'll be down on you like bad news."

Again the unhealthy, relaxed laugh, a corrugated giggle. "Sure they would, but you won't shout." He held something up so Cardenas could see it.

A Scrambler. Military model, banned for private use. Of course, banning was only a legal term. It didn't keep things from falling into the hands of people who wanted to have them. When everything else failed the police used less powerful versions of the same device to subdue juice addicts who outgrabed. It put them down fast but it didn't do permanent damage. Fourth world military types used powered-up models for less reputable purposes. The flashlight-shaped device scrambled nerve endings. The federale issue paralyzed. The military model could break down neurons beyond hope of surgical repair. In hand-to-hand combat it was much more efficient than a knife or bayonet and a lot easier to use. You didn't have to penetrate. All you had to do was make contact.

"Go ahead and shout, if you want to." The flashman calmly touched the Scrambler to Hypatia's exposed left breast.

She thrashed. Hard, but not hard enough to break the secrylic. She whined loud enough to penetrate the slightly porous gag. The flashman showed the Scrambler to Cardenas again, ignoring the heavy, gasping form beneath him.

"See here? No safety. A simple modification." Cardenas bit down on his lower lip hard enough to draw blood but he kept his hands at his sides, his feet motionless. "You shout, you move funny, and I'll shove this between her legs. Maybe it won't kill her, but she won't care."

"I won't shout." Only practice enabled him to reply calmly, quietly. His fingers were bunched into fists, the nails digging into the flesh of his palms.

"That's a good little sponger."

"How long?"

Again the grin. "Since Crescent vacuumed himself. Since the investigation started." He looked ceilingward, toward the low-key incandescents. "One bulb up there's got an extra filament. Records and holds. Can't broadcast each pickup. Security would track it. Just a five-second high-speed burst when a receive-only passes outside the door. Me. Just enough range to clear the room. Not real noticeable, if you know what I mean. I walk by once a day, stop long enough to sneeze, move on. Hardly suspicious. Then playback at normal speed when I'm home. Nothing very entertaining until you showed up."

"You've been monitoring her place, too."

The flashman chuckled. "Sure now. You think I knew she'd be coming here tonight via e.s.p.? Expected you to snore on. Been getting some custom design work of your own?"

He took a step forward. The flashman lowered the Scrambler slightly. Cardenas saw Hypatia's eyes widen, her body tense.

"Ah-ah. Don't want to make me nervous, Federale." Cardenas took back the step, his expression bland, screaming inside. "Glad you started pushing your hypothesis here, man. I would've been in a world of hurt if you'd started down this tunnel over at Parabas. Guess I'm just lucky."

"What do you want?"

"Don't games me. I want whatever's at the end of this tunnel. A subox, resonance, miracle crunch. Access. Same thing you've been after. 'Morphological resonance'. That's wild, man. Immortality? Wilder still. Relax. You'll cramp your head."

"And if you find it?"

The flashman nodded toward the side of the desk. Cardenas saw the metal and plastic plug-in lying there. He couldn't see the cable link but knew it must be present, running to jacks beneath the desk.

"One sequence. I finalize, then do a quick store-and-transfer. Anything valuable and there ought to be plenty." He licked his lips. "Never seen a tunnel like this. Nobody has. Construction crunch alone's worth all the trouble this has taken."

"But you want more."

The flashman smiled broadly. "Man, I want it *all*."

"You'll take it and leave?"

The man nodded. "I'm a thief. Not a vacuumer. Not unless you make me. I get what I've been after for months and I waft." He gestured with the Scrambler. Hypatia flinched. "I'll even leave you this. Memories can be so much fun."

"Assuming there's even anything in there to steal, what makes you think you can transfer a resonance?"

"Don't know unless you try, right? If you can get something in you ought to be able to get it out. It's only crunch. Key the box, key the transfer, and it's off to friends in the Mid East."

"Immortality for the petrochem moguls?" Cardenas's tone was thick with contempt.

"That's up to them to figure out. Not my department. I just borrow things. But they'll have the subox, if there is one. Our farseeing pinkboys are going on another trip. Suppose they can slip in and out of any box they're introduced to? My employers could send them on lots of vacations. A little crunch out of First EEC Bank, some extra out of Soventern. With that kind of access petrochems will seem like petty cash stuff."

Cardenas shook his head. "You *are* crazy. Even if they're in there in any kind of accessible shape what makes you think you can force Noschek and Crescent to do what you want?"

"Also not my job. I'm just assured it can be done, theoretically anyway. But then this is all theory we're jawing, isn't it? Unless I find something to transfer." He turned to the screen. "Starting to narrow. I think maybe we're getting near tunnelend. Stay put." He rose, straddling Hypatia. He wasn't worried about her moving. The Scrambler assured that.

The petitpoint pusher in Cardenas's shirt pocket felt big as a tractor against his chest. The little gun would make a nice, neat hole in the flashman's head, but he couldn't chance it. If he missed, if he was a second too slow, the man could make spaghetti of half Hypatia's nervous system. Thirty years teaches a man patience. He restrained himself.

But he'd have to do something soon. If there was a subox holding a resonance named Crescent and Noschek he couldn't let this bastard have it.

The flashman removed a vorec, still clutching the Scrambler tight in his other hand. He was trying to watch Cardenas and the wallscreen simultaneously. Hypatia he wasn't worried about. As Cardenas looked on helplessly the man spoke softly into the vorec. Patterns shifted on the wall. The steady thrum of the aural playback became a whispery moan, an electronic wind. The tunnel continued to narrow. They were very near the end now and whatever lay there, concealed and waiting. The flashman smiled expectantly.

Teeth began to come out of the wall.

The flashman retreated until he was leaning against the side of the desk, but it was an instinctive reaction, not a panicky one. Clearly he knew what he was doing. Now he would use the key Cardenas had concocted following his own previous confrontation, use it to dry up the power to the psychomorph. Then he could continue on to the end of the tunnel, having bypassed the psychic trap. Cardenas watched as he spoke into the vorec.

The teeth were set in impossibly wide jaws. Above the jaws were pupilless crimson eyes.

The flashman spoke again, louder this time. A third time. The psychomorph swelled out of the wall, looming over Hypatia. She lay on her back staring up at it. It ignored her as it concentrated on the flashman.

"No. That was the key." He turned toward the federale and Cardenas saw stark terror in the man's eyes. "I took it off the filament. THAT WAS THE KEY!" He screamed the words into the vorec. They were the right words, the proper inflection. Then he threw the Scrambler at the opaque shape and turned to run.

The psychomorph bit off his head.

As a psychic convergence it was the most realistic Cardenas had ever seen. The decapitated body stood swaying. Blood appeared to fountain from the severed neck. Then the corpse toppled forward onto the floor.

He stood without moving, uncertain whether to run, shout for Security, or reach for the petitpoint. The psychomorph turned slowly to face him. It was a thousand times more real, more solid than any convergence he'd ever seen. He thought it stared at him for a moment. Since it had no pupils it was hard to tell. Then it whooshed back into the wall, sucked into the holodepths that had given it birth. As it vanished, the tunnel collapsed on top of it.

It was quiet in the office again. The wallscreen was full of harmless, flickering symbology. The speakers whispered of mystery and nonsense. On the floor behind the desk the flashman lay in a pool of his own blood, the expression on his face contorted, his eyes bulged halfway out of their sockets. His ragged nails showed where he'd torn out his own throat. Cardenas searched through bloodstained pockets until he found the applicator he needed. Then he turned away, sickened.

The applicator contained debonder for the secrylic. First he dissolved the gag, then went to work on Hypatia's wrists. She spat out tasteless chunks of the pale green putty. She was crying, brokenly but not broken. "Jesus, Angel, Jesus God, I thought he was going to kill me!"

"He was. Would have." He ripped away sagging lumps of putty and carefully began applying debonder to her bound ankles. "After he'd finished his transferring. Nothing you or I could have said would have mattered. He couldn't leave any witnesses. He knew that." He glanced up at the innocuous wallscreen. "You saw it?"

"Saw it?" She sat up and rubbed her wrists, then her chest where the Scrambler had been applied. There was a painful red welt there but no permanent damage. She was breathing in long, steady gasps. "It was right on top of me."

"What did it look like?"

"It was a psychomorph, Angel. The worst one I ever saw. The worst one anyone ever saw." She was looking past him, at the torn body of the flashman. "Talk about tactile. It really got inside him."

He finished with her ankles. "Don't try to stand yet."

"Don't worry. Jesus." She moved her legs tentatively, loosening the cramped muscles. Behind her was harmless holospace. If you put out your hand you'd touch solid wall. Or would you? Could they be sure of anything anymore? Could anyone?

"Another trap." Cardenas too was studying the wall. "The last trap. Why'd he kill Charliebo? He said he didn't." He found he couldn't look at the pitiful gray shape that lay crumpled alongside the desk.

Hypatia inhaled, coughed raggedly. "He didn't."

That made him look down at her. "What?"

"He was telling the truth. He didn't kill Charliebo. The tunnel did. Or the subox working up the tunnel. I don't know." She rubbed her forehead. "The psychomorph was the last trap, but there was one inserted in front of it. It—it was my fault, Angel. I thought I knew how to protect myself. I thought I was being careful, and I was. But there's never been a tunnel like that one. Part of the tunnel, before the psychomorph.

"I was worried about you, Angel. I thought maybe you were working too hard, too long. You don't see yourself, sitting there, reciting in that unbroken monotone into that damn vorec. It's like it becomes an extension of your own mouth."

"It does," he told her softly.

"So I thought I'd do some tunneling myself. Before the

psychomorph there's ... I don't know what you'd call it. Not a psychomorph. Subtler. Like a reciprocal program. It vacuumed the first thing it focused on." Maybe he couldn't look at the shepherd's corpse, but she could. "If Charliebo hadn't been where he was it'd be me lying there instead of him. The tunnel, the program—it vacuumed him, Angel. Sucked him right out. It was quick. He just whimpered once and fell over on his side. The look in his eyes—I've seen that look on people who've been vacuumed. But I didn't know you could do it to an animal.

"The crunch consumption figures went stratospheric. Maybe it was the same program Crescent and Noschek used to vacuum themselves. I guess they figured that'd be one way to make sure anybody who got this close to them wouldn't bother them."

"Charliebo wasn't an animal."

"No. Sure he wasn't, Angel." It was quiet for a long time. Later, "I cut power and figured out a key to get around the trap. I thought it was the last one. That's when he came in." She indicated the flashman. "But it wasn't the last one. The psychomorph was. There were no warnings, no hints. I never would've seen it coming. Neither did he."

"Not surprising, really. I wonder if it would've made a difference if you or I had tripped it first. Because it wasn't a psychomorph."

She gaped at him.

"It wasn't a psychomorph," he said again. "It was a— let's call it a manifesting resonance. A full-field projection. I asked you if you saw it. I asked you what it looked like. You had a ventral view. I saw it face on." Now he found he was able to turn and look at the shepherd's corpse.

"It wasn't a psychomorph. It was Charliebo."

She said nothing this time, waiting for him to continue, wondering if she'd be able to follow him. She could. It wasn't that difficult to understand. Just slightly impossible. But she couldn't find the argument to contradict him with.

"Their last defense," he was saying. "If you can't lick

'em, make 'em join you. You were right when you called it a reciprocal program. Vacuum the first intruder and use him to keep out anybody thereafter. That way you don't expose yourself. Co-opt the first one clever enough to make it that far down the tunnel. It could've been you. It could've been me. They were luckier than they could've dreamed. They got Charliebo.

"Noschek and Crescent. Couple of clever boys. Too clever by half. I won't be surprised if they've learned how to manipulate their new environment. If so, they'll know their reciprocal's been triggered. Maybe they'll try to move. Somewhere more private. Maybe they can cut the tunnel. We're dealing with entirely new perceptions, new notions of what is and isn't reality, existence. I don't think they'd take kindly to uninvited visitors, but now Charliebo's in there somewhere with them, wherever 'there' is. Maybe they'll be easier on him. I don't think he'll be perceived as much of a threat."

She chose her words slowly. "I think I understand. The first key triggered the reciprocal program and Charliebo got vacuumed. When that bastard tried to go around it . . ."

"He got Charliebo's resonance instead of Crescent or Noschek. I hope they enjoy having him around. I always did." He helped her stand on shaky legs.

"What now?"

As he held on to her he began to wonder who was supporting whom. "I could go back to Nogales, close the file, report it officially as unsolvable. Leave Noschek and Crescent to their otherwhere privacy. Or—we could dig in and try going back."

She whistled softly. "I'm not sure I can take any more of their surprises. What if next time they come out for us instead of Charliebo? Or if they send something else, something new they've found floating around down in the guts of otherwhere?"

"We'll go slow. Put up our own defenses." He jerked his head in the flashman's direction. "He seemed to think his people would know how to do it. Maybe with a little help from GenDyne's box we can, too."

"Then what?"

"Then we'll see."

It took almost a month for them to learn how to recognize and thereby avoid the remaining tunnel guards. Crescent and Noschek failed to manifest themselves when the end of the tunnel was finally reached. There was a subox there, alright, but it proved empty. The Designers' resonances had gone elsewhere. There were hints, clues, but nothing they could be certain of. Tiny tracks leading off into a vast emptiness that might not be as empty as everyone had once suspected. Suggestions of a new reality, a different otherwhere.

They didn't push. There was plenty of time and Cardenas had no intention of crowding whatever the two men had become. It/They was dangerous.

But there was another way, clumsy at first. It would take patience to use it. What was wonderfully ironic was that in their attempt to defend themselves, to seal their passage, Crescent and Noschek had unwittingly provided those who came after with a means for following.

First it was necessary to have Hypatia jumped several grades. GenDyne balked but finally gave in. Anything to aid the investigation, to speed it along its way. What the company didn't know, couldn't imagine, was what way that investigation was taking. And Senior Designer Spango and Sergeant Cardenas weren't about to tell them. Not yet. Not until they could be sure.

Besides which the additional salary would be useful to a newly married couple.

There was uncertainty on both sides at first. Gradually hesitation gave way to recognition, then to understanding. After that there was exchange of information, most but not all of it one-way. Once this had been established not only GenDyne's box was open to inspection but also that of Parabas S.A. and through the power of the Fordmatsu link everything one would ever want to access. Including an entirely new state of reality that had yet to be named.

Cardenas and Spango played with it for a while, kids enjoying the biggest toy that had ever been developed. Then it was time to put aside childish things and take the plunge into that otherwhere Crescent and Noschek had discovered, where existence meant something new and exciting and a whole universe of new concepts and physical states of matter and energy danced a dance that would need careful exploration and interpretation.

But they had an advantage that could not have been planned for, one even Noschek and Crescent hadn't had.

They wouldn't be jumping in blind because they wouldn't be alone.

Hypatia had pulled her chair up next to his. It was quiet in the office. The climate conditioning whispered softly. The walls and door were secursealed. Cardenas had checked every light bulb by hand.

In front of them Crescent's wallscreen glowed with symbols and figures and words, with rotating holo shapes and lines. The tunnel stretched out before them, narrowing now to a point. Only it wasn't a point; it was an end, and a beginning. The jumping-off place. The ledge overlooking the abyss of promise.

They knew what they wanted, had worked it out in the previous weeks. They knew where they wanted to go and how to get there.

Cardenas took Hypatia's hand in his, squeezed tightly. Not to worry now. Not anymore. Because they weren't doing this alone. He raised the vorec to his lips.

"Fetch," he said.

From the Notebooks of Angel Cardenas:

Okay, so I didn't lose a dog: I gained a program. You just have to be careful how you use programs. Handle With Dare. In the old days messing one up cost you some time, maybe a little money, maybe even a lot of aggravation. Programs have changed a lot. Now *they* can mess with *you*. Now one could cost you your life.

Isn't progress wonderful?

I miss Charliebo, but then there are people I miss, too. *Compadres* who never made retirement, ladies who met guys involved in more stable professions, people I've met on the street. Funny thing, about the streets throughout the Strip. They eat people. Gobble them up, digest them, discard them so thoroughly you can't even find the droppings. That's because there's way too much money around. Me, I always tell the ninlocos and the *sararimen* and the floaters that you can't take it with you.

I understand MegaMolly and Sapience France are working on that program right now.

With so much credit abounding and so many diversions readily available, reality tends to get short shrift. I love that word, *homber*. You know the term? As in, "Do you got enough shrift?"

Money drives the Strip. Lights it, feeds it, clothes it, runs it. Everybody wants the stuff. Abstract numbers. Extra zeros. Most people work for it, but some try to take. I try to brake those who take. They say break. You say tomato, I say tomahto, you say potato, I say *patata*. Let's call the whole thing off, otherwise I got to read you your rights. Only, my rights come first, citizens second. Why? Because a dead cop's not going to do you any good.

I don't have to intuit that, and neither should you.

Thirty years on the Strip, you get a feel for people, for money, and for how they interact. Every once in a while you cross a situation where the money's actually incidental to the incident, if you follow my meaning. This time I didn't follow the meaning, and it cost. Not me. Some kids. It always costs the kids.

Near as I can historize, that's one thing that hasn't changed in the last seven thousand years or so.

Heartwired

"CAN' you do nothin' about the little null, Paco? He makes me nervous, the way he lookin' at me tonight."

Her neg glanced back down the street. Sure enough, the kid was still trailing them, his big puppy eyes focused forlornly on Paco's main pos. But the monsoon had stopped for the *noche*, it was an under forty-d night, and he was feeling expansive.

"Just ignore him, 'Nita. All the guys stare at you the same way."

"Yeah, but they just look. They don' follow me around."

He slipped his arm around her waist and pulled her close. "He's harmless. Hey, if it's really bothering you, I'll get rid of him, but he's handy to have around sometimes. Like a shorter in your pocket. Think of him like that; like a tool."

"I guess it doesn't matter." She smiled at her neg. Paco was big, almost as big as Contrario, and certainly the handsomest member of the Teslas. And he'd picked her to be his pos. She leaned against him, feeling the tautness of his body beneath the shirt, content as they splashed through the puddles deposited earlier in the day by the intense July storm, her charged boots keeping her feet and legs dry. Negs, and poses side by side, the gang marched cockily up the street, commandeering the sidewalk from regular citizens as they kept a wary watch out for other ninlocos.

Wormy G hung five meters back, keeping close to the armor glass of the storefronts, savoring each glimpse of Anita up ahead. In his heart he knew he was the only one, the only male on the planet who truly appreciated her. To him, she was more than merely attractive; she was a logarithmic sculpture, the essence of beauty, a magnet for all that was good and fine and clean in this sordid world. He knew that his existence barely impinged on her consciousness, that she hardly knew he was alive. It did not matter. *He* was aware of *her*.

She was the sun: intense, life-giving, pulsing with warmth and light. He was content simply to orbit her.

And there was the little secret they shared.

When by chance her gaze happened to encounter him, her expression invariably turned to one of disgust or indifference. He couldn't understand why. Maybe he wasn't a sinewy elemental force like Paco, but neither was he invisible or disfigured. Nor was he a spacebase junkie. It puzzled him how after having shared their secret for so long, she could continue to ignore him so utterly.

He did understand why they wouldn't let him into the gang. While he wanted desperately to belong, he didn't fit the image of a ninloco. He was too sane, too respectful of reason and logic, if not convention. They let him hang around because his knowledge of locks and vorecs was sometimes useful, because he could build and repair the gadgetry and toys that the gang frequently acquired by illegal means. He was tolerated, but not liked. He ignored their snickering insults because it was the only way he could get close to Anita.

There were at least a dozen gangs that called Puerto Penasco home. The Teslas and Newts, the Comenciados and Vitshines along with the Sangres and Orotoros were the best organized, the ones sane enough to hang together for more than a month at a time without self-destructing. The others disintegrated and re-formed regularly, sometimes under entirely new names. They lived in a condition of colloidal anarchy, battling among themselves as often as with rivals. This made it tough on the local federales, since a gang member one week might metamorphose into an independent skim artist the next.

A blue cruiser went by, its powerful electric engine humming threateningly. Several members of the gang waved gaily at the feds inside. They knew they were invulnerable. You couldn't arrest somebody for being a member of a gang. It would violate the Thirty-eighth Amendment, or some legal thing like that.

Of course, they could hassle you. Nothin' in the Thirty-eighth Amendment against hasslin', homber. Maybe it was the heat, maybe they weren't in the mood, but, for whatever reason, the feds chose not to bother the Teslas that night. Hassling in the heat was no fun, and it was the dead middle of the July Sticky.

Wormy G did not hate Paco. Hate was a mature emotion to be visited only on worthy targets. It would've been wasted on a brain-damaged blob of steroidal mush like Anita's misbegotten neg.

He did envy him his gang tattoo; the electrified coil that danced across his tricep, spitting tattooed blood and sparks. It was too expansive to fit on Wormy's thinner arm, but would look nice on his chest. He'd thought of getting one there and keeping it hidden, like the secret he shared with Anita. His own private gang emblem. A laser wash would take it right off if it were discovered.

What stopped him was the knowledge that Paco and his fellow ninlocos wouldn't allow him the luxury of a wash. They'd choose to remove it themselves. Slowly, with sharp knives, if they found the emblem on him or anyone else not anointed a member of the gang. So he continued to savor the idea while passing on the reality.

He turned off the mike in his cap and fingered the vorec

in the pocket of his shorts. If Anita would put on her Muse lenses, he could send her a song. He tried to gauge her mood. Sometimes she listened, but there were nights when she complained to Paco. Usually Wormy chose to take the risk. Because when Paco and the others were beating him up, he was closer to Anita. Such beatings were hardly ever dangerous. Only painful. It was no fun beating on someone who just hung limp in your hands and didn't even try to get away. Weird. Almost weird enough to qualify for admission to the Teslas.

They hung around Gordo Mike's until late; snacking on ray satay, frijoles, and grouper mole, sneering at the cleanroomies with their oh-so-tricked-out dates. Tomorrow the cleanies would vanish, sucked as if by a giant corporate vacuum back into the hi-tech plants that lined the Bahias de Adair and San Jorge, there to labor churning out products and components for the multinats that were the reason for the Montezuma Strip's existence.

Big money, hi-tech, cheap labor. The Strip drew people from all over Namerica and points south; anybody who could fly, ride, walk, or crawl to The Border. Nursing a crop of doped gallium arsenide or microbio storage proteins paid a helluva lot better than growing corn and potatoes.

Beneath the immense service sector that kept the cleanies happy were the parasites, and below them the undefinables like the ninlocos. The crazyboys. Wormy G brushed stringy black hair off his eyes. Maybe he couldn't match Paco's strength, but at least he kept himself clean.

They didn't have to get rid of him. He knew when it was time for him to fade into the shadows, when his presence began to become an embarrassment to them. He didn't much feel like taking a beating, either, so he left early, frustrated at having been unable to gift Anita with one of his compositions. But she'd never donned her Muse lenses, the thick glasses that delivered vits and sound to eyes and ears. Not in a musical mood tonight. So there would be no sharing of secrets, no interruption of regular programming by the arduously constructed broadcast unit he carried in his pocket.

Sometimes, out of curiosity, she listened. His lyrics were platitudes, uninspired if feverish. He was better at the music, good enough to hold her interest if she was sufficiently bored or indifferent.

Those brief moments, however impersonal, were a form of contact. Wormy playing, broadcasting just for Anita. It was what he prayed for, what he lived for, every day.

He made his way through the night lights and the screaming laser ads and drifting holos that implored him to buy, try, don't be a null-lined guy, down to where the towering codos lined the beach. The factories and assembly plants and research facilities lay to the north and east, the beach having been reserved for the cleanies who could afford to live facing the waters of the Golfo Californio instead of the dry inland desert.

The surrounding security gates kept out the likes of thieves and muggers, but not Wormy G. It wasn't hard to get in. The system was verbally cued. The voices of individual codo owners keyed the gates. Wormy had spent a couple of days with an absolutely faz specially rebuilt Siemens modified directional mike recording the voices of codo owners as they came and went. After that, it took no time at all to install selected settings in his voice-recognition unit.

He approached a side gate, checked to make sure the night patrol wasn't around, and keyed the vorec. Out came the voice of a plump, middle-aged mask sculptor. The gate analyzed, acknowledged, and popped. He made sure to close it tight behind him.

Down under the massive concrete pilings where damp sand stunk of dead sea-things, paint cartridges, spraywall buckets, and salt-resistant polycarb binders, his boat lay concealed beneath a tarp stained with crusted liquid waterproofing. He hit the battery-powered pump and waited for it to inflate. Two minutes later he was dragging it out onto the beach, gazing at the Christmas lights of the towering codos that lined the coast all the way down to Guyamas.

There was little wave action this far up the Gulf. Salt water slapped his legs as he pushed the inflatable into the water.

Jumping aboard, he turned to activate the tiny electric motor. It wheezed to whispery life and pushed him seaward. It wouldn't make much speed, but he was in no particular hurry. His destination lay more than a hundred kilometers nearer than the cross-Gulf town of San Felipe.

Like a fiery medieval fortress, the Puerto Peñasco desalinization plant loomed out of the dark water on immense pilings, adrift on an onlooker's imagination like something from another world. It groaned and complained, the vast metallic guts emitting prehistoric sonorities. It looked as if at any minute it could abandon its footing deep within the sands of the Gulf to stride toward the land, like some monster from an ancient entertainment vit, to smash the codos and their inhabitants to pulp and rip apart the factories that stretched north along the highways.

The plant and others like it supplied fresh water to the states of Sonora and Arizona and the industries they supported along the southern portion of the Strip.

Beneath the plant itself, clinging to the near impenetrable jungle of intake tubes and valves, switching pumps and cleaning stations and filtration tanks, were isolated habitats. Thrown together out of scavenged wood and metal and plastics, they were home to those few individuals independent and resourceful enough to eke out an existence underneath the facility.

If you could work fast enough and camouflage your place well enough to avoid the attentions of company Security, you had access to free sewage in the form of the Gulf below and plenty of fresh water, which could be unobtrusively drawn off from the check taps on the major pipes that snaked toward the beach from the east side of the plant.

There was food, too. Fish congregated near the surface, away from the disorienting sonics that made underwater life around the deepwater intakes untenable. Except for the threat of an encounter with Security, you were safe. But you had to like the salt smell of the Gulf, the perpetual dampness, and be able to tolerate the rattle and boom of the plant, which never stopped, never shut down.

Wormy G tied his boat up beneath the gaping maw of an old, broken piling that looked like a leviathan's half-extracted tooth. It was too much trouble for the company to tear down, so they left it hanging and rusting for future maintenance specialists to worry about. He took the weighted end of the rope he carried aboard and threw it up and over the lowermost pipe. The weight pulled the rope, which was attached to a nearly massless nypron ladder. After securing it with a quick-release clip, he ascended. Legs straddling the pipe, he flicked the release and pulled the ladder up after him.

Monkeylike, he made his way up through the dense, rusting forest of pipes and conduits until he reached a service walkway. A quick glance revealing that it was unoccupied, he vaulted the railing and hurried along homeward.

His shelter was constructed of plastic panels epoxied to the circular interior of an old transfer pipe. It was tall enough to stand up in, and the opening could be closed by a hinged section of pipe he'd cut out with a borrowed torch long ago. No passerby would suspect that someone was living within.

After latching the doorway, he turned on the air cooler. Out in the Gulf this time of year, there was no need for heat at night, only cooling. As always, it was humid and sticky. Tomorrow he could look forward to another day of temperatures approaching forty degrees and humidity up around ninety.

The cooler struggled manfully. Eventually he slept.

He spent the morning working on the bioprobe he'd invested six months in rebuilding. When his eyes began to hurt, he decided to go for a visit, carefully avoiding maintenance and tech crews until he reached the big globular float that hung suspended from a single cable over a patch of dark, roiling water. Three times he rapped softly on its eggshell-white flank, paused, then repeated the pattern.

The unsuspected opening in the old float's side gaped, and he was greeted by a wary Taichi-me. He had his glasses on as usual, Wormy noted disapprovingly.

"You got to cut down on the vits," he told his friend as he climbed inside the converted float. "I keep telling you, you spend too much time sucking that slop. Your brain's gonna turn to tapioca."

Taichi-me wore a sheepish look as he removed the Muse lenses. He owned at least a dozen pairs, all tuned slightly differently, including a powerful Keemsang arc unit that Wormy had reluctantly helped him to restore. It could pick up direct Sat broadcasts instead of just the local air pollution.

Next to his friend, Wormy G loomed large. Taichi-me was a skinny, bony half-Korean, half-Mex kid who kept himself in vit wafers and food by selling ashore what he could fish from the waters beneath his float home. Not seafood, but industrial salvage that drifted down with the current from the plants farther north. Sometimes he even came up with stuff that had made it all the way out the mouth of the Colorado. It wasn't much, but Taichi-me didn't need much. He hardly ever even went ashore anymore, preferring to lie snug and secure in his float, mezed by his glasses, bungoed out on vits.

He was also the nearest thing Wormy G had to a best friend.

"So how'd it go, G?" Taichi-me never called his friend Wormy. "Did you get to see her? Did you get to talk to her." His eyes got wide. "Did you get to *touch* her?"

"Fair. Yes. No. Are you kidding? I just tagged along the way I always do." He lowered his voice to a conspiratorial whisper. "She *did* look at me once, and I know that she saw me, and she didn't say anything to that stupid neg Paco."

"Hey, that's great, that's plus, that's *muy* solid!" Delighted, Taichi-me leaned back on some of the moldy pillows that lined the interior of the float.

"Better than getting beat up." Wormy grinned.

Taichi-me turned to rummage through a pile of smelly equipment, produced a box of five-centimeter-square LCD screens.

"Look what I netted this morning. What do you think, G?"

Wormy took the plastic container and broke the seal. Most of the screens inside had sustained some water damage, but those in the center of the pack had been protected by the ones on the outside and might still be capable of accepting a charge. He told Taichi-me as much.

"I thought they might be worth a couple of bucks." The skinny kid sounded hopeful. "Are they color?"

"Let's see."

Wormy moved to Taichi-me's box and plugged one of the salvaged screens into an unused vit port. It flickered but lit. The resultant picture was serviceable but not good. The second one was better. The rest were useless.

He had to explain it all because, as an infant, Taichi-me had lost his sight in an accident, and the cheapjack job his long-since-gone parents had bought into provided for the cheapest of replacements. So Taichi-me's thirdhand prosthetic lenses permitted him to see the world only in black and white. He retained a few pitiful early-childhood remembrances of color, which were fading rapidly with age.

Wormy agreed to take the two usable screens into town and sell them at Moritake's. Since they were color, they might get as much as three dollars for the clean one, a buck for the slightly damaged. Come evening he bid his friend good-bye, then boated back to shore to conceal his deflated craft and hunt up the Teslas.

He had a new song for Anita, but first he played back his favorite wafer for his own enjoyment. He always did that before broadcasting to her. It was his little secret. Theirs revolved around the songs he composed and transmitted only to her. She was the only one who could hear them because he aimed his directional transmitter only at her glasses. He knew she received them because, when each had ended, she would turn to glance back at him. Occasionally she even smiled.

He lived for those smiles, for the sight of her backturned face with its reflective eyeshadow highlighting her beautiful green eyes and the thermosensitive lipstick whose color intensified with the minutest rise in her body temperature. Wonderful were those special moments, as if the two of them were playing a private joke on the rest of the gang, on the whole world.

Because only Anita could hear his songs. The little device he had built, had cobbled together out of bits and parts and scavenged knowledge and the skills inherent in his small, delicate fingers, was that precise. She could be leaning right up against that crazy Paco, and he wouldn't hear a thing. Only his Anita.

He eased it out of his shirt and aimed it, using the little add-on telescopic unit to line it up, and then he transmitted. He saw her twitch once, glance back in his direction, then look away. Her glasses rode her face. She was hearing the wafer, he knew. Hearing the song he'd composed only for her.

He never knew if she liked them, but she must have liked something about them because she didn't complain, didn't send Paco or any of the other ninlocos back to smash the sender. He always trembled slightly when he was transmitting for fear she might do just that someday, or that he might otherwise accidentally offend her. But what was there to offend? He was careful not to reach too far, too high in his lyrics, not to make demands or even requests. In the songs he sent, he did not exist. Only her. They extolled her beauty, that was all. Her grace and her light. What girl could find such compliments displeasing, irrespective of their source?

He followed at a respectful distance as the gang ducked under a particularly insistent clot of ambient advert neon. Tendrils of light reached for them, clutching at their hearts and their pockets. They ignored it and strode through, the advert colors illuminating their slick shirts and brazenly colored shorts and boots, reflecting metallically from the receiver suspenders the guys wore.

Suddenly they halted, as if on command. Wormy frowned. Unified responses were alien to the gang. Surely they weren't reacting to an ad. He approached closer than usual, trying to see what had so caught their attention.

When chaos took over, he found himself swept up in the middle of it.

Sangres. A dozen or so of them, out for a night's mischief stroll, looking to cause some midnight miseria. There was no time for talk, for discussion, for reason. Clever homemade weapons magically appeared on both sides; the knives, the delicate little vibratos the girls carried in their culottes, the blue-and-purple titanium-niobium jewelry honed to razor sharpness for double duty.

Wormy found himself caught, swept up in the *terremoto*, unable to break clear. He hunted desperately for a way through, simultaneously trying to protect himself and his precious, irreplaceable transmitter, his one link to his beloved Anita. Spotting a garbage bin, he managed to slip the transmitter under its support rack, where it would be out of harm's way.

Someone must have smashed him from behind, or maybe he was tripped and he just hit the pavement wrong. In any case, he went down hard and out.

When the sleep went away, strange faces hovered like orbiting satellites above his own, haloed by bright lights. But they were no angels. They wore blue cool caps with integral snap-down, light-amplifying nightshades, short-sleeved blue shirts, and tropical blue slacks over running shoes. Federales.

One of them held an object in a Teflon glove. Half of it was clotted with something like stale honey. The pointed half.

"Why'd you do it, kid. Won't you crazies ever learn?"

"Do what?" Wormy mumbled dazedly. He sat up slowly, gaping dumbly at the knife.

There were a couple of speedbikes and a cruiser nearby,

and lights. Lots of lights, which did nothing to illumine the intimidating mutter of adults talking in low tones. The Teslas were gone. So were the Sangres, except one. He lay on his back, one leg crossed comically across the other, arms splayed on the pavement. Fleshy archipelagoes in a sea of his own blood.

"Come on, *niño*, let's go." Strong hands under his shoulders, lifting him up. As consciousness returned, he began to make connections.

"Hey, that's not my knife," he told them anxiously. "I don't even own a knife, homber. I don' kill nobody. You the ones who are crazy."

Another fed showed him a micropolaroid. "Prints on knife. Your prints. Knife in your hand. Sorry, *niño*. We got a match. You got shit."

Wormy was waking up real fast since someone had started running his guts through a garbage disposal. "Hey, that's crazy, homber! That don' make no sense."

"I didn't think you ninlocos liked to make sense," the tech replied. "I thought you liked to make crazy."

"No, hey, no." He began to kick, to howl, but he had about as much chance of breaking free of the big fed as he did of winning the Sinaloa lottery.

They threw him in the back of a cruiser and let him scream all he wanted to in the soundproofed compartment, let him pound on the opaqued glass and dig at the nyproy upholstery. By the time they reached the station, he was exhausted from fighting, unable to cry.

He let them lead him through the bureaucratic maze, refusing to respond to questions, ignoring the faces that poked into his own with varying degrees of concern, hostility, boredom. Let them book him for murder. Allowed them to put him in a holding cell, where he ignored the cheers and jeers of fellow juvie inmates. The other occupants of his cell ignored it all in favor of continued sleep. It was late. One rolled over, squinted indifferently in his direction, coiled back to sleep.

Wormy stumbled into the farthest corner and stood there,

staring at the smooth, antiseptic polystyrene wall. He was still numb, he was not cataleptic. His brain continued to work.

Some Tesla had gutted the Sangre. Then they had unconscioused Wormy and planted the bloody knife in his hand for the federales to find. That much was simple, obvious enough. Of course, there was no hope of the federales believing such a story. It was a tale any ninloco would tell to try to save his skin. No one would listen to a dumb street kid's excuses. They had his prints on the knife; that was all they needed. There were no witnesses to the killing except the members of both gangs, and why should they say anything to save him? He wasn't even a gang member. Just a goofy citizen unlucky enough to be in the wrong place at the *equivocado* time.

They would send him to Hermosillo, to the juvie farm there. With luck he might get out in four years. If the other inmates didn't make tacostuff out of him first. Wormy knew he'd have nothing going for him in facility, nothing to offer except his body, which wasn't particularly attractive. It wouldn't matter. They would chew him up and spit him out, and nobody would give a shit, nobody at all.

Paco. It helped to think about the sneering, good-looking neg. Maybe Paco had put the knife in his hand. Paco would do something like that. Maybe he was even the killer. Wormy felt better. It helped to have something to hate (he discovered he could hate Paco now). Something to focus his tormented thoughts on. He concentrated on Anita's neg; on his grinning, handsome, ugly face; on his arm, which was always around *dulce* Anita. The muscular, powerful, tattooed arm that Wormy often envisioned feeding to the hammerheads that haunted the pilings beneath the desal plant.

A bored voice approaching. "Danny Mendez; let's go." Wormy turned. A tired guard stood outside the grille. Probably just getting off shift; indifferent to his surroundings, thinking of home. "C'mon, *niño*, get your lazy ass in gear."

Wormy's eyes flicked to the occupied bunk bed. Its occupant slept soundly. Instinctively, he moved forward. It was dark; the guard was into himself. This probably wouldn't go any

farther than the gate, he knew, but he had nothing to lose by
finding out. Maybe a kick or a fist in the groin when he was
discovered, but he could deal with that. It lay in the future.

The guard hardly glanced at him. ''Got your street clothes
on; good.'' He pivoted.

Wormy followed, hardly daring to breathe. Was there a
chance? Everything had happened real fast. Time enough
for confusion to linger. This wasn't an adult prison, wasn't
maximum-security *nada*.

The guard led him through the gate, into the jail's outer
offices. Danny Mendez, Wormy told himself. The name blazed
itself into his brain. I am Danny Mendez, and I need, want,
deserve to get the hell out of here.

He tried to keep his head down without being obvious
about it. The checkout clerk was equally busy, didn't bother
to look up from her box screen. She assumed that the guard
knew what he was doing. The guard assumed likewise of the
clerk.

They had him sign for the personal effects of the innocent
Mendez. Wormy accepted them without protest. A little
money, a credcard he could jerk around, a cheap Indonesian
watch. A packet of thermosensitive condoms, a half-pack of
sense sticks. He pocketed it all.

The guard led him to the back door of the jail, mumbled
something about staying out of trouble, and nudged him out
into the night.

Wormy stood there a moment, staring at the damp, humid
back street. Then he started walking. Not too fast. Probably
they wouldn't discover the mistake until Mendez awoke or
somebody expecting him on the outside started making
inquiries.

Only after he hit the alleys did he start running. He ran
until his heart threatened to burst through his sallow chest,
ran until he had to stop because the pain in his throat was
choking him. Then he cautiously began to retrace his steps,
until he was back at the scene of the fight.

The feds were gone, along with the corpse of the unfortunate

Sangre. The transmitter was where he had secreted it, untouched and unharmed. He slipped it back into the front pocket of his shorts and headed for the beach.

Taichi-me found him in his pipe, working under a battery-powered light. "Hey, G, I ain't seen you in days, homber? What you doin'?"

Wormy said nothing, did not look up. He didn't have the right equipment, didn't have decent parts, and it was hard doing what he was trying to do. But he'd thought about it a lot. It was possible. He could do it. Paco was his inspiration. Taichi-me moved close to peer over his friend's shoulder.

"That's your girl toy, ain't it?"

"Shut up," Wormy muttered.

The younger man backed off. "Take it easy. Didn't mean nothing." He looked hurt. Wormy sighed.

"It's Okay. I'm just having a hard time." He turned back to the improvised workbench. "I'm going looking for somebody. Not Anita."

"Sure." Taichi-me shrugged. "You let me know if I can help, okay?"

"You can't. Not with this. I just need time."

"Sure, homber. I'll wait. Vit you later."

"Yeah, right."

He knew the feds would find him eventually if he stayed in Penasco. After they realized their mistake, they'd start broadcasting the holos they'd taken of him. Sooner or later somebody would recognize one and call him in. Except for Taichi-me, he knew he couldn't rely on the discretion of the desal plant's inhabitants. Not where real reward money was involved. He had to find out what he needed to know before that happened, had to finish some things while he still had time.

It took him plenty days and still he wasn't sure it would work. But he didn't see how he could make it any better. He went looking for the Teslas.

He didn't find them, and when he went later that night to talk it over with Taichi-me, his friend was gone. Where the big float that the kid had converted into a home had hung, there was only a frayed cable, dangling in the humidity like a severed nerve. Flying fish darted through the Promethean pilings below while the moon hinted at the ghostly presence of mantas.

"Taichi-me! Goddamn it!" He wrung his hands. Had they pried him out first or just cut him free, not realizing that there might be a living, breathing human being inside? Had the float been salvaged or just dumped?

"He's okay, *niño*." Wormy whirled. Two big desal guards stood on the catwalk behind him, blocking his escape. "We got him out first. Trespass is a misdemeanor. He'll be out in a few months."

"Had to scrag his junk, though." The other one made a sniggering noise. "Should have seen him cry over that crap."

Wormy knew that that crap consisted of all Taichi-me's earthly possessions, everything he'd been able to scavenge or buy with his pitiful earnings over the past three years. Junk. That's how they think of us, he thought. We're just junk, barnacles to be scraped off the pilings and fed to the bottom dwellers. Garbage.

One of the men started toward him. "Come on, now, *niño*. Don't make no trouble for us, we won't make no trouble for you."

Wormy started to retreat, fumbling for his transmitter as he did so. "Go play in the ooze, *pendejos*."

The man's expression darkened. "Don't get smart with me, sperm trash." He glanced meaningfully at the calm, receptive water below. "You could have an accident."

"So could you," Wormy stammered with false bravado as he desperately aimed the transmitter.

The man stopped as if he'd run headlong into a ten-ton block of ice. Then he screamed and grabbed his ears. His partner looked on in shock. Wormy turned and ran, sliding down a pipe to the next catwalk below, jumping a three-meter gap to dig his way into a maze of piping and tubing. Security did not pursue. His last sight of the man on the catwalk showed him kicking and moaning as his dazed companion bent over him. After a while he looked over the side of the catwalk, but by then Wormy was away and gone.

His greatest fear was that they would send a boat out after him. His little inflatable's radar silhouette was slight enough to be overlooked, but they might trap him with a spotlight scan.

While almost silent, his craft's tiny motor was not very powerful. Knowing that they could catch him easily, he was a writhing knot of anxiety until he finally beached the inflatable beneath the massive codos that lined the shore. Without thinking, he went through the motions of deflating and hiding it, wondering as he did so if he'd ever be able to make use of it again.

He'd hurt a guard, maybe badly. The modification of his transmitter had been driven by a theoretical notion of its potential. Now he had some idea of what it could do. So would the feds once his unfortunate victim was examined. He was no longer just a juvie parasite on the desal plant's backside. He was a genuine threat. They'd leaven the search for him with some real intensity.

Hugging the transmitter like an injured baby, he hurried off into the city.

None of the locals knew Cardenas personally, but he didn't have to introduce himself. His reputation preceded him. Besides, any federale who survived into his fifties automatically acquired the respect of his colleagues.

Cardenas wandered into the room, his blue eyes searching. His big black drooping mustache saddled him with a perpetually hangdog expression. Not that melancholy wasn't present in his personality, but it was a consequence of his job, not his appearance. He considered the doctor, the local lieutenant, and the man lying in the hospital bed.

They had asked him to come down from Nogales because they had run into something they weren't familiar with and couldn't explain. Whenever this happened, people usually

found their way to Cardenas. It was a responsibility he
accepted with resigned grace. After so many years on the
force, he had long since grown used to the attention, the
sideways glances, the whispering behind his back.

At least his unglamorous appearance (he did not look good
on the vits no matter how they photographed him) allowed
him to maintain a low profile. This pleased him. It was his
experience that federales with high media exposure had a
tendency to have their careers violently cut short by excitable
ninlocos or runners in search of revenge, reputation, or both.

After thirty years of working the Strip, he'd seen a lot, but
nothing quite like the report on this little coastal contretemps.

He gazed down at the guard. The man was twice his size,
massive and muscular. He looked competent enough. Then
he spoke to the lieutenant. "Some kid did this?"

The officer nodded. "That's what the comedown says. They
were excising squatters from the Desal Tres out in the Gulf;
the pipes out there are home to antisocs and weirds of every
kind. This guy and his partner were in the process of netting
another one, when suddenly the ninloco points some piece of
box junk at him, and his head goes berserk."

"I read the report." Cardenas looked back at the man in
the bed. "Music, wasn't it?"

The lieutenant nodded. "Nothing remarkable about that.
According to our man here, what he could make of it sounded
like your usual babbling contemp trash. It wasn't the music
per se that was responsible for the injury, though. It was the
way it was broadcast. Or maybe received. It was more than
just directional. His *compadre* never heard a thing. The lab's
been working on possibilities, but they're still baffled. Presum-
ably the ninloco knows how he did it, but he got away."

"And now he's out in the city somewhere, and everybody's
nervous he might decide to play with his toy again."

"*Exactamente*, Sergeant." The officer looked down at his
stocky colleague. "The other guard got a good look at him.
We've got a POV holo out. Interestingly, it coordinated with

that of a ninloco booked earlier for murder who was released by mistake from Eastside station."

Cardenas peered up at the lieutenant, blue eyes gleaming. "By mistake?"

The officer made a face. "Bureaucratic foul-up. They were supposed to release somebody else from the same cell. It was late; this ninloco had just been booked in; nobody did their job."

Cardenas shook his head. "And he was in for murder?"

"Sand fight, just a miseria; nobody knows. Found him unconscious with the murder weapon in his hand. Said he didn't do it, of course."

"Of course." Cardenas returned his attention to the man in the bed. "Anything else?"

The lieutenant sighed. "Damn little. Kid gave his name as Wormy G, wouldn't tell us his real name . . . if he has one. No ID number. No card, no bracelet. Typical ninloco outer. Didn't look like much. Skinny little twerp."

"Dangerous skinny little twerp," Cardenas added. "Anybody check out his claim that he didn't kill anybody?"

"Can't do much without the prime subject to question."

"Questions make these kids nervous."

The lieutenant grunted. "If you want to see it, I've got the file in my box."

Cardenas patted his shirt pocket where the police portable rested. "Already transferred. I'll call you if I need you."

"Don't you want backup, a cruiser?" the lieutenant asked him.

Cardenas shook his head. "Not right away. I know Peñasco pretty good. Been here a few times on other business. Be easier trying to find one kid melted into the wallwork if I can melt in a little myself."

"Suit yourself." The lieutenant watched the sergeant depart. He was glad when he was gone. He didn't much like Intuits, not even department types. They made him uneasy. Knowing how hard it was to lie to one kind of crimped normal conversation.

He wanted to ask the security guard some more questions, but couldn't until they were printed up. Because the man in the bed was now stone-cold deaf.

Wormy kept to the back alleys and the service ways, away from the lights. He spent the next day in a big recycle dumpster, not daring to return to the desal platform. Probably his little cozy had been discovered and vacuumed by now, its hard-won contents dumped into the Gulf alongside poor Tai-chi-me's possessions.

They might as well go ahead and dump him, too, Wormy thought bitterly. The kid was too vit bungoed to last a month in juvie hold. He'd go over the screen inside, never come out intact. He had been the nearest thing to a real friend Wormy had had, and now he was gone, too.

There wasn't much left to try to scavenge except maybe a little truth.

He found two of them, Carasco and Gray Leena, outside Compieradas's Emporium. They were leaning against the wall, sharing a sense stick and laughing and giggling. Wormy sidled out of the shadows, nervously watching the street for signs of federales.

"Hey, Carasco?"

The big Tesla turned, frowning. "Who asks?"

"Me. You know me, Carasco." Wormy stepped farther into the streetlight.

"Hey, ain't you the little freak who keeps following Anita around? Paco finds you, he's gonna grease you good, *camarón*."

"Wait a minute, Cary." Drogged by the sense stick, Gray Leena was trying to focus on the new arrival. "How come he ain't in jail?"

"Yeahhh." Carasco seemed to remember something. "How come you ain't in jail?"

"They let me go." Wormy looked past them, eyes on the street. "I got to find Anita."

Carasco laughed. He was a big kid, full of wildness and

the usual juvie sense of misplaced immortality. Nothing could hurt him; nothing could frighten him.

"Get gone. Waft. *Jojobar, camarón.*"

"I got to know. I got to ask her something." As Carasco started to turn away, Wormy made a desperate grab for his shirt.

Carasco reached around to swat him with the back of his hand, disdaining the effort required to form his fingers into a fist. Wormy went staggering back, stung. The bigger boy's expression went mean.

"You touch me again, *camarón*, and there won't be nothing left for Paco to grind."

Wormy's lips tightened. He extracted his transmitter. "Tell me where she is. Tell me now."

Carasco squinted at the device. "Or what? You gonna grease me with your box?" He took a step forward, reaching out with a massive hand. "About time somebody got rid of that piece of junk."

Wormy retreated, holding the transmitter in front of his chest like a shield. "Don't, Carasco. I don' want to hurt you."

The big Tesla laughed and continued to advance.

Wormy touched a contact. Carasco suddenly whipped around almost in midair, as if he'd been hit by a heavy-caliber slug, to land screaming on his back holding the sides of his head. Beyond, a couple of patrons about to enter the Emporium had stopped and were staring in the direction of the noise.

"Jesus!" Gray Leena bent over her neg, who was kicking and crying like an infant. She stared fearfully up at Wormy G. "What'd you do to him?"

"He was gonna hurt me. Where's Anita?"

"Try the Tiburon pier. She said somethin' about spendin' the *noche* out there with Paco." She touched her whimpering boyfriend, drew her fingers back as though his skin had suddenly acquired toxic properties. "What did you *do* to him?"

Wormy spun and ran into the night, leaving behind the lights of the Emporium, the street sounds, and the whine of an approaching siren.

Tiburon pier extended triple fingers out across a shallow portion of the Gulf. It was a mixing place, old and seedy but full of life and lights, a grand spot to stroll away a hot summer night. Rich administrators and cleanies, assemblers and maskers mixed freely on the pier with ninlocos on good behavior, poor truck farmers from inland, recycle monkeys and spacebasers. On the pier, nobody cared who or what you were. Darkness and damp dissolved away daytime discrimination. All that mattered was the soothing sound of the Golfo Californio slapping against the pilings beneath your feet, the noise and laughter and smell of greasy seafood frying in dozens of tiny shops.

Wormy was glad of the crowd. While the pier had its own private security force, patrolling federales occasionally put in an appearance.

It was busy tonight, active as it always was in the summer season. Plenty of *touristas* as well as locals out trying to beat some of the heat. Good pickings if one were inclined to a little petit larceny. But not this evening. Not for him.

He found them almost by accident, as he was about to give up and start back from the tip of the southern finger. They were standing to the left of the fishermen who methodically cast their lines over the sides of the pier more for the activity than in hopes of catching anything. Farther out on the dark sea lay the ambulatory stars that marked the location of cruising ships, pleasure craft, and shrimpers orbiting the brighter constellations of the desal plants.

Paco and Anita's embrace rendered them oblivious to such sights. Their faces were pushed tightly against each other, lips and tongues pressing, probing. Paco had his hand on the back of her glazed culottes, and she had both arms around him.

As always, the sight was almost too painful for Wormy to bear. Another time, another night, he would have fled in despair. Tonight he could not.

He stepped out of the dark place where he'd been hiding, his voice tremulous. "Anita?"

They separated, startled. Up the pier the fishermen, intent on their lines and conversation, ignored the confrontation. Paco seethed.

"What do you mean scaring us like that, you stinking little shit?" He straightened slightly, remembering. "How'd you get out of jail?"

"Luck and accident." Wormy was watching Anita, not her threatening neg. "I got to know what happened."

Paco smirked at him. "You killed a Sangre. Congratulations, *camarón*. Now waft before I call the feds."

"I didn't kill nobody. You know that." He was speaking to Anita, who regarded him the way she would something that had just spilled dead and slimy from a fisherman's pail.

"The feds think you did," said Paco. "That's good enough."

For the first time since he'd found them, Wormy locked eyes with his tormentor. "Then you know I didn't do it. You know I don't carry a knife. Who did it, Paco? Carasco? Ellioto? Sad Jerry?"

The big ninloco grinned at him. "Maybe me?"

"And you put the knife in my hand so the federales would find it."

Paco just laughed and shook his head. "You poor *camarón*. Why don't you just waft now? Maybe the feds don' find you if you can make your way as far as Hermosillo." He took a step forward. "Go on, creep, waft!"

Wormy raised the transmitter.

"Don't come near me, Paco."

"I think that's about enough."

The three of them turned in the direction of the new voice. The short man with the mustache who was standing nearby was overdressed for Peñasco's climate, sweating in his long shirt and sandals and slacks. He looked sad and unhappy, like somebody's grandfather escaped from a pension home. Older than his years.

Wormy retreated and pointed the transmitter in his direction, trying to keep an eye on Paco at the same time. "You a fed?"

"*Sí*. And you are not a murderer."

Uncertain, Wormy lowered the transmitter a little. "How you know that, mister?"

The man stared back at him, his transplanted blue eyes unblinking. His gaze was almost hypnotic and it held Wormy still. He searched the shadows behind the man, but there was no sign of other federales. It made no sense.

Then he understood. "You're an Intuit, aren't you?"

The man gestured diffidently. "I have been doing my job. Listening to what all of you have been saying, to the nuances and shadings of your voices. I know you did not kill that other boy." His voice tightened slightly. "You did hurt that man on the desal rig, though, didn't you? And the boy back in the city?"

"What are you talking about, homber?" Paco inquired, lost in the conversation, unhappy at being ignored.

"I didn't mean to," Wormy mumbled. "I didn't mean to hurt nobody. But they were gonna put me off the platform, and I had to do something, you *comprende*? I had to do something."

"It's going to be okay now. I promise you. I'll speak up for you in court. Besides, I know who killed that other boy." The blue eyes regarded Paco sadly.

"Hey, fed: you crazy, homber. I don't kill nobody. You can' prove nothin'. I don't care if you are a weird. I heard about you guys. You hear things in other people's voices, see things in their faces. That's *toro mierde*, homber." He was backing toward the railing that edged the pier.

"You put the knife in my hand," Wormy said accusingly. "You did it, Paco. You!" He raised the transmitter.

Cardenas judged the distance. He was much faster than he looked, but the boy was still far enough away to swing the device around and bring it to bear on him. Having lived six years in the kingdom of the blind, he was genuinely afraid of possible deafness. The biosurges had given him back his sight. He had no desire to go through that again at the expense of a different sense.

"You nasty little *camarón* shit! Leave him alone!" Anita stepped in front of her boyfriend. "*I* put the damn knife in your stinking stupid little hand, who do you think?" She sneered down at him." Always following me around, like a little dog. I got tired of trying to shoo you away. Then that happened, and I saw a chance to get rid of you and help somebody I loved besides. What did you think I would do?"

The younger boy stared uncomprehendingly at her. "You put . . .? But what about our secret? I thought you . . .?"

She laughed sharply. "What, those stupid little songs you kept sending through my glasses? You can't even sing. I always told Paco about them afterward. We had some good laughs."

The kid's voice was as dry as the Sierra San Pedro Martir, a sick, unhealthy rasp. "You told him? You told *him* my songs, our songs?"

"Shit, what you think, *camarón*? Why you think I didn't have him take that toy away from you and throw it into the Golfo the first time you pull that? Because you kept me laughing. Because you were so funny. But not so funny that I didn't think you'd look better with the knife in your fingers when the federales congealed."

"Oh." Wormy stood there, swaying a little, as if keeping time to an unheard tune. Then he touched a contact on the top of the crazy, cobbled-together mass of components and wires and wafers he carried, and raised it. Too ignorant to know better, the girl just stood there, as if her sheer beauty were shield enough. Her boyfriend shrank down behind her, trying to conceal himself, trying to hide.

Cardenas moved, but he was too late. The boy's thumb convulsed on a second contact.

As he reversed the transmitter and pointed it directly at his own skull.

It was as if a giant fist had struck him under the chin. His small body arched up and back, and he did a broken half somersault, striking the ground hard, writhing and twitching like a worm on the end of a hook. Blood exploded from the sides of his head.

Cardenas kicked the transmitter out of the boy's fingers. As it went skittering across the plastic pavement, the twin LEDs on its surface winked out. The febrile, feathery wiring at one end snapped, a couple of sparks flared, and a crack appeared on the side of the case.

Breathing hard, Cardenas looked down at the skinny kid, whose twitching was already beginning to slow. He spoke without glancing up. "Don't move, please. You are both under arrest."

Paco bolted toward the bright lights of the middle pier. Cardenas pressed a switch on the police box in his pocket. The ninloco would not make it back to land.

The girl had better sense. She stood there, angry and upset, not glancing in the direction of the younger boy at all.

The parameds got there fast, but not fast enough.

"He's gone." The middle-aged woman looked up from the pathetic corpse. It was no longer bleeding from the ears. "I mean, his body's still alive, but that's all." She tapped the side of her head meaningfully. "He blew in his ears. There's pulverized bone all mixed in with the blood. I did a quickscan. The cochlea is gone on both sides, along with the ossicles, the utricle and saccule, and some of the surrounding supporting bone. The force of it drove bone fragments into the brain and caused immediate hemorrhaging. He's a vegetable."

When the lieutenant arrived, a tech was gingerly examining the transmitter, poking and prodding the damaged device. Finally he picked it up and walked over to his superiors. There was plenty of disbelief in his voice as he spoke to Cardenas.

"That kid made this?"

"So we believe," said the sergeant.

"You know how Muse glasses work? You watch the vit images in the lenses while the arms deliver the accompanying audio to the eardrum by direct transduction. The power is kept way down so that nobody can overhear and you don't

disturb others when you use the glasses in a public place."
He tapped the transmitter.

"This son of a bitch is a tunable *broadcast* transducer. It
works just like glasses, except no physical contact is necessary.
It's also overpowered by a factor of a hundred or so. No
wonder he blew his brains. His ears must have imploded. I
don't know how the hell he worked out the necessary logs
or frequencies, but me and the guys back at the lab are sure
as hell gonna find out. He made it out of junk, too. Scrap I
wouldn't give twenty bucks for." The tech looked down at
the body.

"Poor scared little *niño* was a freakin' genius. Hey, I've
rigged it with a speaker wafer. Want to hear what he killed
himself with?"

Cardenas said nothing, but the lieutenant nodded. The tech
held up a DiData control nodule he'd attached to the damaged
transmitter with an optical pass cord.

A female voice emerged from the tiny wafer grid that had
been hastily glued to the top of the transmitter. It was cracked
and disjointed, but audible. Someone had set it to crude synthesized music.

"I love you so much, baby . . . oh, do that to me, please
. . . I can't hold you tight enough . . . squeeze me harder, lover
. . . melt into me. . . ."

A shriek made them turn. Two blues were loading the girl
into a waiting cruiser, as she whirled to stare furiously at
them.

"The little shit! The dirty little *camarón*! That's me! That's
my voice. He stole my voice! Alla time he was following me,
he was stealing my voice."

They shoved her into the cruiser, shutting off her hysterical
tirade. The tech regarded both men.

"His pockets were full of stuff. Among other things, he
had a compact directional mike on him. He must've eaves-
dropped on her conversations with her boyfriend and edited
him out, cut out the parts he didn't like, added music, and
made himself his own little private fantasy chip. Something

he could listen to real intimatelike, via Muse transduction when nobody else was around. Like she was saying all those sweet things to him. His own little secret. Pretty sick, huh? The kid was pretty sick."

Cardenas looked past him to the bloodstained pavement. The parameds had already removed the crumpled rag of a body. It would not go on life support. There was no reason, no anxious relatives. No money.

"No," he muttered. "He wasn't sick."

The tech spoke up. "How would you . . .?"

"Sergeant Cardenas is an Intuit," the lieutenant explained quietly, interrupting.

"Ah. Right." The tech gave Cardenas that familiar look, the one that always slipped out before people realized what they were doing, and left, carrying the broken transmitter like a cache of precious jewels.

When he was gone, the lieutenant turned to the older officer. "You that sure he wasn't sick, Sergeant?"

"No, but it wouldn't have mattered. He died before he turned his handiwork on himself." Hard blue eyes gazed past the blood, to the dark, indifferent sea. "Over the years I've come to believe that emotions can be conveyed all kinds of ways. Call it verbal transduction if you want. The techs, they always have to have names for things." He inhaled deeply of the bracing salt air.

"The kid . . . his soul imploded before his ears did."

From the Notebooks of Angel Cardenas:

So what, you say. There's a surplus of kids. Even smart ones. Yeah, but smart and inventive are two different things. Society at large doesn't seem to prize inventiveness, originality, quite the way it should. It's only recognized when it makes money for the big companies, I guess. Sometimes I think the insignificance of originality is a canard they propagate so they can hire away all of it for themselves, and patent it, and manufacture it, and market it, and make us feel like it's something we have to have even though we obviously don't need it.

That's modern advertising. As in, "play your best canard."

I try to watch what I buy. I think I'm pretty good at it. Why, I estimate that of all my worldly possessions, no more than seventy percent are actually irrelevant to my continued happy existence. That's how I know advertising's good for me.

Actually, it's all a Jewish conspiracy. So many of the members of that tribe I know are born with guilt, or have it slathered on by relatives. The way I understand it, they take your foreskin and give you guilt in return. It's a cultural tradition. The rest of us poor *schlemiels* have to acquire our share through advertising, so we can keep up. You know the Spanish for "guilty," don't you? It's "culpable." Pronounced, "kool-pable." Two weird languages, I tell you. So near and yet so far.

One thing about some of the people I have to arrest. They never feel guilty about what they do. To them it's just business, *comprende*? They'd gladly pay taxes if the Namerican government would just leave them alone. Most of the time, they insist nobody gets hurt. Besides, is Namerica a free market, or what? They only supply what the people want. Isn't that the ancient cry of businesspeople from the beginning of time?

Why somebody buys something, and why somebody else objects to them buying it, always boils down to a fight between money and morals. Ninety percent of the time in such contests, money wins.

Sometimes even when morality wins, it loses.

Gagrito

I

AS the sifaka sang the final chorus of "White Christmas" in its creamy, ethereal tenor it dropped to one knee and spread both thin white-furred arms wide, imploring applause. The delighted heavyset woman in the stylish beige thermosuit obliged. Acknowledging the compliment by placing its right arm across its powdery white chest and executing a deep, fluid bow, the half-meter tall lemur concluded the performance by scampering back up to its blackwire cage and shutting the door behind it.

"It's breathing very hard," the woman observed uncertainly. Cuffs trimmed in brown diamond dust flashed as she gestured with perfectly manicured fingers. "Are you sure it's okay?" The light from the Gee-ee tenplus carbonide on her ring finger seemed to increase the illumination in the back of the store. Her round face bore the distinctive Ponce glow of recent collagen sculpting.

The master of the establishment appraised the sifaka professionally. Squawks and screeches issued from the multitude of cages piled three and four deep against the storeroom in which the imprisoned crawled, crept, flew, and squirmed in perpetual quest of appropriated freedoms. Some paced restlessly, their expressions motile friezes of ambulant desolation. Others snatched at fitful sleep. Despite the insistent respiratory hiss of the automatic deodorizers the atmosphere in the back room was unavoidably thick with clashing musks.

"She's fine." The owner turned to his customer, smiling reassuringly. "Their bodies adapt quickly to the necessary contortions, and they are of course unaware of the existence of the installation itself."

"That's what I've heard." The woman appeared unconvinced, but willing to be.

The merchant reached up to tap on the blackwire. The black-and-white inhabitant of the cage was too tired to flinch. "You never see the stim wires because they're laid right on top of the muscles. Loading access for the neuromotor and the voicebox is on the right shoulder, just to the side of the spine. There's a small bump, but the animal's fur hides it completely. First-class installation, brand-new animorph components. You won't find better."

"It's not the tech that concerns me." The woman eyed the sifaka hungrily. "I thought all lemurs were on the endangered species list?"

"Only certain species, and then only in parts of Namerica," the store owner assured her. "Sifakas breed well in captivity. This one's surplus stock from a Sinaloa zoo. Comes with a notarized license, all registered and legal. You can take her home without worrying."

The woman still hesitated. "I don't know. . . ."

The advocate smiled encouragingly. " 'White Christmas' is just one of a dozen traditional favorites included in the holiday song pak, and there are twenty song paks for this model available on the open market. I just happen to have the holiday pak in her now. You saw some of the tricks she can do. There's a gymnastics pak . . . sifakas are very agile

. . . and a kidkin pak, and a household assistant pak. They have opposable thumbs, you know. Very handy if you do a lot of cooking and take the kitchenaid option. You can't get that with a puppy."

"I know; but puppies are legal."

"I'll show you the certificate of release from the zoo, if you want. Of course," he added, pursing his lips and turning away with studied indifference, "if you're not interested . . ."

"I didn't say that," she said hastily. She approached the cage, which rested atop a much larger enclosure containing a quiescent golden tegu. The sifaka gazed mournfully down at her out of vast, vacant eyes.

"She's so pretty. And so much more . . . unique than a puppy."

As it was clearly no longer necessary to exert any pressure, the owner relaxed. All that remained were the formalities. "I understand you're from New York?" The woman nodded. "Imagine the reaction of visitors to your home. None of them will have anything like this."

"Dr. Fonsecu's wife has a black cockaded cockatoo that sings Italian opera while playing the piano, but I think a primate is just so much more . . . versatile."

"Very right." He reached up to unlatch the sifaka's cage. The lemur did not try to run. It had done that once before, and remembered.

A small electronic pad reposed in the owner's left hand. "Do you have a notex?" His customer nodded. "I'll transfer the instruction book and command controls." He indicated the cage. "You can manipulate her manually or via the prepro-grammed sequences. The holiday song pak comes with the purchase."

Having made up her mind, the woman gave way fully to her desires. "I'll take all the accessories you have. The kitchen pak, all the song paks; everything."

"That's going to be expensive," the store owner warned her, quietly gleeful.

"It's already expensive. Let me worry about that."

"As you like. I suppose you'll be wanting a travel cage for her, too?"

She nodded eagerly. "Something subdued and tasteful. My husband and I are at the Cantana in Tucson. I drove over this morning. Had a hard time locating your shop."

"A common complaint, but my customers always manage to find me. Being situated in an industrial district sometimes has its disadvantages." A noise from the front of the shop made him frown. In expectation of this special referral he'd closed early, and had no further appointments scheduled for that evening. "Excuse me just a minute."

He was halfway to the door that separated the front of the shop from the back when it burst inward, sending him stumbling backward in surprise. The woman blinked in confusion.

"Gluey, Twotrick, get the cages."

At first the startled owner thought a woman had spoken, but quickly saw that it was only a spanglo girl. Not more than sixteen, if that. She was skinny and blond, with eyes from which the pale blue had been drained as if by a siphon. Her skin was the color of fossil ivory, scorched in places by brown cancers that were the inevitable result of living too long beneath the merciless southwestern sun. Bony hips were all that punctuated the nervous angularity of her body.

Of much more interest was the peculiar suit she wore, gray-black like sooty steel. Including gloves, boots, and hood, it covered every part of her body except her face. A multitude of silvery wires had been woven into and were integral with the dark fabric. Gleaming, diode-spotted components were strapped to her limbs, giving her the appearance of an ambulatory entertainment center. A thin black vorec curled from the edge of the hood toward her narrow lips, bobbing like a questing worm when she moved.

Of the two boys who accompanied her one was slightly younger, the other distinctly older. Twotrick was tall, muscular, and black, with a distorted prognathous jaw that gave him the aspect of a dead pharaoh and a rumbling nose that had suffered through too many street fights. The much smaller

Gluey was stringy-haired and afflicted with the cherubic visage of a feral baby. Tiny flecks of black floated in the whites of his eyes like pepper on fried eggs, sure sign of a longtime desdu user. He blinked incessantly despite the subdued lighting.

The owner's blood pressure soared as the boys began opening the cages. Initially hesitant, animals were soon pouring out. They frolicked about the storeroom, screeching and cawing, pounding on their former enclosures, generating a din suggestive of a chorus of the recently damned.

"Gluey, get the back door." The girl's voice was unexpectedly resonant. Her stunted cohort sniffed as he ran to key the egress. As the door slid aside it revealed the interior of a large van that had been backed up to the rear of the store. Little of the access alley in which it was parked was visible. The boy's taller companion began shooing freed animals into the waiting vehicle.

The owner took a step toward him. His gun was latched under the counter, out front. "Hey, you can't do that!"

The youth whipped something short and nasty out of his back pocket, snapped his wrist. The ten-centimeter-long cylinder promptly quadrupled in length. It looked like a teacher's pointer except for the slide trigger set in the base. "Fade, animonger."

The merchant swallowed, correctly assuming that the power injector was loaded with something other than copasceptic. He was reduced to looking on as dogs, cats, birds, and exotics were alternately cajoled and guided into the truck.

"Some of them need special diets, special care. They'll die on you," he muttered accusingly. "You can't expect them to survive in the Strip."

"We'll do the best we can," the girl responded matter-of-factly. "At least they won't have to spend the rest of their lives dancing and performing to the stim of some goddamn program for some rich kid's amusement. Some of 'em will make it. There are people who'll help and won't ask questions." Her pale eyes flashed. "You've been mongering dan-specs."

"What do you care?" Helplessly he watched his priceless inventory fly, run, crawl to freedom. "Damn loco *niños*!"

"*Seguro* miro." The one called Gluey giggled as he tweaked the lock on a black macaque's cage with a pair of snips. The primate hesitated, then swung free. Twotrick urged him toward the van. Night heat poured into the storeroom, Strip fierce and unrelenting.

"Little bastards. You'll pay. I have friends, too. You'll pay."

The girl ignored him as she opened the sifaka's cage and murmured encouragingly. "It's okay. Come on out. C'mon." She extended a hand. The lemur eyed her gravely, then climbed out onto the perch of her arm.

"As we came in I heard something singing. This one?"

The shop owner sniffed derisively. "It's sold."

"Not anymore." The girl turned to the terrified older woman. "You don't want her anymore, do you?"

"N-no. Look, I don't know what's going on here. I just want to leave. Please let me leave. My husband's waiting for me back at the resort. He'll be worried. I told him I was going shopping, but it's getting late." She edged toward the doorway that led to the front of the shop, away from the rear entrance that was filled with escaping animals. "Just let me go."

Pale blue eyes considered as the girl addressed the lemur. "What do you think, little preman? Should we let her go?"

The sifaka had been preening its long, black-striped tail. Now it stopped to stare at the woman. "Kill the bitch," it said distinctly in its liquid tenor.

The matron's eyes widened. "No, it can't, you can't."

"Tear out her womb. No, let me." The lemur leaped, land-ing gracefully on the now-empty cage nearest the woman. She screamed and bolted.

"Can't you see the girl's controlling it?" But his terrified visitor didn't hear. She stumbled over a pile of bagged pet food and fell to the ground. The sifaka landed on her back, clawing at her expensive clothes. On hands and knees the woman scrabbled toward the doorway. Behind her Gluey was cracking up, his machinegunlike laugh only half natural. The girl in the suit wasn't smiling.

Bloody gouges appeared in the matron's back as the lemur's claws dug deep. She moaned as she staggered to her feet and clawed weakly at the door latch. The girl whispered something into the vorec that hovered at her lips and the sifaka released its grip on the woman's shoulders, pivoting to race toward the van on all fours.

Sobbing, the would-be customer stumbled through the portal. An instant later the merchant darted after her, thinking of the gun secured to the underside of his front counter. Twotrick uttered an oath in spanglish and Gluey's maniacal giggling ceased.

The girl reacted, the sensors proximate to her arms and legs, hips and head automatically transmitting her movements to the nearest magnified animal. The reticulated python whipped out and caught the shop owner around the legs, bringing him crashing to the floor in an explosion of supplies and empty cages. The girl's lips moved.

"Too late, *ladrón*." The python's voicebox had to work hard to generate an intelligible wheeze. "You sell no more magic animals."

The merchant flopped wildly as the python threw a coil as thick as a man's arm around his neck. It was an unnatural movement for the big snake. Ordinarily it would slip its coils around its prey's chest, patiently constricting as the quarry inhaled, suffocating it. But for the moment its muscles functioned in obedience to the girl's movements.

"Please!" Suddenly the shop owner was pleading, no longer threatening but frightened, really scared now. "You've already ruined me. Enough!"

"No," the girl murmured tightly. "No, not enough. Not this time. Not anymore, enough." Slowly she brought her arms across her chest. As she did so the snake's coil, taut as steel cable, tightened convulsively around the man's neck. He screamed. But it was late, and dark, and the buildings on the other side of the alley were silent and deserted.

Gluey giggled when the man's spine popped.

The girl turned away and rubbed at her eyes, too-tired orbs that seemed to belong to anyone but a sixteen-year-old.

"Let's finish it," she muttered determinedly. Twotrick gazed solemnly back at her and nodded.

Too much stimmed dancing had damaged the young orangutan's leg. It took the two of them to help it out of its cage and into the waiting van. City noises, Strip sounds, drifted into the empty alley. The merchant lay on his side, eyes gazing blankly at the ceiling of his storeroom, his head screwed 'round at an impossible angle. At the best speed it could manage, the python slithered off him and headed toward the alley.

II

"We've checked with the San Juana, Nogales, and Yumarado district SPCAs and the big regional animal rights activist groups. All of 'em deny any knowledge. As usual, nobody knows nothing. But some outfit in San Luis calling itself the Protectors of the Wild got a whole truckload of critters dumped on them the morning after the homicide. Half of 'em were danspecs, endangered species, and nearly all had been magified. Enough violations to seq the guy for twenty years if he hadn't already been nulled."

"You think they're telling the truth?" Cardenas gazed out the window.

The lieutenant shrugged. "Fanatic animal freaks, who knows? Usually they're about as cooperative as last week's hash. But we don't have a thing on any of them and the Yumarado office can hardly drag people in on suspicion. Some of them say that they're willing to answer questions. So Yumarado asked for my best questioner. That's you, Angel."

Cardenas didn't turn away from the view. Focus of law

enforcement on the Montezuma Strip between East San Juana and Elpaso Juarez, the Nogales Police Complex leaned west toward the distant green monument of Tumacacori. North to Phoenix, south to Guyamas, east and west to the sea, the *maquiladora* plants of the Strip ingested raw materials and basic components from around the world and through application of massive quantities of skill and labor transformed them into consumer goods, unwanted excess heat, and enough nighttime light to drown out the desert stars.

Millions of people worked in the Strip's vast multinat design and assembly facilities; mask sculptors, compilers, fabrication artists, whitecoats from all over Namerica, each hoping to rise through the ranks, each aspiring to a codo in Phoenix or Guyamas, San Juana or Felipe. In the rush to achieve, to succeed, to survive, there was little time left to devote to abstract moral crusades. Those remained the province of the truly idle, the entertainers and industrialists of LaLa or the Big CMC.

To sate their consciences they gave money, and time when it was convenient and efficacious. Then they hurried back to their sumptuous homes and careers, content that they'd done their humanitarian duty until the next TV headlines made them uneasy afresh and they sensed it was time for their next egalitarian fix. Celebrities shot up on moral rectitude.

The true animal rights activists were more dedicated. For them convictions were more than a hobby. They fought, and marched, and struggled to put across their philosophy.

But to the best of Cardenas's knowledge they didn't murder those they disagreed with. Until, possibly, now.

"What about the woman who was in the store?"

The lieutenant shrugged. "She was pretty shook up. Managed to get a quick statement out of her before her husband hustled her out of Tucson. He's some fancy doctor back East. You saw the transcript. Three crazy kids, animals that went gonzo, one that attacked her. Not much detail on the kids. One black, one white, one spanglo. Since when have ninlocos started taking an interest in animal rights?" He shook his head. "Doesn't make any sense. There's nothing in it for them. Too bad she didn't witness the actual homicide. From her description none of the intruders was big enough to have killed the owner, but that doesn't make him any less dead. Maybe there was a fourth party she didn't see. Given her state of mind at the time it's not an unreasonable assumption."

Cardenas nodded. The coroner's pictures made it look as if the shop owner had been strangled with an anchor chain.

III

He hopped an express induction shuttle west, the crowded high-speed public transport following the approximate line of the old U.S.-Mexican border. The plastic car smelled of disinfectant and spanglish fast food. The local from Yumarado Central dropped him off two blocks from the station, where a bored investigator went over the details of the murder with him one more time and finished by pumping the official line into his notex. The crunch included the address of every local organization with an interest in animal rights and endangered species.

He checked out the Friends of the Earth office first, then the Nature Conservancy people, then the Yumarado arcomplex SPCA. No one he talked to expressed much sympathy for the dead pet store owner. All were violently opposed to the semilegal concept of magimals, whether the involved was a representative of a rare species or just a common mutt. They thought the concept barbaric. Cardenas didn't argue with them; he just moved on.

He'd saved the offices of the Protectors of the Wild for last, since it was on their doorstep that the animals liberated from the pet shop had been deposited. The young man who agreed to talk to him wore the beatific expression of the self-anointed. His office was cantilevered out over the lower Colorado canal. As Cardenas took a seat an ocean-going freighter went plugging past, headed downriver on its way back to the Golfo de California. The docks where it had dropped its cargo lay farther upstream. In this part of the arcomplex the canal was lined with offices and expensive codos.

"Nice place," Cardenas commented, taking in the posters of big-eyed animals and lush rainforest that filled the walls.

"We're fortunate to have a sponsorial legacy," the young man told him. "We've already told the local police everything we know."

Cardenas smiled. He was a small man, deceptively muscular. His drooping dark mustache, flecked with gray, and his deepset eyes gave him the appearance of a commiserating basset hound. Behind that harlequin visage lurked skill, talent, and a glittering intelligence.

"I know. I don't mean to take much of your time, but just to satisfy the people in Nogales, tell me. Please." He smiled hopefully.

The younger man sighed. It was midsummer and he wore a white thermosensitive cool suit. It was ten A.M. and already the temperature outside had risen to forty-seven Celsius, on its way to a predicted forty-nine.

"Nothing much to say. The lady who opens for us every morning found one of our transit enclosures filled with new animals, each group neatly separated into compatible cages. The note pinned on the gate just said, 'Refugees: take care of them.' That's what we've been doing."

"I understand most of them have already been dispersed?"

The man nodded, looking pleased, as though he expected Cardenas to challenge him. "Police wanted them impounded as evidence, but we got an animal habeas corpus fast. Most of them are already at or on their way to appropriate parks or reserves, where they belong. The domestics are being given away as fast as we can do the operations and find homes for them. There are a lot of people who still like unmagified pets. Birds that act like birds instead of stage performers. Cats that don't do housework."

"For what it's worth," Cardenas told him, "I don't believe

in the modifications either. The best friend I ever had was a seeing-eye dog. Nobody had to program him to look out for me."

It took some of the edge off his host's attitude. "I didn't know. We've fought for prohibiting legislation ever since the technique was introduced, but it's a new area of law and getting animal rights codified is a difficult slog. Too many people haven't made up their minds yet. It's tough when your kid gets a dog for Christmas and the neighbor's boy gets a puppy that can fetch water from the bathroom, turn the pages of a book, and sing you to sleep while saying 'I'm your best friend.' It's unnatural and more than a little sick, but it sells." He made a face. "Novelty always sells."

"It hasn't been proved that the magified animal suffers," Cardenas felt compelled to point out.

"Not if it's treated properly, no. Forget for a moment that it beggars the question of animal dignity and human responsibility. We've got files of horror stories; kids overworking their magimals, exhausting them to death. Animals used for illegal purposes. Sloppy installation and maintenance work. Pornography. You name it, I can show it to you."

"We have our own files," Cardenas reminded the man.

"But not our sources. People will come to us who don't want to get involved with the federales. Let me show you just one example." He pulled a vorec from his pocket and addressed it quietly. The wallscreen to his left came to life.

Cardenas was interested. He'd never seen a magified alligator before.

The big reptile had been laid open along the back, the thick skin peeled aside to expose the deep red musculature beneath. As his host spoke, the image zoomed in close to show the tiny controller unit that had been installed atop the gator's spine. Microscopic metallic filaments extended from the unit to the gator's legs, tail, and skull. The program chip had been extracted and lay atop the control unit. It was the size of a pinhead. Nearby lay a tiny plastic square from whose slick black surface four miniature joysticks protruded. Using them, the manipulator could electrically stimulate the animal's muscles to expand and contract according to carefully prepared programs, making it walk, run, jump, or execute any number of complex muscular activities, natural or anthropomorphized. Or the control pad could be set aside in favor of automatic programs.

"The owner had the poor creature fitted with an attack chip," the man explained. "Using the controller he could make it stand on its hind legs and tail and fight off burglars. When he wasn't around, the gator patrolled his place of business according to an exhaustive protection sequence. The talk portion of the chip supplied the animal's voicebox with some pretty intimidating language."

"I still marvel at how they make them speak," Cardenas murmured.

The man smiled grimly as the wallscreen blanked. "If you want your magimal to talk you have to pay for a properly installed artificial larynx. In every higher creature except man the larynx is elevated so the animal can breathe and drink at the same time. That's why unmodified apes and dogs can't say so much as 'hello.' Neither can human babies under three months of age, until their own voiceboxes begin to descend into the throat. But graft in a second, lowered larynx and animals can form words just as effectively as the rest of us.

"Set the control chip to stimulate the second larynx according to preprogrammed patterns the same way it stimulates specific muscles elsewhere in the body and you've got an animal that can 'talk'. Except that it isn't talking any more than the football-playing grizzlies you've seen on TV are playing football. It's all being run by programs or humans manipulating controllers.

"As much as we might've disliked this guy and what he was doing, we didn't have anything to do with what happened to him. Even if the local federales don't believe us."

"I believe you," Cardenas told him. "I'll see to it that you're not bothered anymore." He started to rise.

The young man was too surprised to be thankful. "That's it? You just ask me a few questions and you're sure?"

Cardenas turned. *"Sí."*

His host's eyes widened slightly. "You're an Intuit, aren't you?" Cardenas said nothing and the man nodded to himself. "Yeah, no wonder you're sure. You read my mind."

The sergeant sighed. "An Intuit cannot read minds. We arrive at our decisions based on careful consideration of linguistic peculiarities, semantic fluctuations, subtle movements of eyes and limbs. Experience gives you a feel for when people are telling the truth and when they're lying or trying to hide something. That's all. Because of an incident of violence I suffered sightlessness for many years, until the biosurges learned how to transplant optic nerves and could give me new eyes. During that time my condition forced me to sharpen my skills." He smiled again.

"So you see, I know a lot about modifying operations." He reached the door.

"How're you going to find the people who did this? The federale I talked to said you were looking for a bunch of ninlocos. There are a thousand ninloco gangs in the Strip, plus solos. At least a hundred of them claim members in the Yumarado district."

"I know," said Cardenas simply. "You learn by asking questions. That's what I came here to do, and I've just started." The door closed quietly behind him.

IV

The arena stank of death and chicken shit, human perspiration and dried blood. On opposite sides of the pit miniature grandstands had been cobbled together out of discarded plastic and extruded carbon composites. The pit itself was carpeted with sawdust. In corners and beneath the stands dried blood mixed with the scrap pulp and shreddings to form irregular brown clods. Lightstrips glued to the low, flat ceiling dimly

illuminated the arena while a couple of mobile cold spots
suspended from the roof were aimed at the pit.

From the men and women in the grandstands arose an
enthusiastic babble in a multiplicity of languages, but the
predominant means of communication was spanglish, the
patois of the Strip. Lithe, mean-faced men circulated among
them, taking down bets on battered vorecs, offering false
encouragement to the bettors. They could afford to be accommodating. No matter which individuals won, the House always
got its percentage.

Higher up off to one side several comfortable chairs rested
on a suspension platform. Those seated behind the single
Lexan railing could look down both on the pit and the crowd.
El Banquero spread out in his chair, his attention concentrated
on the steady stream of information that filled his earplug.
Occasionally he whispered into the jeweled vorec trapped
between his thick fingers like a metal cigar. On one gleamed
a fine gold ring dominated by a single ruby the size of his
thumbnail. It was, naturally, bloodred.

Behind him stood a beautifully tanned anglo not quite as
big as the average family vehicle. In the weak light he wore
dark glasses with infrared boosters. His eyes roved restlessly,
professionally, over the milling crowd. A woman not more
than twenty who looked not less than forty sat sideways in
Banquero's lap. His free hand probed mechanically between
her thighs, up under the short neofabric skirt. She looked
unutterably bored.

Cheers reverberated throughout the arena as the spots were
turned on, bathing the pit in their harsh, inescapable glare. Two
men emerged from opposite doorways behind the grandstands.
One was lean, old, hard; a permanent denizen of the Strip
from whom all sympathy and compassion had long since been
wrung out as thoroughly as the moisture from a wet rag. The
other handler was younger, with a bald forehead that gleamed
fleshily beneath the lights. Shouts, suggestions, and ribald
comments from the crowd buffeted them as they took up
positions opposite one another.

They spoke soothingly and continuously to the roosters they carried as they set them down gently on the sawdust floor. The birds were petted, caressed, reassured. Each wore a small blindfold over its eyes and on each leg and wingtip a razor-sharp spur fashioned from discarded surgical scalpels.

As the noise of the crowd rose to fever pitch the men removed the birds' blindfolds. The two fighting cocks saw one another even as their handlers tossed them into the center of the pit. Banquero leaned forward slightly.

Slowly, methodically, the birds began to circle one another, heads thrust forward, neck feathers erected and bristling as they tried to stare each other down. One bird, resplendent in iridescent black and green plumage, was slightly larger than its opponent, whose feathers were tinted a more familiar but no less spectacular yellow and brown. The crowd howled, bellowed, gesticulated obscenely. Vorecs were waved, bets doubled and tripled.

The two handlers squatted on their haunches, each holding a small controller box as they gazed at the clock that hung on the far wall. At the agreed-upon time the controllers were activated. A shudder seemed to pass through each bird. They straightened abruptly, assuming unnaturally erect postures without sacrificing any of their natal alertness.

The yellow-brown bird suddenly leaped, twisting its body to the left and kicking out with its right leg. The opposing handler's fingers moved on his control sticks and his own bird ducked, blocking upward with a wing to effectively turn the blow aside. The crowd roared.

The green-black rooster threw a right jab, then a left as its opponent backpedaled. Spurs flashed, but both blows missed. The two roosters, their movements regulated by the karateka chips embedded in their necks and the controllers of their handlers, continued to throw kicks and punches and blocks as efficiently as any highly trained humans facing each other across a dojo mat.

The yellow-brown was smaller but slightly quicker. A jumping-spinning back kick finally caught the larger bird a bit slow to react and an ankle spur sliced through its chest, sending feathers and fluid flying. The crowd roared: first blood. Stunned, the green-black retreated, defending itself as its handler tried to assess the extent of the damage.

The green-black was very close to him when it suddenly whirled, jumped, and kicked out smartly with both legs.

A different sort of scream rose from the crowd as the handler fell backward, clutching at his ruined eyes. An instant later the other handler, trying to run to his opponent's aid, was brought down by his own bird, which struck with both a leg and wingtip at the man's ankle, severing the Achilles' tendon and sending him screeching into the sawdust.

The noise volume in the arena previously was nothing compared to the panicky tumult that now shook the walls as the crowd surged wildly toward the single exit. They jammed up against the narrow portal, men and women alike finding themselves crushed against the walls or trampled underfoot by fellow frenzied aficionados, those in back moaning or shrieking as they tried to protect themselves from the fluttering, fast-moving cocks who utilized the hysteria as a stage, slicing randomly at flailing hands, arms, and exposed backs.

High up, a frowning, disturbed Banquero rose and started for his office, wondering at the cause of the chaos. The woman who had been attending to him clung to his arm, seeking protection. Banquero grunted once and his hulking shadow ripped the girl free, tossing her over the rail with casual indifference. She stopped screaming when she hit the ground, bounced once, and lay still.

Banquero had his hand on the office door when something snicked across the back of his wrist, causing him to jerk it back. The four-centimeter-long gash oozed blood as he grabbed at it. Cursing, he gazed in furious bemusement at the yellow and brown rooster that perched on the railing, staring back at him.

His bodyguard drew a large-caliber gun from a shirt holster and was aiming it at the bird when a fluttering mass of feathers landed on his head. Spurs dug in. Howling, he reached up with both hands to dislodge the green-black. Avoiding the powerful, clutching fingers the fighting cock struck out as it dropped, kicking hard enough for the surgical steel on its ankles to shatter the dark lenses and drive fragments of sharp carbonite into the hulk's eyes. He screamed and stumbled backward. The railing was insufficient to support his great weight and he fell, still clawing at his face, to land not far from the motionless whore who by dint of his callousness had preceded him floorward.

Banquero reached for the door again and again the yellow-brown struck at his hand, this time gouging deep enough to lay open the tendons on the back of the man's wrist. Hissing with pain and fury he fumbled inside his shirt for the tiny but lethal pistol that reposed there.

Having finished with the bodyguard, the green-black flew straight at Banquero and began kicking. The arena master screamed like a woman, dropping to his knees while flailing feebly at the attacking bird. The other rooster left its perch to join in, the two birds digging and clawing and scratching until there was simply nothing left of Banquero's face, nothing at all. Then they fluttered over the broken railing, trailing blood from their feet and wingtips.

They landed on the narrow shoulders of a young woman clad in a gray jumpsuit. As the rest of the crowd fought to escape the arena, she hurried toward a hole that had been cut in the base of the far wall. Exhausted but otherwise unhurt, the two rumpled birds obediently hopped off her shoulders to precede her through the gap.

V

As Cardenas questioned selected representatives of the various ninloco gangs that drifted in and out of the Yumarado district he found himself watering a ripe field of negatives. No one knew anything. Nil, nix, *nada*; nothing. The interests of the gang members he talked to were wholly orthodox, which was to say they were obsessed with sex, drugs, and music to the exclusion of everything else. Causes moral or otherwise concerned them not at all. What interest they did express in magimals extended only to those that could be stolen and resold.

There was some talk of rare species being smuggled northward for sale from the CenAm states and the Yucatán, but to the best of the gangs' knowledge this was traditional animal smuggling, nothing to do with magifying.

He spent a week questioning, interviewing, following tips, learning nothing. The heat was horrible and he tried to confine as much of his traveling as possible to late night.

The first morning of his second week in Yumarado found a message waiting on his desk when he came to work. Though elegantly phrased it was more in the nature of a command than a request. Something about the signature at the bottom seemed vaguely familiar. He ran it through research and was not surprised when a response was rapidly forthcoming.

His Yumaradoan colleagues were suitably impressed by the summons, which did not extend to the suppression of various risqué comments. Apparently his summoner had something of a reputation.

"I won't have any problems," he told his colleagues. "I'm an old man."

"That's all right," a local sergeant guffawed. "From what I hear she's kind of yesterday's wine herself."

They went so far as to give him a new cruiser to drive. After all, when he returned to Nogales they would have to remain, perhaps to deal with her again, and they wanted him to make a good impression on the department's behalf. So he convoyed in comfort.

He'd been in the governor's mansion in Phoenix once, for an official function. Compared to the house he now found himself approaching, that official residence was little more than a shack. His destination occupied several acres on a bend in the river; the real river, the old Colorado, not the nearby arrow-straight ship canal. The banks of the private peninsula on which the house was sited had been reinforced with flexible cladding to protect it from the rare possibility of flood or, more likely, dam failure on the upper river.

It was contemporary Southwest in design; two stories, artificial red tile roof, inward-slanting walls of faux copper engraved with murals executed by an artist of obvious talent and probable fame. Lush tropical landscaping surrounded the house and covered the grounds, signifying the presence of someone sufficiently wealthy to afford enough expensive desalinated water to maintain the luxuriant trees and shrubs.

He paused at an outer gate, flimsy in appearance but adequately electrified to fry any vehicle that might try to crash through, along with its occupants. The towering wall of ingrown mutated jumping cactus that enclosed the grounds was as green as it was deadly, a bioengineered barrier more effective than any that could be fashioned of concrete or metal. In effect, the house was guarded by a million toxic, attire-piercing needles.

Passing beyond this topiary terror Cardenas found himself greeted at the entrance to the house by an elderly Hispanic of superb bearing and posture. The man looked like a refugee from an old movie, the sort of somber countenance off which Cantinflas used to bounce hilarious bon mots. Overhead misting units lowered the outside temperature from the unbearable to the merely hellacious. He was glad to be inside.

The servant led him across an entryway tiled in black pyrite. One entire wall dripped water over hammered leaves of gold and copper, into a pool filled with glittering cichlids. The man left him in a room that boasted more floor space than Cardenas's entire abode. A floor-to-ceiling arc of polarized glass looked out over the rush-lined sweep of ancient river. As he entered, both of the room's occupants rose to greet him.

Cardenas figured the man for his late twenties. He was tall, athletic, his features perfectly handsome according to current styles, so much so that they verged dangerously on the effeminate. But his handshake was firm and his tone at once reverberant and accommodating. Smile and kind words notwithstanding, there was in his voice an undertone of something Cardenas found disconcerting. No one but another Intuit would have picked up on it.

Despite his presence and good looks it was his companion who immediately drew Cardenas's attention, and not just because a woman's signature had been appended to his summons. She was slightly taller than he but in no way statuesque, voluptuous without being overpowering. Her visage was dominated by a sharp-bridged, angular nose that might have been lifted from a classic Greek amphora. Dark hair tumbled around her in tight ringlets, framing her beautiful face. Cosmetic artisans had been at work there, but only to enhance what nature had given, not to replace or rebuild. She held a tall frosted glass in both hands and wore a rather severe V-necked dress of floating niobium lamé. She was perhaps twenty years older than her male companion and didn't look half it.

"I appreciate your coming to see me, Sergeant." Her voice was like the river beyond the glass, he thought. Steady, eternal, commanding, deceptively gentle at the edges. "Would you like something to drink?"

"No thanks," he told her. "You said you might have some information for me, Ms. Okolona?"

She seemed to hesitate, a gesture as much studied as genuine, as she glanced briefly over at her companion, who had taken a seat on a sand-colored couch large enough to hold seven people.

"Ramón convinced me I should talk to somebody."

Cardenas regarded the man, then the woman, and wondered why she should find the subterfuge necessary. From everything he had been told and had observed thus far, Sisu Sana Okolona was one of those entirely confident individuals who did not require approval of their actions from other human beings. He said nothing.

She began to pace. More for effect, he suspected, than from nervous need. "First it was that pet store owner. Of course, what he was doing was illegal, but he didn't deserve to be murdered for it. Now that other man, Banquero, that was different." Her expression twisted. "By all accounts he was a subhuman parasite, living off people as much as animals. But two other people got killed besides him, and a lot of others hurt." She halted, regarding him with violet eyes the color of fine amethyst. "I don't want anyone else hurt and blaming me for it."

Cardenas's brows rose. "You?"

"Didn't they tell you about me at your station?"

"I know that you're the president of Neurologic. I recognized the name Okolona."

She smiled thinly. "My late husband and I. We founded the company when no one believed in it. Throwing our lives and abilities away on obsolete technology, everyone told us. We built Neurologic up from nothing, Sergeant, with our hands and brains and little else. No technology is obsolete. Only applications. Well, we discovered and developed some new applications. One of which was the magifying controller and concomitant software."

"Ah," said Cardenas, understanding now.

"Of course when Norris and I were working on the process the magimal concept wasn't even a glimmer in our imagination. The neuromuscular stimulation technology that we were interested in was originally developed to enable paralyzed individuals to move their limbs by sending stimulating electrical impulses directly to the requisite muscles by means of ultrathin wires. Originally these were taped to the epidermis. Later they were inserted beneath the skin, for cosmetic purposes.

"But when we started working with the technology the biosurges were just learning how to regenerate damaged nerve tissue. That rendered electrical stimulation technology unnecessary and extraneous. Nevertheless my husband and I continued to work with it. We found other uses for the technology, not only in medical rehabilitation but in research. The magimal concept came about, as so many great commercial developments often do, by accident.

"We oppose the magifying of any exotic animals or dan-specs. The idea originally was and still is to provide children with better pets. Puppies that can talk. Birds that can help out around the house. Pit bulls into which fail-safes can be installed. Steeplechasing horses that no longer have to be destroyed because their riders can better help them avoid obstacles. Guard dogs that cannot only run down criminals but read them their rights and frisk them at no risk to the arresting officer. The magimal concept has been a great success."

"So in addition to regretting the fact that magified animals were involved in the deaths of these people you're also concerned about the possibility of adverse publicity," Cardenas observed succinctly.

She responded with a radiant smile, but it was a cold, controlled radiance of the sort to be found in fireflies and certain effulgent denizens of the deep ocean. "I know that you would not have been sent all the way from Nogales if you were not an unusually perceptive and sensitive practitioner of your profession, Sergeant. I see that additional explication would in your case be superficial."

"My concern is for the dead and injured," he told her, pointedly omitting any reference to a desire to spare the Neuro-logic corporation bad publicity, "and in keeping this from happening again. That's why I'm here. You said you might have some information that would be of use to me. I won't deny that I could use some help.

"We think that some ninlocos may be involved, though for the life of me I don't know why. There's no motive for them. But an eyewitness put three at the scene of the first incident, and several survivors of the abortive *pelea de gallos* gave descriptions of a girl similar to the one seen at the first murder site."

Sisu Okolona paused again, and this time her hesitation struck Cardenas as genuine. She glanced at her companion, who smiled and shrugged. Then she turned back to her patient visitor.

"Neurologic tries to track sales of our equipment, to prevent just the sort of illegal activities that the unfortunate pet shop owner was engaged in. We're not in the investigative business and we're not perfect. We're just concerned about quality and, I admit it, publicity. Components are marked, but as I'm sure you know better than I there's a vast underground market for all sorts of componentry." She walked to a table and opened a drawer, extracting a piece of paper.

"A young woman of interest to us is suspected of frequenting this address. Not being the police, we've had no reason to interfere with her movements or activities. But she is one of a number of suspicious people we do try to monitor. You see, Sergeant, we try to stay one step ahead of the kind of people who have recently been killed. Obviously we are not always successful. You might pay this young person a visit and ask some of your questions. You might get an answer or two."

Cardenas took the paper, glanced at the address. "This would be here in Yumarado."

Okolona nodded once. "In the deep industrial district, I believe. Where once at high summer midday the temperature was reported to have hit fifty-six Celsius. Not a pleasant place. I would not like to go there."

"I don't mind the heat," Cardenas told her. "Although as I get older I seem to have less tolerance. For it, and for other things."

A real smile this time. "You're not at all that old, Sergeant." It vanished quickly. "Be careful if you follow up on this. My people tell me that even though these individuals are little more than children, they can still be dangerous."

Cardenas put the paper in his shirt pocket. "I've taken down important criminals and real locos, Ms. Okolona, but the boy who blew my face away years ago was just nineteen. It doesn't take experience or strength to pull the trigger of a spitter."

"Are you sure you won't have that drink?"

"*Gracias*, but no. I guess I'm a glutton for work."

"Now that," she volunteered in kindly fashion, "will kill you far quicker than the heat."

VI

The address consisted more of directions than numbers, and he had to abandon the police cruiser outside the first alley. The narrow gap that separated two *maquiladora* plants was frantic with people, lower-grade assemblers and toters rushing to beat deadlines and the heat. He'd waited until evening, not only because it was cooler but because he sensed he'd have a better chance of making the acquaintance of the contact at night. Ninlocos tended to sleep as much as possible during the hot day and emerge in the comparative cool of darkness, like any other sensible troglodytes.

Many of the *maquiladora* factories operated twin ten-hour shifts with four off in-between for maintenance and cleaning. With a surplus of labor drawn from CenAm, S.A., and the Mexican states they could set their own hours and standards and many did. Labor inspectors sometimes got paid to wink at substandard practices, but most of the big companies had to toe the line lest they risk a shutdown because of violations. They maintained government standards, not out of altruism but because it was cheaper than having their lines halted even temporarily. But the smaller plants, the independent operations . . . Cardenas had over the years observed conditions in some of them that bordered on the inhuman. They were able to stay in business because there was always a surplus of labor, millions begging for the low-paying, dangerous work. Anything was better than trying to eke out a living tilling a few acres of corn with a mule, or potatoes in the Andes.

As night rode roughshod over fading evening the day shift made way for their replacements, workers moving both ways jamming the warren of access alleys around the plants until the last of the daytime personnel had escaped to the worker's warrens south of the Strip and their nocturnal counterparts were online. There were still people in the alleys and streets, but not nearly so many now, nor all so gainfully occupied. In addition to the massive factories there were cafes and tiny service markets, outlet stores and discount marts that identified themselves by means of drifting holagel adverts and ambient neonics. They clung to the flanks of the plants like whale lice to favored cetaceans.

Cardenas's clothes worked overtime to cool him down, but along the Colorado with its combination of desert inferno and river humidity there was no choice but to sweat.

The combination of directions and numbers led him to a workers' hostel. Only the poorest of the poor, the true bottom-end laborers lived here, in the bowels of the city, because they couldn't afford to get out, couldn't afford the price even of a shuttle commute. There was no live desk clerk; only an automonitor that demanded his room card and had to be satisfied instead with his police identification.

Following directions he rode the elevator to the top floor and exited into a hall that reeked of neglect and stale urine. Someone had managed to etch obscenities into one supposedly graffiti-resistant wall with a cutting laser or similar tool. There was barely enough light to illuminate the hall and its feature-less flush-set doors, the chemoluminescent strip tacked to the ceiling weak and long overdue for replacement.

The old aural stripping around the doors leaked and he could hear sounds from within each apartment as he passed it: children crying, men and women arguing vociferously, TVs blaring. He went to the end of the hall. There was a window, a single fixed pane of transparent plastic. The building's air-conditioning huffed reluctantly. On this top floor it was stifling hot. The lower levels, he knew, wouldn't be much better.

He drew his gun, made sure the tracer sewn into his suit was activated, and thumbed the callthrough. A tinny male voice barked back at him.

"Yeah?"

"Police, open up. I just want to ask you a few questions."

There was a pause. Cardenas's fingers tightened on his weapon. He didn't like this place, didn't like the delay. Much as he preferred to work alone, maybe he ought to have requisitioned backup for this one. But his tracer was on, and the room's occupants had no way of knowing he was by himself.

"Sure, homber. Come on in." Cardenas heard the door seal unsnick.

He found himself in a single room, somewhat larger than what he'd expected. There were two beds, rumpled and used, the cooling thermosheets stained beyond hope of color recovery. An ancient chair squatted beneath a window that was a match to the one in the hall. It offered the same dismal view of alley and buildings. Cotton stuffing bulged from various holes in the upholstery like bloodless entrails.

The walls of the room were an incongruous, immutable pale pink splattered with faded images of butterflies. The choice of scheme was ironic. The dirty, polluted chunk of industrial Namerica that smothered the lowermost Colorado hadn't played host to a real butterfly in a hundred years.

Both boys looked to be in their late teens. One was tall, healthy-looking, dark-skinned. The other had ear-length stringy blond hair and a stunned expression, as though he wandered through life under perpetual sedation. From the look of his bones and eyes his condition wasn't entirely due to drugs though. Cardenas saw that he suffered from congenital mental numbness.

The tall black kid nodded toward the pistol. "You just want to *habla*, frion, why the punch?"

"Regulations." Neither boy was armed nor was there anything lethal visible in the room. Cardenas dropped his arm, letting the gun hang at his side, where they could see that it was still activated. He took in his surroundings. Maybe drugs for sale if not for use, but that wasn't what he was here for.

"You guys know anything about some illegal magimals been involved in a couple of incidents recently?"

The tall boy laughed, his companion chiming in with a

rasping giggle. "*Seguro*, frion. Sure. We monitor the news every day."

"We don't know *nada*, man," added his equally hostile companion. "Anything else you wanna know?"

The combination of ignorance and pugnacious disdain might've been enough to put off a regular federale, but not Cardenas. There were too many pregnant syllables in the boys' phrasing, too many subtle, disquieting, revelatory shifts in their posture. He intuited that they were hiding something, that they knew more than the nothing they were saying. Staying alert, he strolled over to the far bed, eyed the door beyond.

"What's in there?"

"Bathroom, frion," said the tall boy. "You got to take a leak, be our guests. But watch your booties. The pot leaks, too." He laughed again, studiously indifferent but unable to hide the suggestive twinge of sudden anxiety the sergeant detected in his voice.

"Thanks." Cardenas hefted his pistol and pushed through the door.

He was ready for another boy; for a gun, for a stick. He was not ready for the two hundred kilos of distilled lightning and muscle that exploded in his face. The jaguar slammed him to the ground, knocking the wind out of him. Gold dust danced in his flickering vision as he struggled to aim his weapon. The big cat swatted it across the room where the shorter boy rushed to recover it.

Cardenas found himself flat on his back, staring up into the jaguar's face. It snarled, canines that were proportionately the largest of all the big cats a scant half meter from his face. If he moved, if he twitched, it could rip out his esophagus like so much garden hose.

"I ought to kill you right now," the jaguar growled. "A little bit at a time. Bite off your ears first. Or maybe your works. Chew 'em up slow." Nearby, the smaller boy laughed uproariously.

"How'd you find us?" the jaguar asked. When Cardenas didn't reply a huge paw descended to completely cover the lower half of his face. Claws contracted, digging into the sides of his cheeks. Excruciating pain shot through the sergeant as his jawbones were ground together.

"He's scared shitless." The taller boy leaned casually against the wall. "He ain't gonna tell us nothing like that."

"You're right," said a new voice. The jaguar eased off Cardenas. He sat up slowly, his whole body aching from the collision. The big cat squatted on its hindquarters nearby, tail switching nervously back and worth. Its eyes were now closed.

From the bedroom behind the now open door a woman emerged. A girl, really, Cardenas thought. She was slim, even skinny, with a faded, pinched kind of prettiness too much time spent on the streets imparts to certain children. She wore a peculiar silvery suit with the hood pushed back and integral gloves and boots. Hair the color of dirty oak was cut short and bound up on the crown of her head in a samurai knot that more than anything else resembled an antique shaving brush.

She nodded toward the big cat. "I've put him in sleep mode, but I can wake him up fast if you make me. Jaguars are light sleepers."

Cardenas staggered to his feet. The younger boy had the pistol trained on him. "Then I'll be careful to move slowly. You're not very hospitable to visitors."

"You're no visitor," she snapped. "You're a frion, a cop, the chill. How'd you find us so fast?"

Cardenas responded with an accusation. "You were the ones at the pet shop and the cockfight. You caused the trouble."

She shook her head, pushed out her lower lip. "*They* caused the trouble, exploiting animals like that. Not me. Goddamn Neurologic components."

"Magifying animals is legal in the Southwest, except for the Californias. You may not like it, but that's the way it is. Magifying exotics is illegal, though. But you don't kill the violators. Turn them in and let the law take care of them."

"I'd rather take care of them myself." She indicated the

jaguar. "When we found Chimu in San Juana he was being used in a sex show. I won't tell you how. The people who'd had him magified were making him do things no cat was designed to do, making him move in ways no cat was designed to move. Twisting his bones and muscles out of position, hurting him." She grinned wolfishly. "We freed him to react naturally."

"It hasn't come to my attention that anyone in San Juana has been killed by a jaguar."

Her smile lingered. "After I let Chimu null the two *pendejos* who'd been mistreating him he was hungry. They never fed him properly, either. So I let him eat them. Jaguars are very thorough diners. When he'd finished there was nothing much left for anyone to get excited about. Poetic justice."

"You strike me as a very bright young lady. Too bright to be messing around with something like this. How do you program the animals to react and talk like that?"

"I don't. I won't program anything. But I'll borrow. See." She touched one switch among the many on her right sleeve. Almost instantly the jaguar was on its feet, alert and awake.

The girl raised her left arm. The jaguar mimicked the gesture perfectly with its left foreleg. She made a circle with her hand in the air. So did the big cat. When she tilted her head to one side, the animal did likewise. When she took a swipe in Cardenas's direction, he felt the simultaneous *whoosh* of air as the cat's claws missed him by centimeters.

"I don't work through chips," she told him proudly. "I've got a steady-state broadcast unit in the suit that records the actions of my muscles. The animal's controller receives the information and transposes my movements accordingly. My suit reads my movements and gestures and conveys them to the broadcast unit, which passes the action digitally to the Neurologic controller in the animal, which matches my movements gesture for gesture. Unlike in the old paraplegic outfits, the stim filaments in my suit are coded for pickup, not distribution."

"Pretty clever," Cardenas admitted. "So the animals are only imitating your movements, your gestures, and not reacting to some embedded program."

"That's it, frion."

"So they haven't killed anyone. You have."

Her smiled vanished. "You're awfully stupid for such an old cop, but then you were awfully stupid for coming here in the first place. You still haven't answered my question." She straightened and grabbed for him. The jaguar rose on its hind legs and wrapped a paw around Cardenas's right hand. "Tell me, or I'll have Chimu pull off your fingers one at a time."

He could feel the pressure, as if his hand had been encased in a heated vise. "Take it easy. What difference does it make?"

She approached and pushed her face close to his own. The jaguar was right next to her, its fangs wet and sharp. "That's my business." She touched a control and when her hands started going through his pockets, the jaguar did not mimic the gestures.

She found his wallet, which she tossed to the tall boy, and his police vorec, which she gave to the shorter one. Eventually she found the slip of paper containing the directions.

"*Mira* this, Twotrick." The tall boy took the paper.

"*Mierde*! Okolona letterhead." He wadded the paper into a ball and threw it aside.

"I guess I'm not surprised. It's my fault. I should've expected it." Her hands balled into tiny fists.

Cardenas felt the bones in his fingers grinding together as the jaguar's paw contracted. He wanted to scream but clenched his teeth and sucked it in.

"No more of this," she muttered. She looked and sounded suddenly tired. "No more."

"Hey, Gagrito!" The shorter boy looked up from where he'd been playing with Cardenas's vorec. "You ain't giving up, are you? The game's just getting good and started."

"Ball it, Gluey," she shot back. "It's no fun if they know. But we can still endgame, *verdad*?" The shorter boy jammed the vorec in his pocket as he hopped off the bed, nodding eagerly.

When she looked back at Cardenas there was a horrific blankness in her eyes, as if he were no longer there. He knew that look but had never encountered it before on the face of one quite so young.

"We're leaving." Her voice had grown distant, surreal. "You can stay and keep Chimu company."

"Now wait...."

She held up her balled fist and he winced at the increased pressure on his hand. "My range is about twenty meters. As soon as we're on our way down in the elevator the connection will be broken. Then Chimu will be on his own. So will you."

They left hurriedly, Gluey favoring Cardenas with a last nervous giggle as he shut the door behind him. The sergeant stood there gazing at the jaguar, his right hand throbbing with pain in the animal's grip. It could be counted on to react suddenly and instinctively when the girl's control was released. Striking at its eyes might buy him a second or two, Cardenas thought tensely. Probably the three ninlocos were already stepping into the battered, rickety elevator. He had only seconds left in which to do something, anything.

The jaguar's posture, standing erect on its hind legs, was completely foreign to the animal. For the moment it was being ordered to hold on to him, and that was all.

So he kicked it as hard as he could between its hind legs.

The gesture was remarkably productive. The paw clutching his right hand let go and the animal dropped and rolled onto its back. Cardenas sprang for the door and wrenched at the handle as the big cat yowled thunderously behind him. The handle wouldn't budge.

They'd locked it from the outside.

Already the jaguar was scrambling back onto its feet. Having previously been introduced to the taste of human flesh Cardenas doubted it would stop with just killing him. Not that the final disposition of his corpus would matter to him once he'd been eviscerated. He looked around wildly, then sprinted to his right even as the cat was digging into the floor with its claws, gathering itself to leap.

The cheap plastic window shattered as Cardenas flew through it, arms crossed protectively in front of his face, the frame snapping like cardboard, the fragments of inexpensive transparency cutting his hands and arms. The big cat, never hesitating, followed.

The cable he'd noticed from inside the room felt like it was going to slice through his armpits as he slammed against it and convulsively curled his arms, his body and legs swinging wildly five floors above the alley. He felt a claw rip his pants leg. Screeching, yowling, twisting, the jaguar plummeted earthward. The last sound it made was an audible *thud* as it struck the unyielding pavement far below.

Cardenas dangled suspended in the sweltering night air, his muscles aching. He could feel warm wetness beginning to trickle from beneath both arms. Across the alley a window opened and a face appeared. He yelled in its direction. Dimly aware that while his lips were parted and moving, no sound was emerging, he tried again.

The window slammed shut, the face disappeared. Cursing, he began to pull himself hand over hand along the cable, heading for the building to which it was attached. There was a roof there, lower than the room from which he'd so precipitously exited. His progress was agonizingly slow, but steady.

VII

They wanted him admitted to the hospital but had to settle for patching him up. Via vorec he supplied the night shift with a thorough description of the three ninlocos as well as their modus. Then he called Sisu Okolona to warn her that the trio now had her address. Having spoken of "ending the game" the girl called Gagrito might decide that the best way to punish Neurologic was to try to take some sort of revenge on its corporate head. Okolona assured him she would take the necessary precautions and not to concern himself because her home was quite inviolable. An army of ninlocos couldn't force their way in.

Thus reassured somewhat, he allowed the biosurges to go back to work on him. They repaired the bones of his right hand, though it would be in a cast for some weeks, and sealed the wounds beneath his arms where the cable had cut. By midafternoon of the following day he'd pulled rank to get himself discharged.

The first thing he wanted to do was talk to Okolona in person again. He should have called for assistance when he first saw the gate in the cactus fence slightly ajar, but decided not to. Probably it simply hadn't shut all the way after its last use and Okolona had assured him with confidence the previous night of her home's impregnability. Such technocratic xanadus generally were.

No servant appeared to greet him, but when he identified himself the door clicked open to grant admittance. Only when he stepped inside did he feel the gun in his back.

A familiar giggle sounded behind him. "You oughta be dead, frion. Why ain't you dead?"

"I'm quicker than you think, *niño*."

"Not quicker than your own gun, I bet. Waft." Cardenas started forward.

They were all in the big room that overlooked the river. Sisu Okolona sat on the big couch, with her edgy paramour close by. Twotrick leaned against an exquisite Victorian sidebar, picking at his nails with a titanium stiletto. Her silver suit dirty and greasy, the girl Gagrito stood confronting the couple on the couch.

The manservant who had greeted Cardenas on his last visit lay sprawled in a hallway nearby, his blood filling the grout lines between the black pyrite tiles.

The girl glared at him. If she wasn't insane she was borderline, Cardenas saw instantly. There would be no reasoning with her.

"You officious prick. What've you done with Chimu?"

"He's not hungry anymore," Cardenas told her quietly, looking for an opening.

"Mierde." She turned back to the couch. The mistress of the grand house looked utterly self-possessed, as always. "That's the last animal whose death you're going to be responsible for."

"I am not responsible for the death of any animal," replied Okolona tightly. "Neurologic only builds the components, the majority of which are given over to perfectly legitimate uses."

"Legitimate, yeah. Like making hamsters jump through flaming hoops and parakeets recite Shakespeare. Forcing animals into unnatural activities that age them prematurely. You cold, heartless bitch; you wouldn't know a 'legitimate' animal if it jumped up and bit you on the ass." The fury of her response startled Cardenas.

Okolona was unruffled. "I cannot supervise every application of every component the company manufactures. It is an unfortunate but inescapable fact that this world is home to some immoral people."

"Unlike you, of course," Gagrito practically spat.

Cardenas felt a need to try to direct the conversation. "It's the suit," he informed Okolona. "It conveys her movements to the controller units and the animals mimic her gestures."

Okolona shook her head. "That's impossible. The controller sequences are all heavily encoded. Two Cribms working in tandem couldn't crack them." Her gaze shifted back to the girl. "You couldn't."

"I didn't have to." Gagrito grinned. "Somebody gave them to me."

Some of the color left Okolona's face. "Only half a dozen people have access to the encoding sequence, and you wouldn't have anything they'd want badly enough to trade for it."

"He did." With great delight the girl pointed to the man sitting on the far end of the couch.

Okolona gaped at him, then slumped slightly. "It's true, isn't it? She's telling the truth. *Why?*"

"Because I gave him what he wanted," the girl declared triumphantly when Ramon declined to respond. "I gave him *everything* he wanted. Did you think he was so fine, so pure? Isn't the fact that he was interested in you proof enough to the contrary? You're old. Well preserved, as well preserved as money can preserve, but under all the attitudes and work and experience you're *old*. Too old to satisfy him all the time. I'm not, and your boyfriend, well, while he made it clear that you were his main foodline, he wasn't averse to availing himself of a little willing young stuff on the side."

For the first time Okolona's composure was shaken. "You gave her the coding sequence for the controllers?"

"I didn't think it would do any harm." Ramon was on the verge of babbling. "She obviously wasn't an industrial spy. She said she just wanted it for herself, to fool around with, that it would help her with her hobby. She showed me the suit, told me what it was for, what she was trying to do with it. She said the coding sequence would help with some algorithms, whatever those are. I didn't see the harm. . . ."

"You didn't see . . . ?" Okolona lowered her voice. "You didn't see. Of course you didn't."

"Isn't that what you always told me?" Gagrito paced the floor like some gangly, predatory bird. "That to get what you wanted, to achieve your goals, you had to do whatever was necessary, give up whatever was required?"

"I never meant . . ."

"Just like you never meant to kill Squirt." The trembling in the girl's voice belied something deep, Cardenas sensed. Very deep.

"You two know each other," he said flatly. It more than explained how she'd been able to gain entrance to the mansion.

The girl whirled on him, her expression a maelstrom of fury and revulsion. "She's my goddamn mother, frion. I had a cat once, a long time ago. A long, long time ago. A cat and a father. She killed them both."

Okolona's voice rose, shaky but still vibrant. "Your father died of a heart condition!"

"Which you aggravated; pushing him, driving him, always reaching, always striving, always. You didn't just help him into an early grave; you shoved him in."

"He wanted success as much as I did! He wanted Neurologic!"

"*You* wanted Neurologic," the girl snarled. "Daddy wanted food, and a roof over our heads, and maybe, eventually, some recognition for all his years of slaving. But that wasn't good enough for you. You had to be on top. You had to be bitch queen of neuronics, a duchess of the Strip. So you kept pushing him, and pushing him, and finally he just gave up and died. It was a way out.

"And Squirt. Why'd you have to take my cat?" She was crying now, crying and accusing all at once. "Why couldn't you have found some other animal to try your damn rotten stinking controller on?"

"That was an accident. I've explained it to you over and over. An accident. It should have worked perfectly. It had been tested repeatedly. I thought you'd like Squirt better after it was done, thought you'd be pleased and surprised with what she could do. The only cat in the world who could do such things. The only one."

"I just wanted a cat!" Gagrito screamed. "My cat! Squirt. An ordinary, smelly, warm, furry cat. Not something that could do highwire tricks and navigate the fucking car. Just a cat. And you killed that. Squirt wasn't good enough for you the way she was. You had to try and improve her. Like you had to try and improve everything and everybody else."

"I did it for you," Okolona insisted. "It didn't work out, it was a tragedy, that cat, but I did it for you."

"*Mierde*, you never did anything for anybody in your life except yourself. You were always improving things. Nothing was ever good enough." She grinned nastily then, and her expression bore more than a little in common with the dead jaguar's. "I learned a lot from you. I studied real hard. I designed this suit, and Twotrick helped a great deal. They threw him out of medical school, and we found each other, and he helped. I can make improvements, too!"

Cardenas tensed as she touched a switch on her sleeve. But no animals leaped into the room, no big cats, no large fanged dogs, no poisonous snakes or hulking bears.

On the far end of the couch, Ramon twitched. His eyes became small moons. Gagrito raised her right hand, clenched the fingers into a fist. Ramon mimicked the gesture, gazing in horror at his own, out-of-control extremities. He gaped at her. "What . . . Nilaa . . . what?"

"When you were asleep." Her tone would have iced lava. "Twotrick rented a place, equipment, assistants. He did it. I drugged you, you woke up and never realized. He did it." She pirouetted and he rose from the couch and duplicated the movement with fluid masculine grace.

"The stim wires. You're full of 'em. They're all in your legs and your arms. In your hands and your feet. It wasn't hard. The system works just as well on people as on animals. The controller's in your back, up high where you can't feel it. No voicebox, though. We didn't give you a second voicebox. You're such a smooth talker on your own."

"But *why*, Nilaa! Why?"

"Because you were with her." The girl gestured at the paralyzed Okolona. "Because I was only an amusement for you, a diversion, a compliant perversion you could wallow in whenever you felt the urge. Because I knew she'd marry you eventually and I couldn't really see myself calling you daddy, now could I? But mostly because she wanted you, she liked you. So I thought I'd help, to her way of thinking, by improving you. God knows you could stand some improvement. Just as she improved poor little Squirt." Eyes blazing, she stared at the suddenly broken woman slumped on the couch.

"How about it, Mother dear? How do you like your new and improved fiancé? Isn't he elegant? Isn't he graceful?" She twisted and bent, jumped and kicked. An expression of

ineffable horror on his face, Ramón mimicked every one of
her movements as earnestly as his older, male body could.

Entranced, perfectly focused, she drew her knife and tossed
it to him, clutching with her hand, making him grab it. He
gawked at the blade in horror, wanting to let go, to drop it,
to throw it aside, but unable to command his fingers, unable
to let loose. She turned toward the couch.

Okolona started to edge to her right, trying to divide her
attention between Ramon and her daughter. "This won't bring
your father back, it won't bring back your cat, and it won't
slow production at Neurologic."

"No, no," agreed Gagrito in a tone turned unexpectedly
gentle, mesmerized by her own audacity, "but maybe, just
maybe, it'll let me sleep without any more nightmares, without
too much thinking. Maybe it'll put an end to some of the
remembering." As she approached the couch so did Ramon,
struggling with his own legs.

"Nilaa, I'm your *mother*."

The girl halted. Behind him Cardenas heard Gluey giggling,
"Go on, do it, do it, Gagrito!"

"No." She retreated. So did Ramon. "No, she's right. I've
hated her for so long I can't hate anymore. All I can do is
finish it. Somehow. Endgame."

"No!" Cardenas took a step forward. Eager Gluey jammed
the pistol into the small of his back.

The girl made a sweeping motion. Casual, relaxed, as if
she were dancing in her sleep. Okolona screamed.

Emitting a terrified croak, Ramon simultaneously brought
his hand up and around and in flawless imitation of the girl's
gesture neatly cut his own throat.

"*Ramon!*" Okolona abandoned the couch and ran toward
her lover, who, shaking violently, collapsed to the floor.
Silently the girl wrapped her arms around herself. In imitation
the flopping Ramon drew Okolona to him, blood spurting
from his throat, splashing her in the face, the neck, the chest.
Gluey and Twotrick looked on raptly, utterly captivated. The
boy giggled uncontrollably, tracing slow circles against Carde-

nas's spine with the muzzle of the gun. He intuited something in the boy's laugh; a moment of distraction, an instant of indifference, preoccupation with the gruesome scene being played out before them.

He was small and old. And deceptive.

Spinning with unexpected speed, he chopped down on the boy's wrist and sent the gun flying. It hit the tiles and slid under the second couch. Twotrick rushed forward, blade at the ready, but Cardenas was ready for him. He blocked the half-wild, undisciplined blow and kicked out straight, crunching the boy's knee. Twotrick howled and went down, dropping the stiletto.

Gagrito whirled and pantomimed an advance. Shoving the hysterical Okolona off his chest a vacant-eyed Ramon rose and staggered toward the sergeant, blood pumping from the slash in his throat, the dripping knife held high.

Retreating, Cardenas fumbled in a pocket until his fingers locked around the spare power cell he carried for his vorec. Activating it with a flick of his thumbnail, he threw it at the girl. It struck her in the stomach.

There was a brief, brilliant flash, bright as a mystic visitation, and she screamed as the stim wires woven into the suit conducted the open charge, shorting out the entire system, feeding back to her muscles. She fell, collapsing, twitching uncontrollably as the system went crazy, throwing her own muscles into mad spasms. Freed of her influence Ramon folded, clutching at his throat.

Cardenas scrambled to recover his pistol from beneath the couch. By the time he sat up Gluey was already gone, fled through the double doors. Twotrick lay on his side on the floor, clutching his shattered knee and bawling like a betrayed virgin. Gradually the girl went immobile. A few wisps of thin, acrid smoke rose from her body. He couldn't tell if she was dead.

He tore off his shirt and jammed it into the hole in Ramon's neck while Okolona cradled the head of her lover in her lap, rocking back and forth and wailing softly.

"Call for help," he ordered her. "Ambulance first, then police. Do it!" he shouted when she didn't react.

Her eyes came up to gaze dumbly into his. For a long moment the madness and the sorrow held sway. Then it receded as a fragment of the iron will that had built Neurologic reasserted itself. She rose and stumbled toward a phone.

Cardenas stayed there, holding the rag tight against Ramon's throat. Later, much later, he was told that the parameds had somehow managed to save him. The sergeant was neither pleased nor disappointed. By the letter of the law the man was guilty of nothing but bad judgment and being a lousy human being.

The girl was in a coma. Cataleptic shock, the biosurges said. As much self-induced as the result of feedback from her damaged suit.

Cardenas methodically filled out his report. It took a long time and he had to stop several times, leaving and then returning to the extensive, impersonal form. When he'd finished he inquired one more time about Nilaa Okolona before starting back to Nogales. He didn't ask about the mother.

No change, they told him. Vital signs steady, nervous system unresponsive. Did he wish to be kept apprised of her condition?

He did not. Experience had taught him that it's not good for a frion, a cop, to become too involved in his work, to get too close to people.

Especially to a ninloco girl who would choose to nickname herself the screaming kitten.

From the Notebooks of Angel Cardenas:

So you see, some things you can't buy. I don't care what the new merchants say, there's no such thing as virtual love. Or maybe it's all virtual. That definition thing, again.

I've loved, and I didn't think there was anything virtual about it. Love's as ethereal as the heat in Sonora and as substantial as the sauce at the *Casa de Mole*. For those of you who don't know, that's mole as in "moh-lay" the chocolate sauce, not as in the subterranean rodent. Though I suppose you could serve mole *mole*. You might; I wouldn't.

The Strip not only manufactures, it sells. Anything you want, *hombre*. That in addition to all the stuff you don't want. Remember what I said about advertising; just don't spread it around. It's considered unpatriotic, and I'm looking forward to an uncontroversial retirement.

Want a slave? Oh, I know slavery's officially banned, but when was the last time you read the fine print on the contract for the last big appliance you bought? I mean the *really* fine print? That's what I thought. If you can indenture a machine, you can indenture a person. Usually it's voluntary. A good slave can make a lot of money. And in these days of rampant overpopulation they're not all that expensive. It's the liability insurance that puts most people off.

Didn't used to be that way. Funny how morality changes with time. I find myself upholding laws that didn't exist fifty, a hundred years ago. Sometimes only the details seem to change. The fine print.

Yeah, you can sell anything on the Strip. But that doesn't mean it's always legal to buy it.

Hellado

*H*EY, don' give me no silly smile like that, man. You want to hear the *verdad* story, I'm giving you the *verdad* story. Why would I make something like that up? I ain't that smart. Besides, no way could I make up something worse than what really happened.

Sure I'm sad. Like, Chuy, he was a friend of mine, *sabe*? Good friend. BTS amigo, you know? But the way I see it, what happened was his own fault.

If he hadn't been so smart, he wouldn't be where he is.

I met Chuy in the Hermosillo juvie Rehab. He'd been there almost a year and they had to let him go because he was gonna turn eighteen. Personally, I think they were getting rid of him because they couldn't make him, you know? He was so damn smart. Street smart, the psychys said. Too smart to waste. So they kept sending him home, and he kept coming back. They'd warn him, and he'd smile, and promise he wouldn't get in no trouble, and in a few months he'd be back.

Me, I was in for lifting galads from cars. You know: gallium arsenide storage batteries? *Stupido*. Too heavy work for me, the federales said when they caught me trying to fence a load, and they laughed. *Pendejomadres*. Chuy and I met in the Rehab library. It was inevitable. Good word, inevitable. There was nobody else there. Rehab citizens tend to fill up the bigscreen vit room, and the mess hall, and the athletic facilities, but they got this tendency to avoid the library. So there was just the two of us, and we saw each other and started talkin', and when Chuy found out I was BTS, too—that means you're from Bahia Todos Santos harbor, Ensenada Arcomplex—it was easy natural from there. Turned out we'd even scoped some of the same neighborhoods.

I knew right away Chuy had plenty of cerebro, and not just because he was getting out. He talked smart, could speak English and Spanish as well as the patois, and he had money. The federales could send him to Rehab, but not his money. He knew several fences, but he was the one who'd taken the kosh—you know, kosher cash? Laundered money?—and stashed it down in Panama. You don't expect a mouthy little bayboy to know about stuff like that. I was pretty impressed.

When Chuy found out my hobby was singing the credit electric, we easy started talking some heavy work-release program, you know? I knew stuff he didn't, and he knew the street a lot better than me. Problemo was, he was getting out soon and if I wanted to scope with him I had to do the same.

So I started paying serious attention to my situation, which meant I had to start listening to Trisha Varese, my case worker, instead of just mumbling "chure" to everything she said while concentrating on her tetas. I can say "sure" as well as any pure anglo, but they think it's cute when you say "chure."

Man, you'd have been proud of me, I was so damn repentant! I mean, I expiated all *over* the place. And "chure" enough, they let me out a day *before* Chuy. I was there waiting for him at the gate when they let him out, and I ream-rawed him pretty good about it. He handled it with a grin—that was one of his talents—and then he took me to an AT and used a card and drew out about a thousand Namerican dollars. That shut me up real quick.

We caught the first commuter out of Hermosillo nonstop back to good old BTS. I got to admit I choked a little when we banked over Point Banda on approach to Ensenada, seeing the big bahia spread out all pale blue like coconut flavoring against the rusty rim of docks and container tracks and cranes, with the city and the mountains in the background and the yellow sand stretching south toward Cabo Colnett like a Zapotec carpet. But I kept it to myself. You can't call yourself a Big Tough Shit and bawl on a commuter vertiprop in front of a bunch of sponge-faced cleanies.

My mother was glad to see me, but it wasn't much of a reunion. She was late for work and it didn't leave a lot of time for talk. You know what the Strip's like, man. There's eight million cleanies workin' the *maquiladora* plants and five times as many as that in places like the CenAm and Colombia and points south would sell their sorry selves for a chance at the least of those jobs. So *mi madre* said hello and hugged me and excused herself so's she could maybe make the seven-quarter induction shuttle north to work. My kid brother and sister were in day school; not that I'd hang with them anyway.

Don't mis*comprende*; I love my siblings. But a BTS wouldn't be caught dead tending no kids.

No, first thing, I went looking for Lita. She's no vit star beauty, my Lita, but she's easy on the eyes, and kissing her is like chug-a-lugging a half liter of salsa. More important, she likes me. Actually, I think maybe she loves me, but I'm careful not to wade in those waters.

"Hey 'Stebo, when they let you out!" Then she throws herself in my arms, which is hard for me to handle 'cause she's bigger than me and it would look bad for me to stagger, *comprende*? We talk, and go cruise the Pershing Villa Mall, and I buy her dinner, and we talk some more, until the moon is startin' to work on the second half of its shift. Then when things are all nice and warm and settled we waft on down to

Ostras Beach for a little Californico Sur body surfing, you know what I mean? Just beach; no *agua*. After those months in Rehab I was more than ready for a little slip 'n slide.

Later we lie on our backs on the sand thinking how nice it was of God to make the moon pretty as well as functional.

While Lita talks I lie there all tired and warm-worn an' let her voice run all over me like saguaro honey. The words I try to ignore.

"You gonna get a good job, 'Stebo. Make some honest money. You so smart; I know you can do it."

I listen to this with my ears and my eyes, but my mind is someplace else. See, Lita, she likes me a lot, and I think she wants to get married and have a house and kids and all that cleanie stuff. But me, I don' want that. What do I want a couple rugrats hanging on me all the time? I argue with her, and then I just give up and nod. It's easier that way, man, and it makes her happy.

We find another wave, and paddle like mad, an' this time I wait for her.

Next morning she's all smiles an' winks when she goes off to her crummy job and I relax 'cause I can forget about the *otra*. 'Til next time. I mean, I'm a BTS, man. I don' need no family mucking my business.

But as the hot days pass she keeps buggin' me, so I start thinking about it serious. Until Chuy come looking for me, and I explain to Lita that I got to go with him. My friend needs me. And just like I'm afraid she will, sure enough she starts crying and yelling.

"What kind of friend can you make in Rehab, you dumb schmuckito? You don't need to be hanging with no ninlocos! This Chuy guy, he's gonna get you screwed all over again and then what am I gonna do?"

She's really makin' rain, so I try to comfort her and reassure her, explain that Chuy's no ninloco, he's smarter than that, smart enough not to get involved with no street gang. Maybe he's an antisoc, but what's the big deal with that? Half the people in the Strip are antisocs. At least he ain't no weird.

But she pulls away from me and tells me to get out, go on, get lost, I ain't gonna amount to nothing because of the people I hang with. I know she'll get over it, she always does, but it's hard, 'cause see, I really like her. Deep.

Chuy takes me in this old car that he drives around in even though he could buy a Shogunner because, he explains, the federales would start hanging right with a young guy in a Shogunner, spizzing him and making him crazy, and while this heap may not look so good, it's a hell of a lot more sophic. It's late, and we head for the back of the docks, where the light induction assembly yards are.

They're big, the induction yards. Container and cargo ships from all over the Pacif off-load their cargoes there. Carriers from Old Nippon, Taiwan, Thailand, Malaysia, and China swap components and chippies and assembly packs and wafers and take on finished goods, cables and connectors, and agriblocks for transport home.

The containers slide right off the ships onto flexible maglev loading arms. You've seen 'em: big stelacrete and fiber-composite tentacles, four to an operator's cabin. The containers are already content and destination-coded and those macho operators, the real good ones, can toss ten-ton containers around like square baseballs.

Most of them end up in the distribution yards, waiting for a slot out. The yard 'puters stack them into trains for redundancy value and when they've got enough headed in more or less the same direction, they send them off north to San Juana or Agua Pri or Yumarado or Elpaso or the Navahopi nation. The already assembled, finished goods that come pan-Pacif go straight to Frisco or LaLa.

The Bay and Ensenada City are the harvest ground for the whole western two thirds of the Strip. All those fancy vits and consumer electronics the cleanies hunger for are assembled in the Strip, using Strip cheapa labor and Zonie engineering. It's a helluva place. *Mi madre*'s job is up there. She does okay considering my stinkin' run-off *pendejo* of an old man never sends no money to her. Okay, yeah; but she has to work like a dog. Ten people waiting to get her job.

We pull into one of the big public cleanie commutee lots and start to cruise, slow and easy. Chuy knows where he's going, I can tell, and the closer we get to where he's going the quieter he gets. Maybe his mouth's shut, but his eyes are moving all the time. Bright black eyes, like dancing ball bearings. He's real serioso now and so I keep quiet, trying to watch for I don' know what.

Then this little smile spreads over his face. If I forget everything else about him I'll always remember that smile, like a guy on a date who's spent a lot of money and has worked real hard to sound sincere and has just figured out he's gonna get laid. He pulls over next to a nice, shiny Sodan coupe, maybe a year old. I flash the two guys in the front seat, one a slant and the other a big blond anglo who don' look like he belongs within a hundred kims of the place. They're flashing me back like they're trying to swim the Golfo from Guyamas to San Blas and I'm a weight tied to their ankles.

The anglo looks unhappy. I keep my expression carefully neutral, but I already hate him for his good looks. "Modal, Chuy. Who's the buffo?" I stiffen but say nothing.

"Take it easy. We hung in Rehab together."

The other two relax a little. So do I. "Oh. I guess that's okay, then." He sneers at me. "What can you do besides make goofy expressions, buffo?"

Before I can reply Chuy steps in. "He's mode. I think he's a tweek."

The Sodan drivers exchange a look. It's clear this they don' expect. I'm inordinately pleased.

"We don't need no stinkin' tweek," the slant mutters.

"Just because we never had one before don't mean we can't use one," Chuy tells him. I can tell he's getting irritated. So can the slant, because he doesn't say anything else. Chuy climbs out, locks his boost-a-wreck. I notice it's got a cute little peapod gelplug under the ignition that'll blow the fingers off anybody dumb enough to try and skrag it. I imitate his withdrawal. We pile into the Sodan.

I check out the interior, note the origin stains: stupid, easily bypassed dash security; elaborate satellite mapping system above the CD player, revolving token holder for the toll highways. I refract this ain't the anglo's cruiser, and I say so.

"Where'd you skrag this gordo, goldilocks?"

The anglo looks angro for a second, then nods in grudging approval. "Not around here. You think I'm a buffo like you?"

"Naw," I reply, displaying a bravado I don't feel. The anglo is twice my size, stuffed full of steroid-rich cereal. "I think you're a buffo like yourself."

It's his turn to stiffen, but it's hard to unload on somebody when you're in the front seat and they're in the back. Then he grins and extends a hand back toward me. The palm is soft, like a vitwit's.

"I'm Kilbee. You know? Like the killer bees?"

From behind the half wheel on the driver's side the slant sniffs. "It's really Kirby, but you know these anglos. Delusions of grandeur. I'm Huong. Long Huong to my lady friends."

"In what *faevela*?" I shoot back, and just like that I'm one of the pak, no longer an outsider. Huong starts the Sodan and the big reviviscent electric motor purrs like a telenovela tart wound too tight. We ease out of the lot, heading toward the main induction distribution yard on the eastern fringe of the Arcomplex. I've already got it figured, but Chuy explains anyway.

"Don't like to leave our real transportation too close to our place of business." He's smiling, but tense now. Getting close to work time, I figure.

We pull up to the deserted four-lane gate. Faking a high, Huong weaves as he sticks a card into a read-only. While we wait nobody says anything. A moment later the reo regurgitates his card and the gate pops sweet as an electric cherry. I see them all relax.

"Card cost a lot of money," Chuy tells me as we roll in. "Kilbee got it in LaLa."

"My folks are never home," the anglo explains. "Took me weeks to set up delivery."

"Where do they think you are, your folks?"

"Studying business at UC Escondido. They're out of town so much they could know less. Much less care." His expression was not fraught with filial love.

We pull as far into the lot as possible and Huong parks next to half a dozen empty vehics. Kilbee reaches under his seat and extracts a big package. He opens the top and hands me a soft lump.

"Left side, near the bottom," Chuy elucidates as he slides to his right. "You can find it with your fingers. Be ready to slip out as it expands."

I eye the lump, find the switch. "You're kidding. What the hell's this?"

Chuy gestures to his left, toward a steel tower on the far side of the lot. "Spy vit up there, covers the whole tarmac. It'll show at least two people in this car. Have to be two here at all times. Probably don't need it, but I don't like to take chances if there's a better way."

"Ready, it's swinging." Huong is looking casually to his left. "Now!"

I flip the switch I've been fingering. The lump hisses like a dreaming gila monster and starts to bloat. I frantically follow Chuy as he scrambles out the right side of the coupe and onto the pavement. Behind me, a pair of inflatable drunks expand to fill my seat and Huong's. They are extremely good likenesses. By the time the spy vit swings back past the Sodan they will be blown up to human size and occupying their seats. I can't repress a grin.

"Who thought this one up?"

"I did," said Chuy. "Got the idea off a vit. Hasn't failed so far. It's a redundancy, in case anyone at central security happened to have noticed us pulling in and gave a damn. This way it'll look like a couple of cleanies using the safe confines of the lot to sleep off a binge. Come on, and stay low. Not everything in here's auto. They have regular patrols, too.''

As the camera swung back again, patient and ignorant, we scrambled toward the yard.

Hundreds of induction container cars rested on surface tracks, a labyrinth of composite stelacrete, plastic, composite fibers, and metal. Chuy and the others seemed to know pretty much where they were going, though they stopped once to confer. I just tried to keep up and out of the way, watching and learning. At the north end of the yard the network converged into the heavy-use lines that ran toward the Strip. All around us was the constant hum of cars moving, disengaging, assembling into trains or breaking away, the sounds of maglev rails being switched on and off, clicks and buzzes, and pungent above it all the sweet jumbled stink of lubrication and ozone. I felt as if I'd stepped over a gap and fallen into a machine, wayward as a free electron.

We stopped outside a wall of six connected cars pointed north. Chuy kept watch while Huong and Kilbee plugged a battered notex into the access slot on the loading door and sped through combinations at twenty a second. I tried to look alert.

"How you know which car to pick?"

"Got to be one headed north. That's the easy part. The rest is experience, practice. Also, I got contacts. Tricky business." I was shuffling nervously back and forth and he indicated my feet. "Watch your step."

I knew what he was referring to. The center rail, where the exposed conducting magnets ran the length of the track, was fully charged. If I stumbled into it, made the slightest contact with it while it was pos, I'd be a long pig taco faster than tequila evaporates downtown on a national holiday.

The container cars sat on their track, vibrating infinitesimally as they awaited orders to move. The damn door finally clicked open. Chuy rose up and stepped back. "Move it, hombers!"

Huong and Kilbee disappeared within. Moments later they

were tossing out long, flat rectangular boxes no thicker than slats. They were made of opaque molycite, carefully labeled. I didn't waste time trying to read them. When Chuy and I each had one the intruding pair descended and we started running, fast and low, back to the lot.

Once there we waited, timing our rush to the Sodan. When Chuy gave the word we moved, into the coupe, deflating the balloon drunks and replacing them with our own selves. Huong drove sedately out of the lot.

At the city lot we abandoned the stolen coupe for Chuy's beat-up Mord. Only when we were back on a main street in town did the boys start whooping and hollering, exchanging raps and cries.

"Let's see what we got," said Chuy. He took a prier from a slim toolbox stored under the front seat and started working on the molycite carton. The lid slid off smoothly and we saw that it was full of densely packed NISC optical leads. As were the other three slats. The last one we cracked contained doublet Mahatmas, gold-sealed and ready to install, each worth sixty Namerican dollars apiece wholesale underground according to Huong. There were fifty leads in the slat.

"What do you think, 'Stebo?" Chuy was beaming. "Not bad for a couple hours running around in the dark, eh? Better than snorting desdu, and safer."

"You did okay, buffo," said Kilbee grudgingly.

"Thanks. Then stop calling me buffo, okay?"

For the second time that night a big hand reached back over the seat.

It went like that week after week. We were doing pretty damn good. One night in July, when it was too hot even for the spy vit to move very fast, we skragged a whole box of custom-augmented lumin plates. Twenty-five of 'em, a thousand dollars a plate. Huong got so boned we had to pass him around three different moray holes just to get him hosed down.

But we each could've packed out a box. It bothered me. I thought I knew what the problem was, but I waited 'til I was

sure before pushing it on Chuy. I was doing a lot of thinking
since I'd been accepted into the troop, and I wanted to be
positive.

"Yeah, we coulda taken four boxes," he told me over a
couple of self-chilling Cabos at his place. It was out on the
Point, in an expensive neighborhood, but not too flamboyant,
if you know what I mean. Not right on the Pacif, but you
could see it from his rooftop. Chuy himself, he never used
the sundeck. That was for crazy anglos who wanted to get as
dark as the people they were always railing against.

"Then why didn't we?" I asked him. Looking out the
second-floor window I could see Huong and Kilbee down in
the compact high-walled garden-yard, sitting under the misters
with a couple of girls they'd picked up outside the International School of Management. Huong's lady looked like she
was from Finland or something. Her skin was as pale as
underwear on washday. The slant was partial to tall Europeans.
Kilbee wasn't partial at all, so long as they had a waist.
Friggin' equal-op employer.

"Because of the way the yard security's set up. We're like
mosquitoes, 'Stebo. You draw a little blood here, a little there,
your target gets up irritated but not furious. You take too
much at one time, you get squashed." He slugged cold Cabo.
"I seen it happen. *Compadre* of mine, Esquivel Figuerito,
borrowed a six-wheel sloader. Slipped into the yard and filled
it up with twelve crates of Miashi and Davidano thrummo
components, real class noise-makers, that he took off a container from Surabaya. Skrag weighed about two hundred kilos,
I guess. They busted him before he was halfway to the barrier."

"How?"

"*Mierde*, homber, those induction containers derop around
on magnetic fields, right? So the weight of each container is
checked and double-checked and recorded when it's off-
loaded from a ship, and the weight goes into the monitoring
'puters along with the rest of the stats. Yard Security Central

has a mass-weight record of every container as soon as it comes off the ship from whatever Slantland it calls home. They're monitored twenty-four hours a day. A container's weight suddenly drops, even a little, and it sets off an alarm in Security that records the amount of weight loss even as it's identifying the specific container. The yardeyes swarm that container on foot and speedbikes so fast you don't have time to sneeze. Nobody gets out.

"That's why we never skrag more than twenty kilos of anything. It allows us about a ten-kilo margin and we don't go over one decagram. Never. That's why I never been caught since I developed this little game. We take too little to miss. Sometimes we don't get much. A couple hundred. You seen it, you been in on it. But it's a gamble every time. I'd rather mess a guess and suffer a few sterile nights than end up busted and back in Hermosillo, or worse. Haven't been lucky. Just been careful.

"Other guys, they get too greedy. We take just a little at a time. Sometimes we don't get nothing. It's a tradeoff."

I nodded. "I been thinking, Chuy."

" 'Bout what, amigo?"

I sipped at my beer. "What if we could get around the weight problem somehow?"

Chuy frowned. "Don't get no funny ideas, homber. We do it my way or not at all. You want to freelance?"

"No, no. I'm as reticent as you. But what if, like, what if I thought of a way where we could vacuum not a few kilos of compo, but a lot more. More than two hundred kilos. A whole container. How much could that be worth?"

Chuy belched, then blinked. "A whole car? Man, you crazy."

"Maybe, but I don' mind bein' rich an' crazy."

Chuy chuckled. "If my guy can't make two hundred kilos, a smart like him, how you gonna take a whole car? You'll set off every alarm in every induction security station between San Juana and La Paz."

I did a little B&D on my enthusiasm. I was pretty confident, but still . . . "By convincing the system that the car isn't being skragged."

Chuy shook his head. "Now just how you gonna do that, homber?"

I sat up straight. Below, rising sounds indicated that Kilbee and Huong were deep in the hearta Mexas. "VR."

Chuy smiled. "That'd maybe fool the box vits, if you're good enough. But it doesn't affect the underlying analytics."

I leaned forward. "I'm not just talking virtual reality sightwise. I'm thinkin' virtual *weight*."

Easing back in his chair, Chuy glanced amusedly out and down to where Kilbee was all over his girl. Kilbee always got all the best-looking ones. Damn anglo. "What the hell is virtual weight, man?"

"Something I been playing with, thinking about ever since you introed me to our faz night games. See, before I got interested in splitting finitives, I wanted to be an artist. I can not only make a car look real through VR, I think I can make it feel real, too, if I can get into the distribution yard main box."

Chuy was thinking hard, still doubtful. "Even if you can fool the yard box into thinking something's still there that ain't no more, the place's still gonna be full of yardeyes. You've done enough slipos to know we got five, maybe ten minutes at the most to pull the old in-and-out before some Eye shows and makes us. So maybe you can work this thing and maybe you can't. It don't matter un ratass because we ain't got enough time to make it worthwhile. And even if you did, we can only take what we can carry. We can't drive a van into the distribution yard, much less a truck. Esqui tried that and I told you what happen to him. The Eyes'd be all over us for unauthorized entry in a minute, even before you could start setting up. Best we can do is get a set of riffy wheels into the employee vehic lot, like you seen."

"We don' need ten minutes to skrag a container," I told him, having thought it all out as best I could before opening my mouth. "And we don' need a truck. We're not gonna vacuum the damn thing. You won't have to carry nothin', neither.

"The Eyes and vit cameras don't track the containers after they've been sent on their way and left the yard, and there ain't no vits on the mainlines. Only box sensors. No point in tryin' to follow real-time pictures of containers snappin' past at three hundred per, so they just put up representations. Schematics. Virtuals. We can substitute our own damn virtuals, man. I can do virtuals like you never seen. That's the easy part. The trick's insertin' them into the network, foolin' the sensors when you sub the dupe, and givin' it staying power 'til we've safely skragged our load."

Chuy pondered some more. Then he chugged the rest of his Cabo, wiped his lips, and smiled that little hard smile of his. "What you need to try this, miracle man?"

I told him. He repeated the list to himself, though I didn't know how sophisticated his knowledge was or indeed if any of it would be famlliar to him.

"Zenitrov portable, Komitsu modem, Digibm peripherals. The other stuff I don't recog. Sounds like you got expensive tastes."

"I didn't say it would come cheap. The Zenitrov's the only portable with enough crunch to handle the VR mass and the graphics." I waited.

Chuy watched condensation creep down the sides of his gold beer bottle, blotting the droplets with a fingertip. "You're talking a lot of money. What if Huong and Kilbee don't go along?"

I shrugged, feigning indifference. Inside, I was excited not merely by the possibilities but by the chance to really make use of the natural talents I'd developed in Rehab.

"Well, Kilbee's always boasting how he can skrag some real money if he ever needs to. Maybe he'll make up any shortfall." Chuy leaned forward. "But you better know what you doing, amigo, or else start looking for an easy route over the mountains."

I smiled, but I didn't feel that way inside. Chuy wasn't
screwing around. Chuy never screwed around where money
was concerned.

It took longer to set up the program than to acquire the
necessary equipment, even though I'd spent weeks working
out a lot of it in my head. Kilbee grumbled and Huong looked
downright skeptical, but Chuy persuaded them. I spent a lot
of time in the basement of Chuy's constricted, three-story
codo, accessing the arcomplex library under an assumed code
and designing the probe.

When I thought I was ready I did some practicing on small
stuff and it all seemed to work, but cracking the inventory
box at Nick's Liquor and Narcotics wasn't the same as what
we were going to try.

There was no need for everyone to go along. In fact, with
just Chuy and I we'd be that much less conspicuous. Huong
and Kilbee watched doubtfully as Chuy and I rumbled off
beneath a quarter moon in a stolen Solarmax.

Kilbee's fancy card got us into the employee lot at the
distrib yard, like always. I made sure the backpack was secure
on my shoulders. Then we blew up our drunk dolls, slid out
of the car, an' started into the yard, absenting among the clicks
and hums of the hundreds of induction containers.

I kept waiting for Chuy to pick a likely target. It seemed
like it took him hours to make a decision, but inside he was
as nervous as always, though not as nervous as me. Finally
he stopped me next to a container with simple graphics.

"Don' look like much to me."

"Hey," he whispered in my face, "you leave the picking
to me. Now do it, if you're gonna. If you can."

I nodded and moved to the front of the container, searching
along the edge while Chuy kept a restive, silent watch for
roving Eyes. When I accessed the interlock I broke the seal
and found myself looking at a heavy-duty but pretty standard
communications module. I slid the backpack off and took out
the Zenitrov, fumbled clumsily with the peripherals while
Chuy cursed me, my ideas, and my mother under his breath,

trying not to nerve me but at the same time uneasy at hangin'
in one place for so long. Containers rumbled and drifted
around us.

I got in pretty fast, if I do say so myself. The distribution
yard box was big, lots of volume. What you'd expect for so
complicated an operation. I munched the stats on this particular container right away, because I was plugged into it. That
was the easy part. I floated around inside the box space,
orienting myself until I felt comfortable. I knew I didn't have
much time for sightseeing. Not with Chuy constantly prodding
me in the ribs.

I worked the Zen's tactiles until I knew everything there
was to know about the container I was into. It seemed pretty
promising, but it was a little early to start gloating. We didn't
have anything yet except a little access. First I subbed the
program dupe I'd shaped and that zeeped into the matrix
smooth as lotion on a beach bunny's buns. So far so *bueno*.

Implementation was a lot trickier. It's one thing to shape
a program and insert it, another to get it up an' runnin' in the
box. I grabbed the shipping info from the container and
inverted it, got a good look at the structure, and dumped it
into the waiting template I'd so carefully installed. Then I
made kind of a silent prayer and plugged the template into
the ass end of the container's up-and-run.

Chuy was tugging on my shoulder as I ran a couple of
redundancy checks. "Come on, homber! If you ain't done it
by now, you ain't never going to. Let's get out of here."

I pulled out, leaving nothing behind me in the distrib yard
box but empty crunch, nothing to trace the tickle. I was
fumbling to get the Zenitrov back into its holster as Chuy
half led, half dragged me back through the yard. As we ran,
making no noise in our expensive pylon skimmers, I could
hear the voices of two Eyes just passing behind us and a chill
went up my back. Too close, man.

Chuy didn't say nothing until we'd orphaned the stolen
Solarmax and were back in his clunker. "So? How'd it go,
'Stebo?"

"I don' know."

His tone turned unfriendly. "What you mean, you don't know?"

I looked earnest. "No way to know if it worked until Thursday."

"Why Thursday?"

"I thought I explained it to you. Everything depends on the container's shipping instructions. Its stats said it's programmed to join a train heading north on Thursday at five P.M. It won' move 'til then."

Chuy looked thoughtful. "So we can't do nothing but wait until then."

I nodded. " 'Til later, really. For when I set the template."

He sucked in a deep breath. "Amigo, it gonna be three nervous days."

He wasn't half as nervous all three days as I was that first hour.

Thursday *noche* found the four of us hanging near the receiving yard behind the Garcilasco Mall. Nothing unusual about that. The delivery area was bare except for a couple of empty containers. At two in the morning there was nobody around, not even an Eye. No reason for a patrol here. Even the Ensenada police didn't come around often. They didn't need to. There were easier places to break into than an armored, fully alarmed mall, with its thermosensitive vits and animorphed Dobermans. As for the loading dock, there was nothing there to steal.

Kilbee had actually rented the off-loader transport. If some federale did stumble accidentally onto us, we'd tell him we were just waiting to move a friend the next morning and couldn't sleep, so we'd decided to lay out for the night and suck a few sense sticks. Chuy an' Kilbee decided the story would sound better if it didn't come from four guys sitting in a stolen truck.

Huong tossed his stick stub through the window and glared at me. "I think you've just been pissing wind, 'Stebo. This ain't gonna work."

le a million and a half and this time you didn't have to
ch the vit news to find out about the skrag. It was all over
the general broadcasts by the first of next week. You
smell the Intuits the company hastily hired searching
clue, a hint, anything. Even our tough-ass purchaser
r a *rapido* vacation down Sudamerica way as soon as
l was done-did, it having gotten too hot suddenlike in
la to stick around. We just hung at Chuy's place and
all the noise.

me I'd added a little fillip to the riff, too (by now I
n' pretty cocky). Instead of putting in a VR-VW
at would remain locked in the box, I had it dissipate
of the desert halfway to Tucson. For days the vit
dense with shots of frustrated federales swarming
patch of cactus and sand out in the omphalos of
re the container was supposedly plucked off the
g along beneath the maglev tracks, sweating and
s unhappy. The only thing they found was an
e couple from TSU and a couple of poker-faced
We laughed ourselves silly.

was getting *caliente* serious, and we talked
huy made investments for us all, and we had
n the Isthmus to last each of us a lifetime.
and habled it for half a year, and finally
he game one more spin.

k back at that time I think it was for the
You get addicted to success. Theft is its
munerations aside.

yard three times before we decided to go
security had faded away in the months
After the furor over the fiber filch had
pretty much back to normal. The ennui
t. Chuy and I went in as usual, lookin'
t this time. One more big skrag and
v and its damning peripherals and my
iddle of the Golfo. One more.

to avoid a trio of Eyes, waiting half

I checked my watch for the fourth time in the past half
hour. "It's not time yet, Huong. There could be unexpected
holdups in the network, extra traffic. All week I've been
watching the vit news. No thefts reported from the system,
so nobody's found my artwork. Abstain, man. Everything's
workin'." I spoke boldly. I didn't have no choice.

Kilbee was fondling his vibrato. "You talk real big, 'Stebo.
Maybe you think you're smarter than us 'cause you can fold
a little crappy box work?"

"Ease off," said Chuy. He stared single-mindedly at the
two maglev lines that led to the big loading dock behind the
mall. "Give it time."

"Yeah, sure." Kilbee turned to gaze tiredly out the window,
resting his head against his closed fist and slumping in his
seat.

I sat up fast. "Something's coming." Everyone forgot about
everything else and sat up straight to look.

It was a container, ambulatin' smoothly according to program, heading toward the back of the loading dock. I tried
to see past it but there didn't appear to be anyone following
it on the track or on the street nearby. I felt a hand squeezing
my arm hard. Chuy, his eyes glittering.

We piled out of the truck and just watched while the container, neat as you please, slid down the elevated induction
track and came to a stop exactly as I'd programmed it to.
Kilbee came out of his trance long enough to give me a quick,
totally unexpected hug. Then he was backing the truck around
while the rest of us anxiously scanned the mall's access street.

The container's module obediently responded to the come-
hither call from the standard beacon in the truck cab and slid
inside. Huong and I shut the rear door and away we went,
the whole damn container snugged safely within.

At the abandoned warehouse down in the old harbor industrial district we cracked that beautiful sucker. Chuy had picked
a car destined for the Dai-Syntec Combine works up at Algo-
dones. The container was crammed with all kinds of good
stuff: sense-screens, blank moto paks, expensive nodulators.

When our private little fire sale was fully concluded and fenced two weeks later we gleaned about six hundred thousand, including an unexpected eleven thousand for the vacuumed container itself. Remarked and calligraphed, with a brand-new identifying module, it was sent cruising surreptitiously south toward Salvador and a new life.

Mi compadres were more than a little spizzed, you know?

There was nothing about our abscond in the vits for three weeks. Then I found a small item in the Strip financial section, had a hard copy made, and showed it to the gang at Chuy's.

"Dai-Syntec Corporation today announced the disappearance—see, man, they don't say theft—of a container load of valuable componentry. Insurance adjusters are investigating, but the loss is believed due to box error." Box error my ass, I half shouted, and everyone had fine words, mostly obscene, for the investigators at Dai-Syntec.

I could imagine the consternation in Company Receiving when their container arrived—and there was nothing there. Their box screens would show the container, whose simple rectangular appearance and markings I had artfully duped in VR, right where it belonged on the delivery track. Instruments would dutifully register its arrival weight as six point two tons, including cargo. But when they'd go out to the unloading dock to look for it, there'd be *nada* there. The boxman would check his stats and visual and there'd be the container, big as life. Except there wasn't nothing in actual reality. Only in virtual reality. A ghost container. No wonder they were sayin' the loss was due to box error.

As soon as the real container had deviated from its original programming and split from its northbound train, my template had kicked in and subbed a virtual one in its space. All the way north, at all the checkpoints, monitors would've recorded the virtual substitute according to the eager feed from my art and indicated nothing amiss. Meanwhile our container had turned sharply south and wended its merry way to the mall dock. If anyone had actually flown over the train as it was speeding north and run a real-time inspection they'd have

seen a container-sized gap between a Simas m and one from China. The whole business worked in the twentieth cen, when a train of cars dragged along by a single energy the front. But with each induction contain ered, it worked just fine for us.

All the poor sucks at Dai-Syntec en of virtual confusion.

We celebrated for a week, and ther of money, too much for Chuy to nobody was hurting for kosh. We ran out and bought six cars an' had our fun, but quietly, even Cocos Annex; soaking up the fems in their tight diving suits heads.

Six months later we did realized about a hundred a good one this time. A didn't push it, though. or leaving a trail for another three month tried a completely

Chuy like to sp

"Holy Virgin half chokin' on have a clue, b I know my e

Huong dir up a handfu is this stu

"Supe

"They run th earth shit c

Huong

an hour until we were sure they were long gone. Then Chuy called me over to a cold car. I waited and watched while he studied the markings, the design.

"I don't know what the hell's in here," he whispered to me, "but it oughta be interesting. Says organics under cold."

"Shit, Chuy," I muttered, "we gonna steal a load of chickens?"

"C'mon, omber. Where's your curiosity? It's got the profound max security seal, which means it's full of valuable Bio. We can get rid of anything before it degrades." In the galvanic darkness of the yard, his eyes were shining. "Let's try skragging something a little different."

"What the hell." I got into the spirit a little. Chuy's enthusiasm was always infectious. "Let's do it." I unpacked the Zenitrov.

We greeted the diverted cargo in a low-level container rental facility south of the city. We never loaded one into a truck from the same place twice. Meanwhile its Virtual Dupe was racing north toward Greater LaLa. The destination alone indicated that the contents were valuable. Otherwise why ship through Ensenada instead of LaLa direct? I admit I was curious.

Thirty minutes later Kilbee backed the truck into the warehouse space he'd rented under a fictitious company name. Chuy had set it up, real legal and fancy. We even had stationery and holoed business cards, just for this one skrag. It was all part of the game.

We dropped the rear end of the truck and went to work on the container. A blast of cool air rushed out to envelop us when the door finally hummed aside. We went up and in. It was chilly in the container, but well above freezing.

The shipping crates were a light polypropylene mix, sealed instead of locked. We had to wait while Huong hunted up the right tools to open them. After all, we didn't want to damage our valuable cargo, whatever the hell it was.

The lid snapped off a bright red crate the size of a desktop. Beneath was another lid, transparent. Inside, nestled in a cushioning bed of puffy insulation, was what looked like a dead parrot.

"It's not a parrot." Chuy ran his modified notex over the embedded lading slip. "It's a blue and gold macaw. From Ecuador. Destination: Haute Animale Pet Emporium, Bel-Air, LaLa."

"Well shit," muttered Huong. "A frozen bird." Equally put off, I remembered what I'd said to Chuy back in the yard about skragging frozen chickens.

Chuy, however, didn't seem too disappointed. "First off, it ain't frozen. It's in an anabiotic state."

"Say what?" Kilbee made a face.

"Don't you guys never read nothing? They can ship anything alive this way and it gets to its destination unspoiled. They substitute a special kind of trehalose for the glucose in the body. That lets the cell membranes shut down safely. Then they chill it to near freezing, slow down the metabolic rate so that the body uses about twenty-five times less oxygen. Swap the trehalose for normal glucose, float the body in warm water, give it an adrenaline boost and back it comes, squawking and screeching."

"Why not just ship 'em in cages?" Kilbee asked.

Chuy straightened. "Because a lot of 'em die along the way, and because they take up more room, and need attention, and make noise, and all those reasons make it a lot more likely Customs will find out about them."

"Customs?" Kilbee blinked, looked down at the brilliantly plumed quiescent bird. "You mean this parrot's an Illegal?"

"Illegal as hell. I'd bet my right *huevo* this bird's a danspec." Chuy's expression was hard. He looked around the container's chilly interior. Suddenly I was colder, standing there. "Let's try another crate."

The next one proved to hold something called a capybara, which I think I heard about on a nature vit, and the one next to it half a dozen Amazonian green parrots. A special square box was full of trehalosed red piranhas, and the biggest one in the room held an eight-foot-long black caiman, snoozing peacefully in its reinforced cold bed. We didn't know all the names, of course, but they were on the bills of lading embedded in each crate.

No wonder the polyprop crates had been heat-sealed.

The next crate we cracked contained a whole family of something called white-faced capuchins, but I think it was the margay kittens that finally got to me a little. Except for their exotic markings they looked just like street cats. The lading bill said they were worth fifteen hundred apiece, wholesale to the buyer in LaLa.

We knew we could market the bioskrag with no problem. Magimal sellers would pay plenty for the endangered species, or danspecs, eager to animorph them. Just north in San Juana you can buy and sell anything. The question was, did we want to?

"Each crate is self-contained and according to the instructions can last ten days outside the big container before the contents have to be revived," Chuy informed us, reading an inscription via his notex. "So nothing's gonna spoil if we ship it out by car." He eyed each of us in turn. "Anybody feel funny about this?"

"*Tot lam,*" muttered Huong. "That's swell. If we just forget it, they'll all die."

Kilbee nodded. "I *know* we can move this stuff. We sure can't send it back to Sudamerica, and if we notify Customs, they'll maybe trace it to us."

"Right. So we go ahead. This is gonna be faz. Don't you guys see it?" Chuy indicated the container's contents. "All this stuff's illegal business. So the people we've riffed it from, they can't go to the federales about it. This won't even make the vit news. We're clean." Chuy rose, looked around. "Let's see what else we got before we close everything back up."

We found all kinds of things in that container, man. The 'mals some people will keep for pets. The big constrictor snakes gave me the twitch just to look at them, and Huong and Kilbee laughed at the look on my face. We found more kittens, and a year-old *el tigre*, and a lot more birds.

Chuy found something, too. I saw him standing over the carton he'd just opened, staring down and saying nothing. "Hey, Chuy, what you got there that's so kinky?"

Huong looked over from where he was helping Kilbee. "Hey, maybe it's a movie star."

Kilbee made a vulgar noise. "Better, how about a putasicle?"

Surprisingly, Chuy didn't say nothing. It was like he didn't hear us. He just beckoned, kinda. So we eyed each other wonderingly and walked over, and looked through the by now familiar transparent inner lid.

It was a baby.

I didn't say nothing. Neither did Huong or Kilbee. I mean, man, what could you say? It was a little girl, buff naked, smooth and shiny an' clean as if she'd been polished. She lay in that white cushiony stuff all the crates were packed with and somehow that made it even more gross, you know? Like she wasn't no different from the parrots and lizards and monkeys. She lay on her back, with her head turned to her right and her little thumb plugging her mouth, just like she'd dropped off for a nap. There was some fuzz on her head, but not a whole lot.

I guessed she was maybe six months old. Huong thought as much as a year. Not that it mattered.

"Bastards," Chuy growled. I was surprised at his vehemence. I mean, it wasn't like it was his kid, or that of somebody he knew.

"I heard how this stuff goes down," Huong mumbled. "Poor women in Sudamerica have more kids than they know what to do with. So they sell 'em. Middlemen breed buy them up and smuggle them north and sell them in Veracruz and New York and LaLa and Nawlins."

"Let's check some other crates," I heard myself saying. Nobody spoke as we went to work.

There were twelve babies in all. Seven boys, five girls. The oldest was maybe a year and a half. The youngest . . . nobody wanted to educe the age of the youngest.

We sat down on crates we were sure held only animals and caucused.

"We got to vacate this," Chuy was saying. "We got to let the federales know and just vacate."

Kilbee looked reluctant. "Shit, Chuy, we could move the animals first. I mean . . ."

"No!" Chuy wasn't fooling around. I mean, you could see it in his eyes, man. I didn't know why he was so mad. Nobody was like festive, but he was more than that. Or less. "We turn it all over to the federales, let them follow up on it. I don't want any part of this, or the tribe behind it. We don't want to sift with them. You need money, Kilbee? I'll give you money."

Kilbee, big Kilbee, backed down fast. "No, Chuy, it ain't that."

"Then fuck it. Let's close this . . . let's close it all back up. We'll waft the container back to the yard." He looked at me. "You can do that, 'Stebo?" Not knowin' what else to do, I nodded. "Okay then. After, I'll tip the federales. None of you have to be involved." He hopped off his crate.

"Ice, infants!"

We all turned together. I gaped, but I couldn't get angry at myself. Nobody else had thought of it, either. Why should I be any different?

The homber sitting up in the open crate was ugly. It wasn't just the cold gel that dripped from his face and clothes. He was just plain ugly. He was about my size, skinny, but the automatic Ruzi he held made him look a lot bigger. We stood watching like four dumb kids trapped by the school bully as he climbed carefully out of the open crate and stood, a little shakily, his expression seeping mood. I knew just from looking at him that he'd as soon as kill us as talk to us. In fact, it was clear that he wanted to kill us. But he was confused.

"What the fuck is this?" He peered past us, toward the dark recesses of the quiet warehouse. "You're not Misko. None of you is Misko."

"He couldn't come," Kilbee said hesitantly.

The man flicked the muzzle of his gun in Kilbee's direction and the big anglo flinched. A dark stain appeared on the front of his tropical silks, got bigger as I stared. "Don't dick me, asshole. Where is this?"

Chuy spoke quietly. "Ensenada."

The man frowned, in control but obviously bemused. "Don't bullshit me."

"I'm not. You're in Ensenada."

"Something's wrong. I'm supposed to revive in Long Beach yard. Alarm must've gone off." He smiled: suddenly, unexpectedly, and unpleasantly. "Well, that's what I took the sleep for. Time to earn my kosh. First time for everything." He raised the gun. Next to me Kilbee made a whining noise.

"A meatrunner. A goddamn anabiosed meatrunner," Chuy snarled. He glared at us while I desperately tried to intuit what he was working. "First person cracks the container, built-in alarm program revives him. He checks to make sure the deal's done straight, flies back home. Anything looks menial-venal. . . ."

"You're a swift little fucker, ain't you?" The meatrunner waved the gun, moving away from his crate and backing us toward the wall. If we'd sensed him when he'd first started to revive, maybe we could've slammed the lid back down on him in time. Maybe.

"You sell babies!" Chuy's eyes were bugged and I could see he was losing it. I didn't know why, but that wasn't my preeminent concern of the moment.

"Shit, I don't sell nothing," the man retorted. "I just do what I'm told. I convoy, I pick up the payment and take it home. That's my job. That, and to make sure everything goes down straight. Ensenada, huh? That's a problem, but we got people here. I can weld things." Somehow I didn't think he was gonna be subtle about repairing our presence.

"What about their mothers?" Chuy persisted. I eyed him uncertainly. Why was he going on about it? We were all dead anyway. The guy was clinching a Ruzi, two thousand rounds a minute, full magazine. We were cheese.

"That's not my business. Buy 'em, steal, 'em; I don't give a crap. I do my job." He gestured with the Ruzi. "It's all meat to me. Like you."

"What if one of them was your kid?" Chuy continued, taking a step forward. I winced, but the gun didn't go off. "Stuffed full of synthesized sugar and chilled down like a microwave dinner?"

"Don't got any kids. Don't got a daily woman. Don't want neither." He wiped liquefying insulating gel from his face. "Think I'd take a run like this if I did?" Gel dripped off his forehead into one eye and he rubbed at it.

Before anybody could say anything, Chuy charged.

The Ruzi went off. In the confines of the induction container it sounded like Chinese new year in Frisco. I saw that on a docuvit once. Kilbee screamed and bolted. *Christo*, we all did. Just because Chuy chose to freak didn't mean the rest of us had lost it. Slugs ricocheted all around us as we spilled out the open back of the container.

Kilbee got one in the ass. He bawled like a kid. Huong had one part his short black hair, leaving a nice red trail behind it. That's how the federales caught them; by tracking the essence. We all went different ways, running like wild men from the warehouse. Since I wasn't hit and didn't leave no trail, I was the one who made it to the car and ripped out of there. I was sorry for Huong and Kilbee, but hell, I didn't know how bad they'd been shot or how long it would've taken 'em to make it to the parking lot.

I didn't go to my codo. Lita was sleeping at her place but I woke her *prontissimo*, told her what had happened. At that time I didn't know that Huong and Kilbee had been picked up, and I didn't care. At a time like that you don' hang around waiting for the door to buzz. It might not be your amigos.

We had a pre-arranged place to rendez, down in the Isthmus. I left my *madre* and brother and sister a terse note, told them I'd be in touch soon as I got a chance.

Then I went after Lita.

She hesitated, but she came with me. See, I'd seen a lot

that night and all of a sudden having a family and a real
esposa and some kids and settling down somewhere peaceable
and quiet far, far away from meatrunners and Ruzis sounded
like a pretty sensible idea. After she got through kissing me
(ee-ha: salsa!) it didn't take her long to pack. She didn't have
no job to quit no more. I'd been taking care of her since our
first big success. As we were taking a robocab to the airport
I looked up from where I was all squeezed down on the
floorboards an' asked her to marry me. She didn't have time
to think about it, which is maybe why she said yes. I don'
care why, just that she did.

I didn't relax until we landed in Gatun City and took the
boat out to the island. I waited there, calypsoing the dish all
over the Clarke belt, monitoring the news vits. It was all there
two days later. Not big stuff. I saw that they'd picked up
Huong and Kilbee and the blood placed them at the warehouse.
Mi compadres, sweet little loco senwhores that they are, didn't
implicate me, though. They said it was all Chuy's idea, Chuy's
plan, Chuy's work. That left me virgin and in the clear.

'Cause Chuy was dead.

Six slugs. None through vital organs, he just bled to death
before the parameds arrived. When the old warehouse night
watchman heard the Ruzi go off he naturally called the federales first. The meatrunner was dead, too, Chuy's malachite-
shafted little vibroblade stuck clean through his throat. I
always thought that was a fem's weapon. Guess I was wrong.
Sorry, homber. There was blood everywhere, which the news
vit only hinted at.

Still, I wasn't going back. Too chancy. I had plenty of
money. So did Kilbee and Huong, though it didn't look like
they'd be able to get at it for eight years. That's what the
legals hit 'em with. They blamed everything on Chuy, and
the legals couldn't prove otherwise, but they could sure stick
'em for skraggin' the container. Maybe Kilbee's rich folks
could've got him out sooner, but they washed their hands of
him. Figures.

Only thing that didn't figure was Chuy rushing that guy. It

was a lunatico, stupid move, which is probably the only reason he was able to get in close with his vibrato before he was cut down. I told Lita about it and she couldn't figure out why he did it neither.

I found out a year later, when I went roundabout to tell his *madre* how sorry I was. Took a long circuitous route to get an answer back to me, too, which is how I intended it.

Chuy'd had a little sister. All black hair an' bright eyes. He doted on her, lived for her. One day when he was seven and she was four she wafted. Just vanished off the damn street, in the mid of the day. Nobody saw nothin'. They never found her. No body, nothing. She just evaporated. Maybe she was abused and dumped, maybe she just wandered away and fell off a dock into the bay and the current carried her south, or the sharks got her. Maybe she was skragged, doped, shipped north, and sold. Nobody ever found out.

It stuck Chuy real deep, even deeper than it did the mother. Abyssal visceral, like. Things like that, they never go way, never disappear. They're like mental malaria: just when you think you got it cured, you end up puke sick an' flat on your back all over again.

You think about that, and the twelve trehalosed babies, and you'll understand. Chuy didn't see a dozen babies in that skragged container: he saw twelve wailing *mamacitas* somewhere in Sudamerica. Maybe the deals were all sad but clean, maybe they all did it voluntarily and were glad of the money. But maybe one or two weren't bought. Maybe they were just acquired, like. Abducted, snatched off the streets, out of a carriage or papoose pack. Nobody ever know that, either.

Mierde, I felt sorry for the babies *and* the kittens.

They couldn't trace nothing to me 'cause the Zenitrov had been left in Chuy's car, and when I wafted I took it with me to Panama. Gave me something to do, play around with. No more yard rifling, though. No more shamming with VR-VW simulations. But I practiced plenty. I'm an artist, you know?

It's be nice to share memories and stories and company with Huong and Krying Kilbee. That's what I call him these days, and I know he wouldn't mind it 'cause we're both BTS, now an' perpetual. Of course I can't do that 'cause they're up in federal penitentiary in Chihuahua, paying their debt to society. They can't get out of that stone-cold place because they're tracked and watched an' looked after by the most sophisticated automatic antisoc monitoring instrumentation the Namerican penal system can devise.

They couldn't possibly be down here with me and Lita, swimming and diving off our little private island, bibulatin' beer and siestaing in the sun and troubling the local senoritas. They have to serve their time and homber, that's just what they're doing.

Virtually all of it.

From the Notebooks of Angel Cardenas:

People have no idea the kind and variety of bizarre goods that end up in federale storage. They think it's all stolen vehicles and personal electronics. That last acquisition we made, headquarters had a helluva time disposing of. You'd think we could trace most of the contraband back to the original parents. Except that there were no original parents, so to speak. Test-tubers, the lot. *In vivo veritas*. Police departments don't have the loose change to run DNA checks on unclaimed bio-property.

Not to worry. The prospective adopters lined up as soon as the situation was explained. I thought about putting in my own name. Yeah, I did. I wouldn't mind having a kid, though at this stage of my life raising one would be a project. I know I could do it, though. See, I've been surrogate papa to plenty of street kids. The straight as well as the crooked.

It's just that I know how hard it would be on a kid trying to grow up with an Intuit for a father. A kid's got to be able to get away with a little fib now and then or they'll go loco.

You'd be surprised how many people who work up and down the Strip have religion. Some of them, see, it's *all* they got. Long hours, cold masters, pay that evaporates during the first trip to the allmart or the grocery channel, that can be taken from them.

But not religion. Usually it's clean, and it helps. Like most things, I find that you get out of it what you're willing to put into it. Religion doesn't betray people; people betray religion. When that happens it's the same old, old story. Money's usually involved, or sex.

You never know, homber, how reality is going to get messed up on the Strip. I love the contrasts. An old friend who managed to retire from the force last year with most of his original limbs once said that I live for juxtaposition. Kidding, I asked him what position, and he told me without hesitating, "The juxta one, of course." Said it without smiling. I wasn't sure what he meant. Still ain't.

I think it has to do with my work sort of explaining itself.

Our Lady of the Machine

I

"God had him killed because he wouldn't pay off?"

"That's what the widow told us." Not a hint of a smile lightened the expression on the captain's face. It would have seemed an alien intrusion at best. Pangborn didn't smile very often.

Cardenas dissected what he'd been told as he gazed absently past his superior. From the office situated midway up the triangular police tower he could see a good deal of sweltering downtown Nogales and out into the Strip beyond. Interlinked kinks of assembly and design plants, the muscles of the most powerful industrial connurbation the world had ever known, gleamed fiery chrome and bronze at eventide.

The relentless southwestern sun shadowed them with red and gold patinas. An occasional clutch of desperate, huddled vegetation signifying the site of a park or sardonically set-aside riparian zone put forth a feeble green scream against the tidal waves of heat that were reflected from pavement and wall. Sinews of program roads and the tendons that were high-volume induction strips knotted the energetic coils of commerce together.

Amid such relentless mercantile fervor humans ventured fitfully from building to building, corpuscles and cells traveling via air-conditioned tubes, minuscule individual shapes vital to the continued commercial health of the aggregate organism. Thanks to the interminable inventiveness and energy of such individuals the Strip had grown to become the engine that powered a sizable chunk of the world's GNP.

Inspector Angel Cardenas knew much of it intimately and was completely at home in its smoldering, fevered concourses, where he but rarely encountered anything or anyone truly likable.

The captain was waiting on him. Not an easily unsettled sort, he looked anxious. Cardenas cleared his throat.

"I'm not a particularly religious man, Shaun. But if I was, I think I'd find it hard to believe in a deity that stoops to common extortion."

"Not extortion," Pangborn corrected him dourly. "Failure to contribute to the support of the poor."

"Ah yes. To the poor extortionists." Cardenas's wry grin minutely lifted the drooping points of his impressive mustache. "Do we have anything to go on besides the theological rantings of half-hysterical widows?"

"Damn *poquito*." The captain shuffled through a pile of printouts on his desk like an aborigine digging for edible grubs before finally shoving a hard copy at his guest. Cardenas took it and read deliberately, his transplanted ice-blue eyes missing nothing on the tattle sheet.

"Initially there was a flurry of complaints." Pangborn chewed on a thumbnail. "Then information dried up."

Cardenas sniffed, wrinkling his mustache. "When the federales can't keep citizens from being killed, the survivors tend to go noncommunico pretty quick." He leaned forward to pass the hard copy back. "This is small squash. Local loco. Why call me in? I'm not bored."

Pangborn considered him out of deep-set burnt-umber eyes
that had pushed around plenty of bodies before they'd been
relegated to pushing papers. "You're our best Intuit, Angel.
This isn't your usual cut-and-wasted racket. It looks simple
enough on the surface, but there's something farking sophisticated going on here, and the mibble on the pave is that it's
spreading. You know how this kind of protection-extortion
works; you persuade or vape a few of the doubtful and the
rest soon fall in line."

Cardenas nodded understandingly. He reached down to pet
the dog that wasn't there and caught himself halfway, wondering if the captain had noticed. "Come on, Shaun. Let's have
a little *verdad* here. Why pick on me?"

The captain grunted. "Graveyard shift supervisor at Mondadoroko Tools over in Nog East got a memo on his Dimail
telling him that he and his blessed company weren't doing
their part to help the indigent in his district, and that God was
displeased with this so they'd more or less better shape up
and do their share. Fast."

Cardenas shook his head. "Don't know Mondadoroko
Tools."

"Precision masking division of Wurtemburg Kraftwerk
GBN."

Which explained everything, Cardenas saw. The local precinct feds would be expected to deal with moderate levels of
extortion on the street level, but when small-time operators
started trying to park their kismet on one of the big multinats
like Wurtemburg Kraftwerk, then Regional Enforcement
would be expected to start taking them seriously.

"Somebody's getting a little big for their britches," he
commented.

Pangborn pursed his lips. "If you think you've got God
on your side, why not try and respirate money out of the
multinats? Why limit yourself to restaurant owners and chip
kickers and proteinoaties?"

"They're starting small," Cardenas mused. "Maybe
they're not absolutely sure God's on their side." He shifted

in the chair, trying to focus on what Pangborn wasn't saying. "How'd our unlucky monger downslide?"

The captain looked uncomfortable. "He and his wife were solicited twice to contribute. By a cowled Collar. You know, a padre?"

"So why didn't they?"

"They discussed it with their regular neighborhood priest. He didn't know anything about this guy or the Order he claimed to represent. *'Nuestra Senora de la Machina'*. The priest advised them not to pay, and to call the local fed station. This they did. The padre came back twice. The third time he warned them that God was angry that they were doing so well while others were starving. They told him to waft."

"What happened next?"

Pangborn's tone soured. "Two days later they were locking up around eleven when according to the widow a vision appeared in the middle of their store."

Cardenas ticked off possibilities. "Holomage projection. Static optical diffusion. Coherent-confluent VR. Something in their dinner. There are plenty of plausible explanations."

"Sure," the captain agreed readily. "The widow insists it was a woman clad in flowing robes, all in glowing white. The color and texture of shaded heavy cream, she said. Too soft for sculpture. It wore a sad expression. It floated over to them and rebuked them for their stinginess. Her husband declared himself unimpressed and insisted loudly that he wasn't about to pay good money to protect himself from magic tricks. He turned to pick up the phone to call us.

"The widow says that's when the image put a hand on her husband's head and he collapsed." Cardenas's eyebrows arched. Pangborn stared back at him unflinchingly. "Coroner's report says cardiac arrest. The guy died on the spot. His wife insisted he was healthy as a horse. His medical records support her.

"The image backed off, steepled its hands as if in prayer, and told the widow that while she was sorry about her husband, the needs of the poor could no longer be entrusted to the sluggish whims of mere human agencies. Then it crossed itself and disappeared." He paused. "I'm no holofield specialist and I don't have time to keep up with what's new in the field, but I've only heard of one gizmode that could do something like that."

"A tactile projection," Cardenas murmured. A very small shiver tickled the base of his spine.

Pangborn nodded. "Strictly military ware, and mostly experimental. Except for one official incident, which happened to occur in our district. Which happened to involve you."

"I'm not likely to forget," Cardenas told him. "Have the relevant companies been queried?"

"Both GenDyne and Parabas insist they've barely begun to probe the secrets of the subox tunnel you encountered on that case, much less figure out how to bypass and disarm the guardian tactile systemics their late, lamented, and self-vacuumed specialists left sprinkled in their wake."

"Then it sounds like somebody else has learned how to run and project an independent tactile. Military leak?"

The captain shook his head impatiently. "Been checked out." This time he did smile. "First they insist they're not working on anything like that, and then they assure you that even if they were their security's so tight not even an engraved molecule of information about what they're not working on could slip out."

Cardenas sighed. "So we're back to hypothesizing an independent Designer. Like the two who vacuumed themselves."

"Or something else," the captain muttered darkly. "Something new. Get out on the streets, Angel. Fave the pave. Go down into the *gordo mucho* and parley the mongrel mongers. Find somebody who'll talk back. I'm busy enough as it is. I don't need the Kraftwerks and Fordmatsus and GenDynes on my back. Nobody my age with my blood pressure deserves that."

Cardenas rose to leave. "I'll pray for you, Shaun."

The beleaguered captain didn't grin back.

II

Paily Huachuco had taken a filthy gel-glazed storefront on Twenty-third Avenue and through hard work and pave smarts turned the rat and roach palace into the modest music nest flamboyantly neoned on the outside as Musik-Niche. That had been five years ago. Now there were four garish, glitzy Musik-Niches, sited equally between Nogales del Norte and Sud. Currently Paily was negotiating for store space in the Lochiel and Cibuta malls. A flashman lawyer for a big synergainment syndicate had approached him with talk of franchising. The offer had been tempting, but the concomitant loss of control that would have accompanied it was not. Better to be an independent minimog than a high-salaried castrato.

Ten years down the road, maybe he'd think about it some more. Right now he was having too much fun.

Through the one-way polarized he could look down on the main floor of his flagship store where rapido repeaters and workers and sub-adults and ninlocos on their best behavior jostled with young execs and maskers and assemblers to peruse Musik-Niche's unrivaled stock. Max-sensorial holovits gyrated above their heads, enticing male and female alike with tridi images of boobs and buns and bulges, and sometimes even music.

The execs and assemblers tended to scarf on preprogrammed cubes, while the store's younger patrons were more eager to experiment. They swam through the humming establishment's vast, daily-updated catalog of rhythms and melodies, voices and instruments, mixing their own according to the latest vogue. Everyone a composer, Huachuco mused. Everyone a singer and musician, arranger and performer. Like its competitors, Musik-Niche served up a swirling, boiling musical and visual soup from which patrons could at leisure and in comfort elutriate the bits and pieces of sound that most sweetly vitalized their senses.

Or if you preferred, one of the store's knowledgeable wandering specialists could help you build your own custom cube.

A teaspoon of reggae, half a cup of tamba, guitar, and juiced samisen to taste, bake in ¾ time, stew with drums and synth, and pour when ready. Sprinkle with lyrics from Musik-Niche's immense ROM library and you too can be a star.

Or buy premixed. That was even more profitable than the customized music in which Huachuco's stores specialized.

His door buzzed and Cina stepped in. She was pretty and efficient and had been with him since the opening of his second store. He'd made her a vice president.

She brushed at her blond surgical transplants. "That Collar's here to see you again, Paily. The padre?"

"Cina, I told you to deal with him yourself." Paily indicated his desk. "I don't have time to talk to chariters. I'm trying to pare down the margin on Hokusai's next delivery by another quarter percent and you'd think I was prospecting Mons Olympica without an airsuit. The stinking tight-assed Hivers don't want to cut an eighth on a single *cancion.*"

"He won't talk to me and he won't go away." She waited immovably.

Huachuco briefly considered having the obnoxious solicitor unceremoniously heaved pavewise, but if he *was* a bona fide man of God, however much his approach and timing sucked, someone might see. Or worse, take a recording of the incident.

"*Mierde:* send him in. I'll get rid of him."

Cina wafted. Her space in the doorway was filled a moment later by a short man in a brown business suit. His jacket's integral hood was pushed back off his head to reveal the white collar. He wore his black hair cut short all over and had more Indio in him than the average Strip dweller.

"Why do you keep pestering my people," Huachuco said belligerently. "No, don't sit down. I don't have time for this."

The Collar considered his host calmly. His attitude verged on the patronizing. Huachuco took an instant dislike to him.

"Everyone must make time for God's work, my son," the visitor declaimed solemnly. He had a scratchy, accusatory tone on which words splintered like thin sheets of glass underfoot. It did little to engender any empathy on the part of his impatient audience.

"I'm not your son, padre, and I don't believe in God. I'm a businessman."

"God is also in business: the business of saving souls. Those who avert their eyes from the pressing needs of the poor would do well to look to their own."

"Hey, I look after the poor. We have a big sale at least every other week. Tell you what: why don't you bring your parishioners in next Saturday for our monthly half-off? If you have any, that is."

"We of the Order do not preach in the obscenely moneyed halls of the great churches. We do our work quietly while embracing worthy individuals such as yourself, so that the contributions so generously made in our name may be guided straightforwardly to those most in need."

"Like yourselves, maybe? Go on, get out of here. I have work to do. Go vend your shtick on Centrale. If you show yourself here again my security people will put you nearer heaven for at least three seconds. That's how long you'll be airborne before you kiss the pave." He bent to his work.

His expression stiff as his collar, the visitor stood. "Our Lady does not take kindly to those who mock the Lord."

"That has a nice ring to it. I'm sure one of our pro mixers can set it to trip-trop for you. But if you're not going to buy anything, you'd better get out."

The brown-suit departed. Without any yelling or cursing, for which Huachuco was grateful. Ill-considered obscenity was tiresome. The pave was home to some wild evangelicals, he knew. From the traditional End-of-the-Worlders to the more trendy Oceanics and the Silicon Surfers. He'd really have to take a moment to dictate a formal memo to Security, directing them to be more selective about who they admitted. Though you had to watch it or the Equops would be all over you, claiming you'd failed to provide equal and unprejudiced shopping opportunities for left-handed lesbian Rastafarians with Down's Syndrome, or something similar.

Musik-Niche stores never closed, but the administrative staff worked normal shifts. Except for Huachuco, who frequently stayed at his desk far into the early hours of the morning. That was how you built a business: by being the first one to open and the last to close. It was up to the boss to lead by example. Besides, Huachuco enjoyed his work. He liked drafting memos and scanning reorder sheets and negotiating for store space and licenses.

It was suddenly and unexpectedly much brighter in his office.

She was exquisitely, ethereally beautiful, and she hovered several centimeters off the floor as she gazed mournfully down at him. Her perfect face was unlined and unblemished, the nose sharp and Semitic, the large liquid eyes overflowing with unabashed concern. Her immaculate white robe, pure as unsullied chalcedony, covered her from head to sandaled feet in the fashion of an earlier time. She wore no jewelry or other form of artificial adornment. She needed none.

Huachuco leaned back in his chair and considered the specter. "That's good. That's very good. I have to admit it: you're the best holomage I've ever seen. But then you'd have to be to convince so many people. Or do you think I don't listen to the pave rave? Tell me: where's the projector? Hard to believe it's a portable; you're too dense. Talk about steady-state renewal: I can't see through you at all. They must tap into a building conduit nearby. Do they have to steal crunch as well as power? Sustaining your configuration, not to mention moving you around, would take a *mass*."

"You have no faith," murmured the female figure in a gentle, disapproving tone.

"You're right there." He raised his voice slightly. "Listen, you *vacantes*. When I opened my first store I had some stupid *pendejos* in every other night trying to hold me up for protection money, or just to see what they could steal. After I sent the first couple to the hospital and one to the morgue the word got out on the pave not to mess with Paily Huachuco. I guess you haven't been around long enough to get the word. I'm not some dumb convenio store owner you can frighten with words and holos." Leaning forward, he casually thumbed a switch on his desk. A loud hum filled the room.

"Know what I just did? First, that's a straightline to the local precinct station. My friendly 'hood federales will be on their way here in thirty seconds. Second, it snapped up a scramble cage around me. Anything electronic tries to slip through—holo, virus, bacterium, lethal charge—it gets reducioed like an electric chicken. You want to try gas, I got a mask in my desk I can put on faster than you can spit. I don't see your holo carrying no gun, so I won't even tell you how I handle that." He checked his chromo. "You better get moving. The feds will be here any minute."

The mage continued to regard him with sorrow. At that moment the door opened and the night manager poked his head in. Huachuco hastened to reassure his assistant.

"Check this out, Benny. It wants prayers and money. Bet you can't guess which it wants *primero*."

The older man crossed himself reflexively, much to the disgust of his boss. "You . . . sure it's just a projection, Paily?"

"Not you, too? The feds will be here soon. Be sure and let 'em in fast. If this thing will hang around for another minute or two maybe they can track it to its generator. That'd put a permanent end to the irritating visits from our most persistent local collection agency."

The figure radiated serenity as it drifted toward him.

"This should be interesting," Huachuco said expectantly. "I've got the scramble up. Will it come apart, make lots of pretty sparklies, or just disappear?"

"Paily . . ." the manager began uneasily.

"Relax, Benny. Go back to work. Tell everybody what's sequencing so they won't freak when the feds show up at the front."

The night manager hesitated, unable to take his eyes off the beatific floating figure.

It impinged upon the scramble screen. And drifted through it.

There was no combustive flash of light, no coruscating disruption of the holomage's structure. The figure simply passed through the screen as though it didn't exist. Huachuco's gaze narrowed as he grabbed for a drawer in his desk. When his hand reappeared it held not a gun but a small rectangular plastic box. There were buttons on the end he gripped and LEDs on top. He thrust it out in front of him, a portly Van Helsing preparing to ward off a persistent phantasm.

"You know what this is?" he blurted, his voice still strong. "It's a fed box disruptor. You touch the tip to a box, a board, a vorec receiver, a projection of any kind, and it sends a coherent static charge back through the box net to the control source. Turns it to mush. It makes a scramble screen look like a toy. Now get away from me or I'll sludge your whole operation at one touch." He peered past the incandescent female form. "Benny, see if the feds are here yet!"

The manager found himself unable to move.

A delicate feminine hand reached toward the owner, who started sliding backward in his chair, the now wavering disruptor held out before him. Refulgent fingers closed upon the plastic. One made contact with Huachuco's hand. He felt pressure, slightly warm though cooler than that which would have been produced by a normal human hand.

The disruptor began to melt, the plastic to run hot and liquid in his grip. He flung it aside when it started to burn his fingers.

"Benny!"

The night manager stood staring.

The melancholy expression on the flawless face never changed as both arms reached out to embrace Paily Huachuco. Mouth ajar, he gaped up at it. Then he twitched, just once, and slumped in his chair, his head lolling to one side, seeming to melt a little; not unlike the disruptor.

A trembling Benjamin Martinez fell to his knees, his hands clasped in front of him, his head bent as he began to pray. He prayed faster as the figure turned and drifted toward him.

Outside in the store below one of the sales clerks was debating with the three federales who had just arrived. As bemused customers looked on she turned and pointed up toward the executive offices on the second level.

The seraphic figure reached Martinez and extended a hand. "Please. Please, God," he murmured desperately. "I have a wife and two children."

The Virgo Gloriosa placed a glowing palm on his forehead. He felt an infinitely light pressure tilting his face up and back. The Madonna smiled reassuringly at him. "Those who give to those who have devoted themselves to helping the needy have little to fear, in this world or the other. Least of all from me." The voice was music incarnate, pristine and refreshing as clear mountain waters. Then it vanished, a quick fade to nothingness.

Weapons drawn, the feds burst into the office. One tried and failed to coax Ben Martinez off his knees while the others examined the motionless form of Paily Huachuco. It was a brief examination, lasting only long enough to ascertain for certain that his heart had stopped.

III

The wiry figure in the brown suit slipped the cowl back off his head the better to study the storefront. It was new, the location having been completely remodeled and popped only a couple of weeks ago. There were no windows, but that was to be expected of a shop that specialized in guns and other means of self-defense. If such an establishment could survive in so dangerous a neighborhood, it promised to be highly profitable. Profitable enough, surely, to spare a small percentage of its monthly gross for a worthy charity. He checked his collar as he ambled toward the entrance.

The store's security was impressive. Just inside the outer door armored vits scanned him visually while other sensors checked him for concealed weapons. Only when the system was satisfied was he admitted past the second, warhead-proofed inner door.

The place was much bigger than he'd expected, and full of customers. Most encouraging. The male and female staff looked competent and active. No doubt they were adept at manipulating the same devices they sold. Drawn by her brassy blondness, he chose the most attractive of the female personnel to approach, his mind toying with decidedly impious thoughts.

"Pardon me, but where can I find the owner?"

"Is there a problem, padre?" She was polite without being deferential. He kept his eyes on hers.

"No, no problem. I only wish to speak with him about a contribution to our Order and its program of public works."

She sneered. "Good luck. *Padron* Cardenas ain't real free with the dinero, either his own or the business's."

"I can only try to persuade him."

She shrugged, thumbed a pickup. "I'll find out if he'll see you."

The visitor pretended to ignore the conversation that ensued, until the saleswoman turned back to him.

"He says because we're new in the 'hood he'll give you three minutes."

"I heard. Which way, please?"

She gestured. "In the back, past the bioweapons cooler. I don't suppose I can interest you in a chili gun? We've still got a few left from our opening week special."

He smiled tolerantly. "I have no need of violent devices. Our Lady watches over me."

"Glad to hear it. Good thing she doesn't watch over every-body or we'd be out of business. Now if you'll excuse me, we're on partial commission here and I think I see a mark with money."

He raised an open palm by way of parting. "Bless you, my child." I'd like to bless you for about an hour, on a hard floor, he thought crossly, but that wouldn't quite be keeping in character. Business *primero*.

The black laminate carbide inner doorway was blocked by a huge dark man with an expansive glower. A repeating pistol made a prominent knot on his hip. Collar and cowl notwithstanding, he gave the visitor a thorough once-over before passing him on. There was no need to check for weapons, the sensors at the main entrance having already seen to that.

The inner office was swollen with a surprising amount of tech. There was nothing readily recognizable as a desk; only a chair occupied by a small, muscular man who looked to be in his late forties or early fifties. A prominent, drooping mustache that gave him the appearance of a jaded basset hound underlined startling blue eyes and a small but jutting chin. He wore a neat charcoal-gray business suit with pink vertical stripes down the right side and a matching filigree-pattern shirt. When he gestured, the three huge rings on the middle fingers of his left hand shifted like platinum, not silver. The visitor was much encouraged.

"Have a seat, padre." The owner gestured at an empty chair. "What can I do for you?" His tone was soft and inoffensive, the kind of voice that made you feel instantly at ease. His attitude was friendly and accommodating. The salesbitch had him all wrong. Maybe this one would go easy, the visitor mused as he sat.

"Señor Cardenas, I represent a local religious Order which has devoted itself to serving the poor of the Strip. To those in need we provide food, shelter, medicines, and sometimes a modicum of necessary funds. Since we are not a nationally recognized institution we are forced to survive on the charity of local merchants. Yours is a new establishment in our parish and you seem to be doing well."

"We are," Cardenas informed him.

"Then perhaps you might see your way to contributing on a regular basis to our good works."

The owner looked thoughtful. "Let me tell you something, padre. When I was very young my mother died. I prayed to God to let her live. She did, for months, in great pain from cancer. Only then did her suffering end. My father was killed by a spazzed ninloco on parole from San Luis. It is my feeling that I have no use for your church or any other. So I will not contribute to your Order. You may leave now."

"Please, Señor Cardenas. I ask you to reconsider. For the poor."

Ice-blue eyes blazed unexpectedly. "You have ten seconds to get out before Fennel renders you unable to collect from anybody, much less me."

The violence of the owner's retort caught the visitor off-guard. Not that he was long troubled. He rose to depart.

"Our Lady is not pleased by those who speak so indifferently of those in need. I sympathize with your history . . ."

"Don't," said Cardenas sharply. "Just get out, and stay out."

"God can persuade as well as heal," the visitor declared as he moved toward the thick door. "Though you have not been long among us it may be that you have heard of others in this part of the Strip who have had doubts of a similar nature resolved."

"I haven't been here long enough to hear much of anything except multo *gracias* from my suppliers, and I never listen to street gossip. *Hasta* your lego, padre. Better luck elsewhere." The door shut firmly behind the visitor.

He nodded at the glowering guard outside and strode briskly toward the exit. Clearly this Cardenas was one of those who could not be recruited by mere supplication. But if he were to meet with a fatal condition a venture like the weapons shop might easily fail. That would not be in the best interests of the Order. Dead men made poor contributors.

The gun monger had struck the visitor as a very straightforward type. Skeptical to be sure, but once convinced, forever amenable. The visitor smiled. He and his Brothers would pray over this.

Behind him, the guard and the saleswoman caucused with Cardenas.

"If he's a real priest, then I'm a pedigreed poodle pamperer," the woman announced. "He was mouthing all the right words, but his eyes were on my chest half the time and it wasn't benediction he had in mind. You could see it in his eyes. Hell, you could practically smell it." Her mouth wrinkled at the remembrance.

"Thanks, Darcy," Cardenas told her. "He's obviously had practice. His performance was good, but not perfect. His origins kept showing." He glanced to his left. "Any thoughts, Corporal Fennel?"

"Sergeant Delacroix's right. It's a scam from the *venga*, sir. I'd bet my pension the poor pavers in this part of the Strip don't see a single credit from this guy's 'Order'. The recorders made a good snatch. If his reality's in the active files we should have something on him by tomorrow; a little longer if he's not."

Cardenas nodded knowingly. "Before he left he as much as threatened me with the same kind of fatal visitation that expiated that music-store exec last month."

"Anything we can wind him on, sir?" the big man asked.

"No. He's too clever for that. Everything was implied. But the threat was real enough. I'm never wrong about such things." The officer didn't dispute this. Everyone knew Cardenas's reputation.

The sergeant looked grim. "All the tech's in place, Inspector. If anything weird manifests we'll be ready for it."

"We'd better be," said Cardenas. "The hook's been set. I don't want any casualties on this operation."

"Orthodox, sir." She turned and departed. The chevroned steroid went with her, hesitating at the door only after he was sure that his fellow officer was out of hearing range.

"Inspector?"

Cardenas eyed the officer. "What is it, Lukas?"

"Well, sir, it's just that . . . my family's Catholic, sir, and I was wondering if maybe . . ." He broke off, looking like a man who'd lost a contact lens instead of the right words.

"Wondering what, Lukas?"

The big man gazed back down at him. "This really couldn't be a manifestation of the Madonna, could it, sir? I mean, I've

read the reports and the descriptions testified to by those
who've seen it, especially the night manager at the musik
store. . . ."

"Lukas, do you really think the Madonna would stoop to
soliciting donations on behalf of false priests?"

"No, sir, of course not, sir, but the musik exec had a
scramble screen *and* a disruptor, and they didn't save him.
They didn't work at all. Any kind of holomage, even a tactile,
should drop before either of those kinds of defenses, much
less both."

"Officer Fennel, are you sure you're going to be able to
carry out your duties on this assignment?"

The corporal stiffened. "Yes, sir."

"Then go back to your station and stop thinking so much."

The big man nodded and left, but it was clear he was
still troubled. He might fool his colleagues into believing
everything was okay with him, but not an Intuit.

It was pretty bad, Cardenas thought, when your own people
started giving credence to the utterly outrageous. That was
the reality of modern supratech for you. Virtually convincing.
The idea that a Madonna was at work in the extortion business
was as patently absurd as the notion of one appearing in an
Ajo farmer's pecan orchard, an actual incident that had been
related on the vit not all that many weeks ago.

This part of the world had been reporting such manifesta-
tions for centuries. Madonnas were seen in twisted tree limbs
or in shadows cast on walls, or in the reflections of badly
installed bathroom mirrors. There were Madonna sightings
several times a year, usually by rural folk for whom the
scientific method and common techniques of simple analysis
remained as unfathomable and mysterious as the inner work-
ings of a modern vehicle. When resigned specialists arrived on
each scene to propitiate the inevitable outpouring of misplaced
fervor, a natural explanation for each event was always quickly
found.

This one was more sophisticated than most and would take
a little more effort to explain. The only caveat awaiting its

explicators was that it was also a lot more deadly than a perceived silhouette on a wall or a benignly misshapen pumpkin.

IV

They didn't have a chance to see what the active files held on their insistent padre because the apparition manifested itself before the requested report could be delivered. For a sanctimonious visitation, Cardenas thought, it was remarkably responsive to the complaints of its chosen supplicants.

He recovered quickly from the initial surprise when it coalesced in his sealed and supposedly screened office. That it could bypass conventional security measures they knew from the way it had actively penetrated the defenses maintained by the recently deceased founder of the budding Musik-Niche music boutique chain. As to its appearance, it was exactly as described by surviving eyewitnesses such as the music store's night manager and the shop owner's widow.

It was quite a show, he decided. Traditional yet stirring, more than substantial enough to convince the gullible. And if the reports were to be believed, capable of unique feats of physical manipulation. That was what really intrigued him. In his career he'd had a pair of unprecedented encounters with tactile projections: more-than-virtual electronic matrixes capable of interfacing with solid objects, including people. He had to admit that the lifesize, softly glowing woman in her simulated white robes was as impressive as anything he'd previously experienced.

"You're very well made." His finger nudged the switch mounted beneath the arm of the chair. No one knew how the specter had managed to kill several perfectly healthy men, but no matter what transpired it would not add Cardenas to its list. A touch of the switch would instantly lower the chair in which he reposed to the basement below.

"You mock me." The voice was perfectly attuned to the

figure, but voices were easy to synthesize and mate to a holomage. Active corporeal tactility was an infinitely more ambitious achievement.

"Not at all. It was a compliment."

"You do not believe in me," the hovering Virgo declared.

"I'm willing to be convinced." This was true, as far as it went.

The phantasm turned toward the blank wall that faced the main part of the store. "You deal in violence."

"Does that trouble you?" Cardenas's finger lightly massaged the safety switch.

"Of course it does."

"But you'd still accept money from me that's derived from the sale of weapons."

From beneath brows of graven ivory limpid eyes fraught with imponderables deliberated. "Not I. Those who serve me. For the sake of the poor and needy, yes, I would not turn away such a tithing. Until the time comes for violence to be banished from this world I will take from the misguided to help the needy. There has after all been violence even in Heaven, when Michael and the Host cast out Satan and his followers."

"I don't deal in anything that extreme. You have to understand, of course, that I would need some kind of proof of your divine character before I'd simply turn over the fruits of my labor to those who claim to serve in your name."

The enraptured incarnation did not hesitate. "Come then, and you will have your proof. He who hesitates is lost."

I don't remember that quotation as being from the Bible he thought, but said nothing aloud.

A luminous white hand reached for him and he flinched. While no threat had been voiced or implied, there was no way he could intuit a projection. Reason suggested he would not be harmed; at least, not this time. He'd expressed a willingness to be converted, and a live believer constituted a much more profitable mark than a dead skeptic.

Reaching a decision he rose from the chair, eschewing the

safety it represented, and extended his own hand. The supple snowy fingers enveloped his own. He felt a gentle pressure urging him toward the doorway. The finger pressure was startlingly real, appropriately ethereal, and not the product of some clever subliminal projection. For the first time he felt his skeptical convictions wavering slightly.

But then, a highly advanced tactile program should be capable of that much. So gentle was the grip he felt certain he could pull away at any time. He did not try to do so for fear the action might provoke a less amiable portion of the program. He allowed himself to be led.

Fennel started when the phantasm emerged with the inspector in tow, but at a sign from Cardenas he stayed clear and kept his hands away from his weapons. As man and manifestation stepped out onto the shop floor, murmurs of confusion and then recognition arose from previously preoccupied customers. There was a concerted, agitated rush for the exit that the salespeople, federales all, made no effort to impede.

One officer feigned panic and joined the customers in breaking for the egress. Cardenas complimented him mentally for his quick thinking. Depending on the sophistication of the Madonna's observation and analysis programming, internal alarms might have been triggered if all the customers had fled while every member of the store's staff stood pat. The officer's precipitous flight should reassure the program along with whoever was monitoring it.

The apparition drifted over to a glass case to examine the weaponry within. "So much intricate death. Yet it is not at this moment in time within my purview to ban or interfere. Only to succor the poor." Releasing Cardenas from her feathery grasp the figure reached out. The plainclothes unsaleswoman behind the case decided it was time to move and edged away.

Radiant fingertips touched the glass and melted a hole through the thick transparency. They dipped lower to nudge the arm-and-activate switch on the shaft of a Rugersturm .10 caliber repeating pistol lying on the top shelf. There were gasps and a couple of muted curses as everyone, Cardenas included, dove for cover.

The weapon wailed. Sixty tiny shells splintered the case and tore into the wall, other display cases, and the floor as the ignited but unguided weapon flushed its oval clip in a thirty-second staccato orgasm of destruction.

As the echoes faded Cardenas looked up and slowly slid his hands off the back of his head. Everyone stayed prone, waiting for whatever might come next. The beatific shade pivoted to fix him with a kind but reproving eye.

"So much violence." It drifted toward another display near the back. Two officers garbed as salesclerks scrambled in opposite directions as the figure melted another hole and triggered a demonstration sinus grenade. As irritating gas spread through the salesroom, personnel scattered, clutching at their faces and sneezing uncontrollably while mucus poured from their nostrils. Cardenas rose to join them in the rush for the street but a lambent feminine figure interposed itself between him and the exit.

"Do not be alarmed. You will not be affected. I have spread my circle around you." And indeed, the initial tickle of the gas was not repeated. All around him his tactical team was staggering for the doorway while he stood alone and unaffected in their midst.

A very impressive demonstration, he decided, but not unarguably divine in origin.

"Let this remind you that I can bless as well as rebuke," the exquisite specter informed him. They waited for the fast-acting gas to dissipate. Only when it was no longer a threat to the inspector did the figure begin to fade.

"Help those in need and do not torment yourself with so many questions. You will be blessed." And then it was gone.

Cardenas stumbled through the lingering miasma, sneezing only a few times, and hailed his staff as they wheezed and gasped in the street outside. Curious pedestrians had slowed to eye the mass sinus attack but resumed their pace as one by one the afflicted recovered. The door passed them back in as they flashed their ident cards.

Cardenas gathered them in the center of the floor. A thoughtful officer announced from his assigned station near the entrance, "Surveillance is green."

"I'm not sure that has any relevance to what we're dealing with here," the inspector told his snuffling, red-eyed associates, "but we'll assume for the moment that we can talk privately. You all saw it?" There were nods and a few remaining sneezes. Tissues and handkerchiefs were much in evidence. "Any opinions?"

"Best holomage I ever saw," the pert sergeant commented readily. Her opinion was seconded by several of her suffering colleagues.

One officer was examining the hole the apparition had punched in the first display case. "Melted right through, sir."

"But if didn't pick up the gun," someone else pointed out. "Or the grenade. It just activated them."

"Its touch is very light," Cardenas added. "I don't think it was dense enough to raise either one. It can generate enough heat to melt tempered glass, but not enough to exert lift."

"Ultrasound," someone speculated, "could exert both pressure and heat."

Cardenas nodded, his mustache bobbing. "That's a possible. I'll buy that explanation for the holes in the cabinets, but the touch on my arm was too steady for ultrasound. There was no accompanying heat or vibration, either. There's more at work here. Something new, or at least something that's not on the market yet."

"It propagated responsive verbalizations," someone else remarked. "They didn't arise from a separate source."

"No, that's something else to note. And there's more. We talked in the office before it led me out. It alluded to the battle in heaven between the archangels and Satan's fallen ones. My first name is Angel, but it didn't even mention that. I'd think a Madonna would have commented on the irony. For that matter, you'd think a real spirit would have known that this store is a blind and that we're all feds instead of eager gun mongers."

"The failure to comment isn't conclusive, sir," Delacroix noted.

"No, but it's interesting. Just like its tendency to speak in generalities. A deity wouldn't do that. A modified generic response program would."

"Your average street monger or exec wouldn't pick up on that," the sergeant pointed out. "They'd be too mesmerized by the holo. Is it a real tactile, sir? I've heard of them, but I've never seen one."

"Few nonmilitary have," Cardenas told her. "I happen to be one of the few. They're not magic. Just incredible reciprocating programs that are sustained by an unbelievable amount of crunch." He turned to another officer. "Favour, have the molly moles run another check on all Strip utilities. See if they can spark a hint that somebody's vaping a large aggregate of charity crunch. If whoever we're after's good enough it'll go untracked, but maybe we'll get lucky."

"Yes, sir," the officer replied.

"The rest of you get this place cleaned up. I want to be open for business again by tomorrow morning." Groans greeted this order. It meant picking slugs out of the walls, or at least spackling them over and repainting. It meant fixing the holed display cases and removing all signs of panic. The true glamour of federales work, he mused.

He felt a bulk at his shoulder and turned to see Corporal Fennel peering solemnly down at him. "Sir?" The big man appeared hesitant.

"What is it, Lukas?"

"Well, sir, I wouldn't want it to affect my record but . . . you remember what I said earlier? About coming from a really religious family and all that?" He straightened self-consciously. "Sir, I'd respectfully like to request a transfer off this assignment."

Cardenas's gaze narrowed. "You're serious, aren't you,

Fennel?" The hulking officer nodded. "All right. I'll make the communication. You can report back into your regular precinct tomorrow morning instead of coming here. Now that we know what we're up against I don't think I need to replace you."

"Thank you, sir. It's just that I . . ."

The inspector put up a hand. "You don't have to explain yourself, Fennel. I understand."

The other's relief was palpable. "Thanks, sir." He lingered, as if feeling the need to justify his actions further. "She *was* vivid, wasn't she?"

"*Es muy verdad*, man. But I don't think she was immortal."

"Can't a reciprocating program go on and on, sir? Isn't that a kind of immortality?"

Cardenas frowned. "I thought I knew why you were asking to be relieved from this assignment, Fennel. Am I wrong?"

"Not really, sir. I was just wondering out loud. Thanks again." He turned and hurried off to help with the cleanup.

A moment later Delacroix was at his side, nodding in the direction of the retreating officer. "What was that all about, sir?"

"Caution. Piety. Uncertainty. Sometimes they all go together, Sergeant." He turned briskly. "We'll open on time tomorrow."

"Yes, sir. If you don't mind my asking, what's our next step, sir?"

"We're going to make a contribution to the padre's Order, of course. Just like *she* suggested we do."

She blinked. "Sir?"

"And in return we're going to ask a favor of the blessed virgin's humble servant. We've now been convinced of her existence and involvement, you see. So convinced we want to extend our contribution beyond that of mere money, to one of a more personal nature."

"Oh. I see, sir. At least, I think I do."

"All will become clear, Sergeant." He smiled.

It had better, he thought, or he was liable to start losing

others in addition to the honest and straightforward Fennel.
Or worse than that.

He had not forgotten that this tactile or whatever it was
could kill while smiling.

V

When the Collar returned the next day he was gratified to
observe the expressions of uncertainty and respect on the
faces of the salesfolk. Though he was not privy to the details,
it was clear that the manifestation had been a most efficacious
one. Certainly he was treated with more courtesy as he was
ushered into the owner's inner office this time, though the
ushering was done by someone other than the giant of the
day before. That was fine with him. The big man had struck
him as an armed weapon able to go off at any moment.

"*Buenos* not so tardy, padre," said Cardenas. "You have
a seat and I'll have a moment." He disappeared as the visitor
made himself comfortable.

The owner reappeared a moment later in the shadow of
unexpected company. The visitor was delighted to see the
attractive saleswoman among them, but the looks on her face
and those of her two companions were less than inviting. There
was no apprehension there, either. One of them activated a
previously concealed wall device while another positioned
himself deliberately in front of the closed door. Meanwhile
the woman produced a sleek portable of a type he was afraid
he recognized and began scanning him while simultaneously
checking the readbacks. He shifted his fracturing bravado to
his host.

"What is this, my son? I don't understand."

"Your Madonna paid us a visit last night."

The Collar smiled, on firmer ground again. "Ah. I can tell
by your tone that she remonstrated with you. No one was
injured, I hope?"

"No, though someone could have been. Your Madonna's a little trigger-happy."

"What mere mortal can divine her methods? She works her will as she sees fit, adapting her approach to time and circumstance. It matters not. In the end all are become aware of her omnipotence."

"Truly," Cardenas agreed. "It was a very convincing demonstration."

"Ah. Then you will be contributing to our Order so that we may continue tending to our flock?"

"In a way."

The visitor was immediately on guard. "What do you mean, 'in a way'?"

"You give us a blessing, we'll bless you in return."

"That seems reasonable enough," the Collar conceded guardedly. "What sort of blessing had you in mind?"

"The blessings of information, Padre Morales."

The visitor tensed. "My name is Brother Gutierrez."

Cardenas nodded past him, at the saleswoman. She read from her portable.

"Eduardo Morales. Also aliased as Pablo Mancuso, Guiseppe Mendez, Arlen Roberto Rodriguez, Julio Ixtapa . . . there are a good dozen others. Born borough of Nuevo Montoya, greater Guadalajara thirty-one or -two years ago to Velaz Morales out of Sisipe Morales, maiden name Santiago. Dropped or kicked out of numerous schools; the names are unimportant.

"Arrested three times for burglary, one conviction; three times for assault, no convictions; twice for attempted rape, one conviction; twice for grand theft, vehicular, one conviction . . ." She glanced up from the portable. "You have a lot to atone for, Brother Morales."

"You've got me confused with somebody else."

"Verdad?" She walked over and flashed the portable's vit pick in his face. He blinked and looked away, but not in time. She studied the readout.

''Retinal patterns match, both eyes. Still think we're making a mistake? Want me to pull some blood and do a DNA match? The state'll bill you for it.''

He gazed moodily at the floor, his demeanor having turned distinctly unclerical. ''So what of it? Anybody can reform.''

''Drastically, it would seem,'' Cardenas murmured.

Morales looked up, suddenly grinning. ''Okay, I admit to who I am. What are you going to charge me with? Soliciting donations under a false name? Go ahead, charge me.''

Delacroix checked her portable again. ''We were thinking more along the lines of extraditing you to Jalisco. Or did I neglect to mention that you're wanted there on an outstanding murder warrant?''

The visitor's pupils dilated slightly. It would have gone unnoticed to anyone but an Intuit. ''That whole *negocio* was a frame! Besides, the drool was a snaffler. He deserved to die.''

''Could be,'' agreed Cardenas, ''but that's really up to the Jalisco Municipal Court to decide. You being a multiple loser, they might be inclined to ignore any mitigating circumstances on your behalf. A nice letter of recommendation on my part could do you a world of good, *compadre*.''

The unhappy visitor eyed the inspector warily. ''You'd do that for me?''

''You help us out here, you'd be surprised what a real friendly sort of homber I can be.''

There was silence. The Collar looked up cautiously. ''Won't do you no good, man. She's real, the Madonna.''

''Come on, Morales. We know better than that and you know we know better than that.''

''No, man, I mean it!'' He peered around anxiously. ''I don't know that she's *the* Madonna, but she's real enough. I seen her plenty. Brother Perote, he's the one who pro ... propitiates her. He knows.''

Cardenas exchanged a glance with his associates. ''This Brother Perote, he's your leader?''

''He's the Father Superior. He's the one who decides how

the offerings are distributed. Who gets what. Some of it does go to the poor," he added defiantly.

"Maintaining a cover," commented one of the officers diffidently.

Cardenas nodded. "How about you tell me the routine, Brother? Everyone meet the same place at the same time?"

Morales shook his head. "Same place, yeah, but there's different people at the prayer sessions at different times. Depends who's around, and who's on duty."

"How many Brothers in your 'Order'?"

The prisoner shrugged. "I don't know for sure. Perote doesn't talk a lot about stuff like that."

"I'll bet," muttered one of the other officers knowingly.

"Sometimes I seen twenty at prayer, sometimes more."

"Good," said Cardenas. "Then a new initiate's not likely to attract undue attention."

Morales gaped at him. "You crazy, fedoco. They'll lase you right out."

"Not if I'm properly coached by another Brother, my friend. I have an excellent memory. You run the routine by me once and I'll remember it. Verbatim."

Morales shook his head. "I don't want no federale's death on my vita."

"I'm not going to die. I'll be well tracked at all times, and armed. In any event it's not your worry. Do we have a deal?"

Morales looked around at the other feds. "You're all witnesses. I'm not responsible for anything that happens to this one." He turned back to eye Cardenas speculatively. "It's not Perote you have to worry about. She'll kill you herself. The Madonna. She doesn't like unbelievers."

"I've already met her," Cardenas replied quietly. "I think we can reason together."

"Man, don't you understand? You don't reason with the holy mother. You just do as she says."

Cardenas nodded paternally, as one would to a stubborn child. "Just tell me the routine."

VI

The patterners in Supply cloak-scanned Morales's outfit and cut Cardenas a suit to match overnight, complete to cowl and trim. They had to work fast lest the good and now highly talkative Brother be missed by his brethren. Morales remained convinced Cardenas would be noticed, despite the color changing lenses over his unusual blue eyes. It was critical that the inspector be prepared to provide the right answers to any casual inquiries. But if one of the deacons or worse, Perote himself, happened to challenge him, then the officers who would be tracking his situation needed to react fast.

The directions Morales supplied took Cardenas deep into one of the poorer commercial sections of Nogales Sud. The district was a mix of older structures, some even pre-*maquiladora*, where cheapjack assembly plants loomed over prefab apartment buildings and a few forlorn one- and two-story homes cobbled together out of presswood and formastone. Street lighting was in short supply, ninloco ganglets prowled the corners around heavily armed and protected liquor and food dispensaries, and citizens exhausted after ten-hour days in the plants pretty much went straight home and stayed there. Even the local whores looked lethargic.

As he hunted for the given address Cardenas recycled the information Morales had supplied about the nature and activities of the Order. *Miércoles* was a regular meeting day, during which reports were presented on successful collections, promises to pay secured, reluctant merchants and individuals who required further cajoling, and so on. Occasionally large sums of money were disseminated among the faithful. Cardenas was now Brother Cardenas. So long as no formal roll calls were run, and Morales had assured him they were infrequent, he was convinced he could successfully infiltrate the gathering.

In the event of the unexpected, or the need to wrap up activities in a hurry, a pair of federal VTOLs cruised overhead, each equipped to monitor the electronics that had been sewn discreetly into his brown suit. He holstered a duplicate of the street gun Morales had favored, knowing he would have to surrender it at the door. But for one in his position to arrive unarmed would be like showing up naked at a convention of nuns.

The churchfront was new, a quickie prefab job obviously slicked, sliced, and stamped to order. It had been superimposed on the loading dock of an old warehouse located at the far end of a cul-de-sac, giving the consecrated facade the aspect of a cheap vit set. The deceptive solidity of the burnished copper-hued spires and arched doorway doubtless imparted an aura of reassurance to passersby, though the volume of both pedestrian and vehicular traffic in this part of the city at night was small. The nearest induction tube station was half a kilometer away. The church was not an easy place to reach, which was doubtless how the Brothers preferred it.

He lingered in the shadows until a pair of Collars alighted from an autocab and accelerated to fall in with them. Before they could ask questions he initiated conversation, employing terms and code words supplied by the loquacious Morales. By the time they reached the feign-grained double doorway, with its pseudo brass brads and sham wormholes, he had intuited enough about his companions to the point where the three of them were chattering like confidants, energetically exchanging views on tough sells and eager contributors.

Replicates of the security nodes the techs had found in Morales's suit got Cardenas past the prominent scanner in the outer hallway and into the inner sanctum. Other Brothers were assembling there, in an atmosphere of expectation and unholy conversation. Women, liquor, and the psychowiles of the freshest recreational pharmaceuticals were mentioned far more often than God and service.

When he finally arrived to call the assembly to order anon a blast from a semiserious synthesized organ, Brother Perote turned out to be something other than what Cardenas had expected. But then, they usually did. He was even shorter than the inspector, stocky and unathletic of appearance, probably in his early thirties. Back and forth across the small raised stage he strutted, like a professional street urchin, his arms and hands in constant motion. He looked like an overwound, overstressed antique child's toy, and sounded like one, too.

Thanks to the generosity of local believers there would be a special distribution to the faithful tomorrow, he declared. This announcement provoked the expected hoots of appreciation among the assembled, as well as some enthusiastic applause. Plans for the forthcoming month's work were discussed, with accompanying exhortations to increase collections and solicitations. Several new members were inducted into the Order without a travesty of a ceremony. Perote simply introduced the newcomers, who were greeted with a few good-natured catcalls and obscenities.

The Order appeared to be not only healthy but growing, Cardenas noted, as was to be expected with any successful, profitable racket. Though Perote made an effort to act and sound like one of the boys, he was obviously a good deal smarter than any of the acolytes hanging in the inspector's vicinity. Cardenas was eager to run a check on him, but pulling out a scanner in the midst of the assembled Brothers and aiming it at their leader would be more than likely to bring his investigation to a violent and premature end.

There was some concluding conversation, including an exchange of questions and answers, before the assembly was finally dismissed. Brothers began to file out the door, to waiting cabs or private vehicles. Perote had vanished early. A check of his watch surprised Cardenas with the lateness of the hour. The meeting had gone on longer than he'd anticipated.

He drifted toward the left-hand wall, where empty shipping containers and old crates remained from the building's previous days as a storage facility, and found one unsealed. Slipping inside, he picked his way back into the depths, stepping lightly among bundles of plastic and fiberboard until he found a pack bubble that would support him. Then he sat down to wait.

When his watch showed three A.M. he removed the night goggles from his interior breast pocket and slipped them on.

Very little light filtered into the church, but the amplifying goggles cast his naturally dim surroundings in an eerie twilight. Making no noise, he emerged from the cluster of shipping containers into the assembly area and headed purposefully toward the stage, confident in the knowledge that the shepherding VTOLs were hovering somewhere nearby.

The platform was deserted, the electronics crudely attached to the simple podium powered down. The back of the stage consisted of a false wall erected out of dark quasistone sheeting. Walking around the far end he saw empty floor and a few scattered crates, a small field kitchen that served to feed the faithful on those occasions when food was required, a quartet of portable sanitary booths, and in the distance a back door. Nothing else.

From the belt concealed beneath his jacket he removed a small tube, adjusted the slide controls on one side, and flicked the button at its based. A pair of bright green LEDs came to life together with a small illuminated readout. Covering the LEDs with his gripping hand, he shielded the readout with the other as he followed its directions.

The device led him to the third in line of the four one-piece, enclosed portable johns. There was a lock on the handle and an "Out of Order" sign pasted to the door. He frowned at his handheld, then set to work. Another tool made short toil of the simple lock. He lifted the handle and peered inside.

In place of the expected holed throne a ladder led downward.

Treading carefully, he started down. The steps terminated in a narrow hallway, which soon opened into a large room filled with enough tech of sufficient sophistication to impress even a multinat Designer. Several sealed cases emitted steady, placid hums, indicating that their contents were powered up, or at least in dormant mode. There were a couple of chairs, some well-marked hard-copy maps on one wall, a pile of pornographic printouts heaped indifferently in one corner, a sink and chiller, and a single rumpled bunk.

He started with the obviously expensive, state-of-the-art

tech, beginning with the satellite downlink. It was active and warm. Though the readout was coded he had no doubt that it could be decrypted quickly enough, identifying both the satellite and transponder in use.

He was moving to the next pile of components when he felt a presence and sensed the light. It nearly blinded him and he clutched at the goggles.

She was floating between him and the ladder, her etheric expression full of regret.

"You shouldn't be here," the image said. "You defile the holy places."

"On the contrary," he replied as evenly as he could, "I have tremendous respect for whoever set this up." He tried to see past the conflagrant figure. "Who's controlling you? What alarm did I finally trip?"

"No alarm. And no one controls me. I sensed your presence, and I came to you. You do not belong here. You are not one of the faithful. You come to work mischief."

"Not me. I seek only enlightenment."

The Madonna seemed to hesitate. "You seek it obliquely."

"That's in my nature." He tried to anticipate what the deadly phantasm might do next as his fingers crept toward an interior coat pocket. Within lay the broadcast unit that would instantly summon the VTOLs and help from outside.

"Your inner self remains closed to me," came the cryptic whisper as he felt something prick the back of his neck. Whirling, he saw a cowled shape step quickly back from him. He fumbled for the unit inside his jacket but his fingers didn't respond. Nerves and muscles had gone suddenly and completely numb.

He thought someone stepped forward to catch him before he hit the floor, but so rapidly was consciousness fading that he wasn't sure. Behind him he heard the specter say, "Be gentle with him. He is no less than a sheep strayed from the flock."

"Yeah, sure," came the terse and entirely compassionless male response.

VII

He awoke on a cot not dissimilar to the one that he'd seen in the underground chamber. Muted daylight seeped in through a high, unreachable, and small window set in the stone wall across from him. Real stone, he soon ascertained, not fake.

Furnishings consisted of the cot on which he lay and a simple polystyrene four-legged table on which rested a pitcher full of water and a glass. He poured himself a drink and sipped slowly. His throat was incredibly dry. An aftereffect of whatever they'd doped him with? He found he was shivering slightly. They had taken every last stitch of his clothing.

Words reverbed over a concealed speaker. "Good to see that you're up and about, Inspector." The voice went silent.

Moments later the sealed wooden door clinked as it was dragged aside. A tranquil Brother Perote entered. Cardenas intuited the presence of two very large men flanking the entrance and placed his instinctive first reaction on hold.

Perote leaned back into a corner of the cell and crossed his arms over his chest as he studied his prisoner. His comparative nakedness didn't bother Cardenas, but the situation did. So did his captor's nonchalance. It suggested that he was completely in control.

"Where are my clothes?"

"You're not going anywhere, so you don't need them. I had them carefully scanned. The usual alert and alarm devices, antenna pickups woven into the fabric of the suit; that sort of thing. We put it on a dummy and slipped it onto a high-speed cargo induction to San Antonio. I figure it'll get about halfway there before your baby-sitters get nervous enough to check in on you in person."

Cardenas kept his eyes on his captor as he sat back down on the bunk. He was still feeling pretty dizzy. "Where am I?"

"Not in Kansas." Perote chuckled. "Not in Nogales, either. How'd you find the church?"

"An informant," Cardenas told him. "There'll be others."

"Maybe. We can move quickly if we have to. Who was it?"

Cardenas smiled thinly in return.

Perote clearly had expected that response. "No matter. You'll tell us in due time. An hour's nothing but *una hora*." He paused to consider something. "You'll tell us everything."

"I'm trained to resist all varieties of persuasion, physical as well as chemical. As an Intuit, I can sense what's coming and prepare for it."

Perote's eyebrows rose. "Never met an Intuit before. Heard of you guys, but never expected to meet one. It'll be interesting to see if you're right." His eyes glittered. "We can artery some real graphic juice."

"Won't make me tell you what the noh-man knows."

Perote shrugged. "Then you'll die."

"You'd *muerte* me anyway."

"That's true. I won't lie to you, Federale. Here, I don't need to."

"The satellite downlink in Nogales shackles you to a base station somewhere. Here?"

Perote nodded approvingly. "You're fast, all right. Quick and dangerous. I'll be glad to see you dead. Nothing personal. I can see that you're the kind of federale who could make real trouble."

Cardenas was not to be diverted. "You generate the program at your base station. Here." Perote did not comment, but neither did he deny the surmise. "You use the downlink to relay it to Nogales. Then what? Hiflow short-form antennae fixed in trucks parked outside each business you extort?"

"Man, you *are* good." Perote admired his prisoner's intuition.

"What made you decide to come up with a Madonna? I've seen tactiles before and this is easily the best of the lot. There's more control over form and movement, and you're able to sustain density. Where do you get the requisite crunch and power?"

"For a condemned man you're ripe with questions."

"You'll get the chance to ask yours in short order."

Perote's smile returned. "I like you, Federale, but not enough to let you live. You're an unbeliever."

"And you're about as religious as a lobotomized lemur."

"Do you intuit that about me?" Perote was enjoying this, Cardenas noted, like a sadistic lepidopterist lazing away a contented summer afternoon with his pins and killing jar.

He nodded slowly, his mustache bobbing. "Yes. Also that you're clever enough to set up and run an operation like this, but not smart enough to devise it."

"No shame in that. One of the traits I attribute my success to is never letting ego get in the way of business." Perote stood away from the wall. He was a lot calmer and more controlled than he'd been on the warehouse-church stage, Cardenas reflected. He wondered what the man's drug of choice was.

"I used to supply components, chips, nodules, protein storage cylinders, and a lot more to a nanker named Silvestre Chuautopec. Ever hear of him?" Cardenas shook his head. "He was a little old, little old man who lived outside of . . . here." The grin widened.

"I was fascinated by his work and used to hang around watching him. Eventually he asked if I'd be interested in helping out. There were times when he needed another pair of hands attached to an unquestioning brain."

"I suspect you fit the bill admirably. Why do I think that was a mistake on his part?"

Perote treated the dig as beneath his notice. "Old man Chuautopec slaved twenty-three years for Tamilpasoft Ltd., sculpting mollypaths and box access technology. Then he quit, registered a couple of patents that made him independently wealthy, and set to work trying to realize his life's dream. It took him another twenty years before he vitalized the Madonna tactile. That's the story he told me. I wasn't there for the whole slog, of course.

"I'll never forget the first time I saw it. I thought to myself,

'That's really something. How can I skrag some credit off this?' "

"I'm way ahead of you."

Perote nodded. "I forget that I'm talking to an Intuit. You'll have to excuse me. The grubber Brothers are generally a little slower than you.

"I did some stone thinking before I decided to run the tactile over the kind of simple folk I grew up with. Having seen what it could do, I thought the indecisive could be quickly convinced . . . and used to convince others."

Cardenas shifted uncomfortably against the abrasive, cold fabric. "I felt the tactile pull me, then saw it melt glass and activate a weapon it was unable to lift."

"What'd you expect? Without an available source of malleable collagen all you have to work with is sound, wave, and light matrix. Sound can give you all the heat you need. You can melt things with it, and it adds to the verisimilitude of the human form. The pressure you felt involved coercing a couple of gigabushels of reluctant photons. More than are used to generate the figure. Wave pressure is enough to convince you you're being touched by something, and to activate a sensitive switch, but not to pick up heavy objects."

"Then I could have resisted its pull."

"Easily."

Cardenas's gaze hadn't swerved. "How does it kill?"

Perote casually examined the back of his right hand. "It's all coherent light and electrical fields. It can portage a whale of a subsidiary charge. Enough to induce tachycardia in a proximate subject. Stops the heart. Or it can scramble brain impulses. It's a very versatile program."

"You're responsible for that, not this Chuautopec."

"You know, it's no fun having a conversation with an Intuit. You anticipate all my answers."

"How does he feel about you appropriating his development?"

"I'm sure if he was alive he'd disapprove." Perote regarded his prisoner calmly. "Didn't intuit that one, did you?"

"I would have eventually." Cardenas shivered afresh; not from fear. It was cold in the cell. "How did you know I was in your downlink station?"

"The Madonna told me we had an intruder, of course. Some of the Brothers and I live in the building next door."

"I was wearing security nodes designed to detect and bypass sensors."

"This tactile's too sophisticated for that. It's never powered down, always on a stand-ready alert status. I call her my Versatile Virgo." He grinned. "Our Lady watches over her little flock."

"Why the Madonna? Why not a nightmare monster, or a small dinosaur, or something terrifying?"

"That's what I'd have formulated, but I'm no Silvestre Chuautopec. Nobody is, or rather was. See, he was a deeply religious man, old Silvestre. Uncommon in this day and age. He wanted to give people something to inspire them in their beliefs, to resuscitate the lapsed. I never did find out if his plan was to fraud his tactile Madonna off as the real thing by randomly vitalizing it in a few churches, or simply to edify the faithful by showing what one might look like. While he was working he babbled on and on about how he was going to spark a religious revival among the masses, by showing people that traditional religious beliefs and modern technology could not only coexist but reinforce one another. The old bastard was no phony. He really believed all that stuff.

"I had to make use of what I inherited after I *muerted* him. It's not easy to frighten a mark with a Madonna. It wasn't until I got the idea of loading the tactile with a lethal charge that I hit on a way of intimidating people. The synchronized religious prattle makes it look to witnesses like the wrath of God is at work. After seeing it in action I'm not so sure that it isn't more effective than a monster would've been." He laughed again, an unpleasant giggle. "I'll bet church collections are up all over the Nogales connurb.

"It's a pretty case-responsive program. You can give it a mission—we call it convicting an unbeliever—and it can react and respond as the situation develops, generating cohesive dialogue on the spot. There's no way we could steady-monitor it during the process and still maintain the illusion. Takes too much crunch just to sustain the matrix. And the power requirements! It has to renew itself from one nanosecond to the next. You can imagine.

"The general public being utterly unfamiliar with tactiles, and pretty credulous to start with, most of them accept it as genuine. I don't have to *muerte* near as many people as would otherwise be necessary in your standard extortion racket."

"That must let you sleep easier at night."

"I sleep fine, thanks. Business is good and getting better. But then you were at the last meeting and you know that. You were at that meeting, weren't you?" Again Cardenas said nothing.

"You're not very responsive. We'll fix that presently."

"I still don't see how you suck enough crunch to maintain it."

"The secret'd ring bells and whistles in Nogales, wouldn't it? But we're not in Nogales, and the utility companies hereabouts aren't near as solicitous of their records. The non-wonders of modern communications. We steal what we need here, generate the program, uplink it via a pirate satellite transponder to Nogales, transfer it to our truck, and from that vitalize it inside a chosen location. If my people are intercepted or found out there's nothing particularly incriminating in either the truck or the church you found.

"If the worst happens all we have to do is shift our Nogales base of operations. The equipment there is easily replaced. It's the box here which generates the program that's critical, and nobody's going to find it. Consider yourself an honored, if temporary, guest."

"If you don't mind, I'd rather not."

"Suit yourself." Perote straightened. "I think I've answered most of your questions. Now you can answer some of mine. I'm really curious to know just how much more, if anything, the federales know about this operation."

Cardenas lay down flat on the bunk, slipping his hands behind his head. "Suddenly I'm not feeling very talkative anymore. Maybe after dinner."

"Why waste food on a dying man?" The door opened and the two guards the inspector had sensed lying in wait just outside entered. One held a large gun, the other a power injector. Cardenas lay quiescent, awaiting them.

The man with the injector leaned over him. The policeman smiled, closed his eyes, and as the guard reached for his upper right arm, the inspector brought both feet up to catch him solidly under the chin. He went backward in a spray of fragmented enamel. The gun roared but missed as Cardenas kipped off the bunk and closed with the stumbling, bleeding guard, using the dazed man's bulk for cover. As Perote darted to block the portal, Cardenas leapt and somersaulted, coming up in the extortionist's face with an elbow. Perote went careening, his nose broken.

There were two more guards waiting at the far end of the hallway. Cardenas was in the process of quieting them when the injector slammed harshly into his back.

VIII

He was running down a long white corridor. Slowwwly, with his feet barely brushing the tiled surface. Friends and strangers, casual acquaintances and lawbreakers he'd helped put in prison, reached out to him. His father, who'd died when he was twelve. His mother, who smiled maternally and called him her littlest angel before collapsing into a horrid heaving mass of pustulent fungi. His adventurous older brother Felix, who'd successfully dodged flechettes and bullets in Southeast Africa, knives in Phoenix and Matamoros, only to find a writhing, painful death from the toxin of a stonefish he'd stepped on while wading with his fiancée across a sun-saturated reef in far-off Kiribati.

Friends quickly replaced family, all breaking apart and

crumbling gruesomely before they could reach him. He was on fire himself now and watched helplessly as little flames burst forth from his fingertips and toes, his hair and genitals. He screamed and flailed at the flames, but nothing would put them out. Burning, he staggered on as the hallway before him grew darker. Teeth beckoned at the far end, sharp as scimitars, their serrated edges dripping acid and ichor. He tried to stop, to turn, to run in the opposite direction, but his feet and legs would no longer obey him. While something vast and unseen moaned expectantly, the eager jaws clashed before him like cymbals.

A large dog, a familiar German shepherd shape, raced up behind him and locked its teeth gently on his trailing arm, ignoring the flames that poured from his blistering skin. Whimpering, it tried to slow his headlong plunge, to drag him back from those gnashing fangs.

On the far distant shore of perception he thought he heard voices shouting. "Hold him down! . . . Get his legs! . . ."

The burning went on for hours, but he never did quite slide into the yawning mouth. Then the fire seemed to flicker and die, leaving him scorched from the Id-side out. Pressure on his body and limbs eased, but the voices did not.

"If he doesn't rest," one said, "we'll lose him."

"So?" A crisp, uncaring, amoral voice, hiding the hint of an evil giggle.

"You can't get information out of a dead man."

"I'm not sure it's worth the bother, Doc. But I'll give you one more try. If he dies then, fuck 'im. I can't hang around here forever. I've got to get back to the flock."

Something was placed on a chair that was dragged close to Cardenas's head. "Can you hear me, Federale? I'm putting my vorec here. All channels are open. When you're ready to cooperate just start talking. The whole system here's on auto shunt. Just say you want to start spilling info and a menu will put you on the right path and activate a nice fresh recorder to take it all down. If you're helpful, I promise you your next *vamanos* will be a lot more comfortable. You'll go quietly, even happily. But don't take too much time to think about it, okay? I got a plane to catch."

He sensed bodies moving away. Once again darkness closed in around him and there were new nightmares, but these were almost reassuring in their familiarity.

When he awoke it was dark and glacially still in the cell. A little moonlight seeped in through the single high window. He lay on his back, naked, his wrists, neck, and ankles strapped to the cot. One wrist strap was half torn through where he'd damaged it in his convulsions. The lashing across his neck prevented him from even raising his head to look around. Another, broader belt of metal mesh bisected his belly. The fabric of the cot beneath him was still wet with sweat and his entire body shivered uncontrollably. He was clammy from head to foot.

Perote was right. Cardenas wouldn't last through another session. Unable to wall off his professional side, he found himself wondering what they'd slipped him. A massive dose of Sericol? Senyabutamin? Nudocaine? Maybe a brew; a threatening cocktail designed to emancipate his inhibitions.

Probably in the morning there would be more questions and then, when he again refused to provide answers, a final party. It wasn't that Perote was particularly vicious or evil, Cardenas knew. He simply didn't care.

He wondered if Sergeant Delacroix and the rest of his guardians up in the circling VTOLs and out on the pave had grown restive enough by now at his lack of communication to check in on him in person, only to find his safe suit riding a mannequin to South-Central Texas.

He didn't even know how many days he'd lain unconscious, or how far he'd been transported from Nogales. Far enough, he knew, for his captors to require the use of a satellite link to pursue their work.

Well, he'd had a good life, and a self-satisfying if not especially brilliant career. So he wouldn't see sixty. He didn't mind dying. A federale anticipated that possibility and prepared for it from the moment of graduation from the Academy.

But he could have done without the pain he was presently suffering and perhaps, even more so, the embarrassment.

He was stripped, half dead, and bolted down. No longer a man but a lump of meat. And there wasn't a damn thing he could do about it.

Except pray.

Auto shunt system, Perote had said. Vorec-driven menu channeler. How open was it? How "auto"? Cardenas could play a vorec the way a good contralto could play Puccini. His head ringing with the effort required for simple motion, he turned as much as he was able toward the chair on which the open verbal recognition pickup lay waiting.

"Our Lady," he began, keeping his voice low but enunciating clearly. His optics were too spazzed to focus on the pickup, but he knew it was there. He engaged all the jargon he could remember from a half-forgotten childhood, when his mother used to send him and his brother off to church school in immaculately pressed and cleaned uniforms: the only intact and unpatched clothes the rough-and-tumble boys owned. He struggled to call forth key phrases from the Bible as well as vorec manuals and modulation theory.

Occasionally he paused to rave falsely in case anyone was listening in, trying to buy himself some time. Now and then he screamed, just so they wouldn't think he was entirely coherent and start to analyze what he was trying to do.

Of course there was no guarantee that the vorec was menued in any way to the tactile, but if all the tech for this setup was proximate to itself, even minimally interlinked, and the Madonna program was vorec-activated and responsive to the main auto shunt Perote had mentioned, there was just a chance that his fevered broadcast might key an electronic nerve and activate something besides a monitor whose job it was to oversee a simple recorder.

A tactile that powerful had to be more than situation savvy. It had to be sensitive over a broad area of responsiveness or it wouldn't be able to function effectively, wouldn't be able to react in depth to nonspecific stimuli. Furthermore, it had to be able to acknowledge peripheral vernacular devoid of cryptics. Code words, for sure. Vitalizing phrases. But what kind of code words, which particular phrases?

Perote was smart, but as he'd admitted, he was no Silvestre Chuautopec. How case-responsive had the unknown old genius made his program? Flexible enough, surely, so that it could interact effectively with the most simple, unsophisticated country folk.

Criminals were always talkative when they thought they were safe. They liked nothing better than to boast of their exploits.

His garrulous captor had supplied Cardenas with a short profile of the tactile's developer, unfortunate and devout as he'd been. Such an individual would make use of certain words to vitalize his matrix, his designs. Words from the Bible, pious parlance from the historical notandum of the church. A catholic molly, so to speak.

A warm radiance harmonized in the cell and the feminine device loomed beside him. "You called out unto me, and I have come. Have you repented?"

"Yes. Oh, yes, Holy Mother, I have repented."

"Then I shall call a Brother to hear your confession." The figure started to turn.

"Wait!" It was an effort to raise his voice. Was anyone monitoring this, he wondered, or had he simply activated the proper shunt and not the queued recorder? The door stayed shut. Though he knew not how much time he had, he proceeded carefully. "I need clarification first."

The snowy *mater doloroso* beamed down at him, comely of form, holy of aspect. "I will help if I can. It is my function."

"You're the holy Madonna, the true lady?"

"I am." The program was self-convicted, as it had to be to function properly, Cardenas knew.

"There can be no other?"

"No other but I."

"Then if I gave you a universal replication code you couldn't duplicate yourself?"

The womanly matrix seemed to hesitate. Cardenas tried not to hold his breath, tried not to keep glancing at the ominous rectangle of the door. If anyone was listening, if anyone glimpsed what he was about .... With luck most of them would be sound asleep. At the moment the lateness of the hour was his only ally, the unseen moon his sole source of encouragement.

"If you're the one true holy Madonna," he rushed on, "you should be able to do almost anything, even create another of yourself. But if you can do that, then you're not the one true Madonna and your programmi ... your true self is by definition ambiguous. Try this and maybe we'll both gain some clarification." And he mouthed the codex.

It was a simple and straightforward attempt to lock up the entire extortion program, using military code logic. He had no idea what the result might be even if it worked. But even if it was the last thing he did, he felt strongly that at least he was doing *something*.

Somewhere beyond his cell an intricately folded and very deep box accepted the transmission from the open vorec and fed it into the fiendishly brilliant designs of the late Silvestre Chuaupotec. Circuits flashed. On the far side of the state of Sinhaloa half a small town went dark as a stealth program diverted the community's power allocation to the basement of an old apartment house in a certain village high up in the southern Sierra Madre Occidental.

There was a white flash as the effulgence within the cell intensified. He blinked and a second Madonna stood drifting near his feet. Identical to the first. He held his breath.

The two maters regarded one another. Each said simultaneously, in the same optimal, benign tone of voice, "I am the true Madonna, the holy one."

A major truck recharge station on Transnamerican Highway Four-One flickered as if struck by lightning. The lights inside went out, leaving twenty truckers and a handful of tourists cursing in three languages. The relevant power docks died and a transformer blew on a nearby pole.

Within the luminous cell four Madonnas pulsed brightly enough to make the pinioned Cardenas squint. In unison sing-song the quartet examined one another and individually bespoke, "I am the true Madonna; let none doubt this."

Within the connurb of Tepic all the streetlights suddenly went dark. An abrupt, undamped power surge blew out those on the west side of the city, sending glass fragments flying. Fortunately it was late and few vehicles were on the roads.

The door to the cell was flung aside. Clad in starkly colored underwear and a short-sleeved cotton shirt a half-asleep Perote stood breathing hard and waving a handgun. He and those behind him had to throw up their hands to shield their eyes.

"*Cuando* the shit is this?" he yelled, hesitating in the portal and blocking the view of the gunmen behind him.

The four Madonnas turned to the new arrival and voiced concurrently, "I am the true Madonna, of the holy spirit."

Cardenas clamped his eyes shut tight.

There was not enough room in the cell to hold the eight Madonnas. Several spilled out into the narrow hallway beyond. One impinged accidentally on the guard nearest Perote. The man shuddered and clutched at his chest. His gun fell from his suddenly limp fingers as he stumbled back against the mossy stone wall and collapsed, his eyes briefly pleading and then vacant. Perote fought past the lifeless mass, his expression wild, eyes wide, immediate thoughts no different from those of his less imaginative but equally panicked associates.

"I am the true Madonna," chorused the drifting, refulgent shapes that packed the cell and spilled through the open doorway, "of whom the word is spoken." Eyes still shut, Cardenas turned his head as far to the left as he possibly could so that he faced only the cool, gloomy rock wall.

Sixteen Madonnas flooded the hallway and the rooms beyond. Perote and his minions abandoned the structure, an aged shut-and-shuttered cantina-cum-apartment building, and took to their feet or their vehicles. Sleepy inhabitants of the village, who knew not what the frequent visitors from the city worked at behind their modest walls and gruff security, came to their windows to view the commotion, and lingered wide-eyed to gawk at the multitudinous incandescent Madonnas as they drifted through windows and out doors.

Thirty-two Madonnas formed a ring around the old building. Sixty-four spread out into the streets. Ingenuous artisans and farmers, workers and technicians, alternately slammed shut their doors and windows or fell to their knees with hands clasped fervently in front of them. One hundred twenty-eight luminant Madonnas filtered composedly through the streets, preceding two hundred fifty-six who fanned out into the countryside, astonishing ranchers and cattle and sheep alike.

In Zacatecas all the vit stations went off the air. All of Colima went dark. In Juchipila power to the whole community of thirty thousand evaporated as the supraheavy grid buried alongside the little mountain cantina siphoned energy from the entire west-central portion of the Namerican national power net.

Five hundred and twelve Madonnas marched through the streets and alleys and cobbled byways of the village of Yerba Alto, beaming at the residents, smiling at maddened cats and dogs, thoughtfully bestowing benedictions on wide-eyed, dark-haired children.

Every electrical appliance, circuit, device, shunt, and toy within a radius of two kilometers had exploded, burnt out, melted, shorted, or otherwise shut down. Only the little village was not dark. On the contrary, it blazed with a pale radiance visible to aircraft as far as a hundred kilometers away.

A vortex of one thousand twenty-four Madonnas invoked considerately; to the overwhelmed populace, to those who fled in mindless panic and fear, to the fleeing Brothers of the Order, to their raging master Perote who was swept up in their hysterical flight, and to Cardenas where he lay bound in his cell, his eyes shut tight, facing the wall, the awesome light pressing dangerously hard against his inadequate eyelids.

"I AM THE HOLY MOTHER, THE ONE TRUE

MADONNA, THE BRINGER OF LIGHT AND HEALING," the thousand twenty-four chorused angelically from streets and fields and rooftops as carefully aligned photons danced and the central matrix frenzied.

On the lip of the Pacific just north of Acapulco the parallel power plant at Ketchtec, which tapped gigawatts from the thermocline just off the coast, flickered and flared. Conduits liquefied, safeties snapped, huge transformers wailed. With a great electronic gasp and crackle the plant's safeties congressed and closed. Power to two states was shut off. Towns went dark, cities went quiet, and for a brief while the landscape was as it had been a thousand years before, deserts and mountains and beaches slumbering in darkness beneath the benign simper of the moon.

Emergency lights winked on, portable lamps were dragged from hibernation in cases and cabinets. Everywhere there was confusion, puzzlement, anger, uncertainty, much of it directed at a power company that was quite innocent and equally as perplexed as its disempowered customers.

A thousand twenty-four true Madonnas vanished, the energy they had been drawing upon withdrawn, temporarily cut out of the Namerican grid. Cardenas's desperate, careful reasoning had induced replication, which had finally collapsed under the weight of its own truth.

He lay shivering in his cell for another six hours, well after the dawn had broken, until a passerby on his way to work heard his hoarse, weakening shouts. Hesitantly entering the deserted cantina the man found the naked and blistered Cardenas bound to his cot and released him. Then he went to get some of his friends, because the inspector was too feeble and drained to walk. He was blistered not from his nightmares nor from the drugs that had induced them, but from his extended proximity to the one true Madonna. To all of them.

There was very little left of the box and its support equipment in the basement of the attached apartment building. Whatever half-magical programs it had contained had been fried, not wiped, when the system had overloaded. Only auto-matic sprinklers had isolated the resultant flames and saved the buildings, and Cardenas.

Local federales contacted his friends in Nogales, who immediately descended on the church of the Order of Our Lady to confiscate everything and everyone they found there. They were subsequently guided to the sophisticated relay truck and its baffled crew by one of the more talkative Brothers they took into custody. Brother Morales was not the only member of the Order possessed of a loose tongue.

Perote they did not find, but Cardenas knew they would do so in time, and he fully intended to be around when that collar of a different sort was announced.

Drink and food and rest and medicine restored him. His dark skin had saved him from a far worse burn than the one he'd suffered, though he would have to walk gingerly for days. When he was finally able to return to Nogales everyone in the department was almost embarrassingly solicitous of his well-being, and not just because he was the senior inspector on the force. Cardenas was genuinely liked by his colleagues, irregardless of rank.

"I saw Charliebo," he blurted to Pangborn as the latter was preparing to leave the inspector's apartment after they'd watched the Sunday game together on Cardenas's vit.

"What?"

"You remember Charliebo. My ex-seeing-eye shepherd? The one who got vacuumed last year by that subox tunnel those two self-vacuumed multinat renegades devised. It trans-posed him into a tactile defense mechanism for their system. Poor Charliebo. When I was drowning in the worst of that bad trip he was the only friendly shape that hung with me. He tried to help me."

The captain looked away, embarrassed. "Sure, Angel. Glad he was there for you."

"Go ahead, patronize me. I wonder, though, if he was only in my dream. They still haven't managed to trace the line of the GenDyne-Parabas subox tunnel. Nobody knows where it really goes, what it links to and doesn't link to. Maybe there's some kind of as yet undiscovered crossover seam between all of these cyber things. Nobody really knows. We just build them and vitalize them and make sure they're doing their jobs. We don't know what they do in their spare time. Maybe it wasn't all a dream, all bad trip. Maybe Charliebo was really there, jumping from box to box, using the tunnels and trying to help me."

"I wouldn't know about things like that, Angel."

The inspector leaned back in his chair, feet up, one hand holding a cold Tecate Primo. "Nobody does, Shaun. Nobody does."

The captain looked at him for a long moment, then shut the codo door quietly behind him. Cardenas checked the numerals that floated blue above the vit screen. Twelve-twenty. Time for bed. He had another week of administrative leave in which to relax, recover, or do nothing, as he saw fit. Plenty of time to think, and rethink, and ponder.

His gaze flicked to his home box, which occupied an alcove next to the wallscreen. It was powered up, dormant, waiting for input. With his left hand he reached for the vorec that lay on the endtable next to his easy chair and flicked it on, holding it up to his lips.

"Our Lady . . ." he began. The telltales on the home box twinkled, indicating it was receiving his transmission. He hesitated, then flipped the vorec off and laid it aside.

A week was time to do too much thinking, he told himself. He needed to get back to work, to the reality of the district headquarters, to the clamor and pungency of the pave. He pushed himself out of the chair and headed for the bedroom.

As he turned he thought he saw a flicker of white light flash from the cover of the box's metallic composite case. But probably not.